A MURDER
OF CROWES

ED W. NICKERSON

Order this book online at www.trafford.com
or email orders@trafford.com

Most Trafford titles are also available at major online book retailers.

Printed in the United States of America.

ISBN: 978-1-4907-5295-2 (sc)
ISBN: 978-1-4907-5297-6 (hc)
ISBN: 978-1-4907-5296-9 (e)

Library of Congress Control Number: 2014922701

Because of the dynamic nature of the Internet, any web addresses or links contained in
this book may have changed since publication and may no longer be valid. The views
expressed in this work are solely those of the author and do not necessarily reflect the
views of the publisher, and the publisher hereby disclaims any responsibility for them.

Any people depicted in stock imagery provided by Thinkstock are models,
and such images are being used for illustrative purposes only.
Certain stock imagery © Thinkstock.

Trafford rev. 01/02/2015

www.trafford.com
North America & international
toll-free: 1 888 232 4444 (USA & Canada)
fax: 812 355 4082

I would like to thank my wife Judy and my
friends Sue Manson and Susan Magnusson for
their help and support in my fifth novel.

Previous novels in the Ed Crowe series.

First Flight of the Crowe (Trafford 2009)
Crowe's Feat (Trafford 2012)
Crowe's Nest (Trafford 2012)
Something to Crowe About (Trafford 2013)

CHAPTER ONE

ROME AIRPORT FRIDAY, DECEMBER 27TH 1985, 8:15AM

Reaching down for a pen from her purse saved Carolyn's life. The bullet flew above her hitting the old lady sitting next to her in the head, killing her instantly. For several minutes the world around her was chaotic.

Throwing herself to the ground, she slid under the seat she had been sitting on waiting to be called for boarding of the TWA flight to New York. The old lady's body down slipped next to Carolyn and with considerable reluctance she pulled the dead body close to her for protection.

There were constant sounds of gun shots and then the horrific sounds of hand grenades exploding. But what she would never forget was the screaming of men, women, and children as they cried out for their lives; all to no avail.

Her mind cleared. She reached into her purse, not for her pen but for her gun. Grasping it firmly and releasing the safety, she pushed the body in front of her away, rolled onto her stomach and listened. The shots were coming from in front of her and to her right. The men firing the weapons screamed in Arabic as they sprayed the area with bullets. When she heard shouting in Italian further to her right, she knew she had to move. Adjusting quickly to a kneeling position, she aimed in the direction of the Arabic voice to her left, stood up and opened fire. She got two shots away before the blast from the last hand grenade thrown that day blew her backwards, ripping open a gash in her left cheek and smashing the radius of her left arm. She covered her face with her right hand and collapsed in tears.

For two minutes she lay fighting back her tears as the noise around her changed to shouting and screaming for help, but no more gun fire.

When she opened her eyes the Italian police officer was assuring her that everything was going to be all right. She thanked him in Italian and calmly fainted.

CHAPTER TWO

FRIDAY, DECEMBER 27TH 1985 THE QUEEN'S HEAD, OAKVILLE 6:15PM

E d shivered into the pub from the blowing snow and shook the snow off his down-filled winter jacket. It took him just a few seconds to warm up and feel comfortable in his 'second home'.

The pub was busy, very busy. People were enjoying the Christmas – New Years holidays and the friendly atmosphere of the local pub was in full swing. He made his way slowly to the bar greeting and shaking hands with a number of the happy crowd. Peter was working the bar and waved to Ed to acknowledge him and to let him know his Double Diamond was on its way. Ed removed his jacket and bent down to hang it on the hook under the counter. As he stood someone pushed in beside him. He stood and stepped back gently to let the person in.

She was tall, at least five-eight, with long blonde hair. Her slim figure made her look taller than what she was, and her red top and black skirt helped her stand out in the crowd.

"I know all about you," she said with authority. "I know where you live, where you work, what you read, who you hang out with; just about everything about you." She paused. "What do you have to say about that, Mister Edwin Crowe?"

Ed quickly looked around to see if someone was having fun at his behalf. If there was, he couldn't see them. He smiled to give himself time to think. She was very good looking. Her makeup was flawless and her eyes were stunning. It was difficult not look at them constantly.

Ed replied slowly. "You have very nice eyes, if you don't mind my saying so. I know that much about you. So how do you know so much about me, although I suspect I know the answer."

She took a slow sip of her tall drink. "Really? Pray tell?"

"I suspect you're a friend of Seana and Stephanie since only they and my mother know what I read. And I must say I doubt my mother would provide that kind of information to such a good looking young lady as you without telling me of my good luck."

"Really?"

"Really. Plus the fact that Seana and Stephanie knew I was coming down for a drink tonight. I usually…"

"You usually only come down for a drink on Fridays and here I am." She smiled confidently.

"What a co-incidence." Ed said.

"No co-incidence, just good planning."

Peter delivered Ed's beer.

"On my tab please," she said to Peter. "And I'll have another one please."

Ed took a long sip of his beer. It tasted good, even better with her company. "So do I get to know your name?" he asked.

"Victoria," she replied.

"Victoria…?"

"Just Victoria for now."

Ed nodded. "Your surname's a secret then is it?" He raised his eyebrows and grinned.

Victoria laughed. "Very clever, Edwin. I've heard all about your play on words."

Ed put down his beer and extended his right hand. "Victoria, it's a great pleasure to meet you. This is more than a pleasant surprise. Am I allowed to ask you why you want to know about me; a boring old travel agent?"

"Sure you are, but not here. I want you to tell me all about where you're sending your clients to escape this rather nasty winter. When you've finished your beer, no rush, I want to drive you to your apartment and we'll order out pizza." She leaned forward and for the first time spoke quietly. "No naughty stuff, Edwin, just a more private environment. Okay? Please?"

To his own surprise Ed took a drink of his beer before answering. "Well the majority of people are heading to Florida," he began.

Forty minutes later they were in Ed's apartment. Victoria wanted tea, not a glass of wine which Ed had offered. Tea seemed to make sense when he thought about it as he filled the kettle.

"Nice place," Victoria said, walking around the apartment, opening doors and cupboards as if she was thinking of buying it. She didn't ask to look around the bedrooms, but simply made herself at home. She checked the fridge and pantry, sniffing gently as she did.

"So from what the girls tell me, you're a pretty nice guy," she said, turning to face Ed. "Sounds like you're too nice sometimes."

"Well that's about as big an insult in a positive comment that I've ever heard. Anything else?"

"Hey, no insult intended," she added as she continued her review of the apartment. "Gotta tell the truth now, don't we?"

"Yes, we do," Ed agreed. "Milk, sugar?"

"Nope. I have to go. Sorry." She picked up her coat and headed for the door. She reached the door and turned. "Give me a quick kiss, Ed," and reaching into her purse she pulled out a piece of paper. "This is my number. Give me a call sometime if you want to."

Ed walked to her, gave her a quick kiss on the lips. She turned and left the apartment.

Ed stood for a moment wondering what had happened to his few quiet beers at The Queen's Head. Now he had a full pot of tea to himself. He shrugged, laughed to himself and poured himself a large cup of tea.

Thirty seconds later there was a soft knock on the door. He opened it to find Victoria standing with her coat over her arms and a guilty look on her face.

"Can I come in, Ed?" She spoke almost in a whisper. "I have an apology to make."

Ed ushered her in to the kitchen table, where she sat with her coat on her lap.

"Milk, sugar?" Ed asked

"Just milk please."

Ed used his best cup and went so far as to use a saucer. He placed it in front of her and sat. "I'm glad you came back," he smiled.

They drank their tea for several minutes before she spoke.

"That wasn't me, Ed. I'm sorry. You must think I'm stupid or something. The girls would never believe I spoke to you like that. Please don't tell them."

He nodded. "I promise. Now here's what I know about you, Victoria. You're obviously an Oakville lady. You know Seana and Stephanie, and the Jag you drove me home in was purchased in Oakville. It's not your car. I could tell that as soon as you started it; the seat and steering wheel went to a set position, which you had to adjust. That person is obviously taller than you. Since it is most unlikely you're married, I assume it's your dad's Jag. The license plate is PLK 001, and there's no V for Victoria in it." He shrugged. "Maybe the PL stands for Pretty Lady? You also struggled a bit with the manual gear change. So you live at home with your parents, in a very nice part of Oakville. You're single, well educated, and assuming you buy your own clothes, you have a very good job. You don't drink, at least not much. The second drink you ordered, 'the same again', was a virgin Caesar. I could keep guessing, but how am I doing so far?"

Now visibly more relaxed, she briefly applauded him. "Very good so far. Why don't we stop there?"

"Okay," Ed agreed, "but let me just say, if I may. You are a very pretty young lady, about twenty-three I'm assuming. Why you dropped in to see me I'll never understand, but thank you for doing so."

Victoria smile almost lit up the room. "You really are way too, too nice, Ed."

Ed stood. "Please stand up, pretty lady."

She stood, putting her coat aside. Ed slipped his golf shirt over his head and dropped it on the floor. "Lift your arms please," he asked.

"Oh my," Victoria gasped as she lifted her arms. "I don't know…"

Ed quickly pulled her top over her head. She wore only a bra and immediately covered her breasts. "They're so small," she said, obviously embarrassed.

Ed held out his arms. "Hug?"

She took a quick step into his arms, feeling better that she was now covered. "Oh, my goodness. I can't believe we're doing this."

Ed held her tight around the waist waited a few moments then tickling her back as he did so, he reached up unclipped her bra, then quickly slipped his hand down to her waist and slipped his hand onto the top of her bum, just below the top of her panties.

"Oh, my God!" she giggled.

"Now, Victoria," Ed said slowly, "I just wanted you to know that I'm not way too nice." He pulled her toward him. "And that's not a cell phone you're feeling. Don't worry. I've made my point."

She held onto him enjoying the warmth of his body and his gentle touch on her back. She waited several moments before she spoke.

"Please close you eyes and turn around, Ed. That was very nice."

Ed did as he was told, taking a step away.

She thought for a moment, and convinced herself she should do it. She removed her bra and walked up to Ed's back, putting her arms around his body and held tight. "Okay, I'm not way too nice either. And that's not my bra you're feeling."

He could feel the hardness of her nipples against him, and the wonderful softness of her small breasts. "Thank you," was all he could think to say.

"Please stay as you are, Ed." She backed away from him, and slipped on her bra and top. "You can turn around now, not too-nice guy."

They took their seats at the kitchen table and finished their teas. They laughed at each other, not sure what to say.

"Here's my business card, Ed" she said, reaching into her purse.

Ed looked at her card: Victoria Kilgour, MBA, CLU.

"You're a life insurance agent," he said. "Wow, I'd never have guessed that."

"Don't worry; I'm not here to sell you anything." She paused. "But I do want you to know that I've heard so much about you, I just wanted to meet you. I know the girls weren't working tonight, so this was my chance. I certainly don't regret meeting you, Ed, but I do wish I hadn't put on that display in order to build up my courage." She stood. "Look I do have to go. Please give me a good night kiss, and phone me if you want to…for a date, not to buy insurance."

They kissed quickly and gently at the door not putting their arms around each other, and then she left. They both knew any longer a kiss would have turned into something they both would have enjoyed, but may have regretted the next morning.

CHAPTER THREE

SATURDAY, DEC 28TH 1985 THE NEXT MORNING 8:15 AM

E d turned off the television at the gentle knock on the door. Intuitively he knew it was Victoria, and when he opened the door she stood smiling with two cups of Tim Hortons coffee. "Coffee with a smile," she said walking in and placing the cups on the kitchen table. She wore a light green business suit under her winter coat. She took off her coat and looked around. "You don't have a guest do you?"

"Yes, she's just getting dressed in my bedroom," he lied with a laugh. "No, of course I don't have a guest, except you that is. So how did you get through the security? They're usually rather sticky on letting people in without being buzzed in."

"Two cups of hot coffee and a nice smile gets you a long way – with men that is." She gave him the smile.

"Ha, so the song's accurate then; city girls…open doors with just a smile?"

"It happens," she agreed. "But it's the wink that really works."

He picked up his coffee and they sat. "To what do I owe this special visit from my new friend?"

She reached into her purse, removing a sheet of paper and a pen. "I would like you to answer some questions for me on this application. Okay?"

Ed raised his eyebrows in interest. "Life insurance?"

"Nope."

"Disability insurance?"

"Nope." She kept a straight face.

"Okay, I give up."

Making sure she was looking at him eye to eye, she gave him a sly wink. "It's an application for consideration of boy-friend status."

He almost spilled his hot coffee as he chuckled. "A what?"

"You heard me. Are you interested? Yes or no?"

"Yes," he nodded.

"Okay, I know all the basic stuff; name, age, sex – oops, gender, occupation, etc. You're a non-smoker, correct?"

"Absolutely." He leaned back in his chair; this was going to be fun.

"Marital status?"

"Single."

"Ever been married?"

Ed cleared his throat to give himself a second to think. "Well technically you cannot be single having ever been married. If one has been previously married, then one's status would have to be divorced, separated, or widower."

Keeping her eyes directly on his, she sipped on her coffee. "Ever been married?" she asked again.

"No."

She gave him the slightest of nods and took another sip of coffee. "Ever spent a honeymoon in Paris?"

His head rolled back and he looked for help on the ceiling. "Oh shit," he muttered.

"Is that your answer, Mr. Crowe? 'Oh shit' I mean."

He couldn't look her straight in the eyes any longer. He closed his eyes to think.

"Take your time, Mr. Crowe. I might ask for your autograph, what with you being a T.V. personality and all."

"There are some limitations involved here, Victoria. Why don't you tell me what you know?"

She was referencing the operation he had worked on the previous September in his role as a consultant with British Secret Service - MI6. Operation Remembrance's goal was to bring to light the involvement of the French Vichy government's active role during the Second World War in arresting and sending French citizens to German Concentration Camps, where thousands died in the gas chambers. Ed's role was to spend his 'honeymoon' in Paris with CSIS operative Pat Weston. The operation was more successful than anyone had imagined, resulting in television newscasts around the world of the fights that erupted in Paris as local skinheads fought hand to hand with Ed, Pat and the more moderate citizens of Paris.

Vicky spoke slowly. "My father has always been a worrier about me, Ed, and even more so after a recent major event that disturbed me. When he heard about you from Seana and Stephanie, he was duly impressed. Last week I let him know I planned on meeting up with you as a friend of a friend...well he decided to check up on you." She coughed to clear her throat and let the message sink in. "My father has a lot of friends in many high places, and it wasn't difficult for him to obtain a copy of the news-piece from the CBC about you and your, shall we say, honeymoon?"

"I er..." Ed tried.

Victoria interrupted "Now to be honest with you, he thought it was marvelous and wants to meet you - if I so choose."

"Assuming I pass the test as a potential boy-friend."

She gave him a wink. "Yes, assuming you pass the test. Just one more question."

"Do you want me to explain a little about Paris...so to speak?"

"Up to you, Ed. I know you're not married. I just wanted you to know what I know."

"The lady in the news piece is a friend of mine, and is engaged to my best friend. He lives in London, England, and she lives in Ottawa."

"I know. She's a civil servant, correct?"

Ed nodded. "Yes. She works for Export Development Canada."

"Sure she does, Ed. Now my final question. Do you have a girl-friend? That's an easy question I hope."

"Sure, that's easy," he muttered. "Let me think."

Victoria put down her pen, picked up her coffee and drained it. "Take your time. I've got all day." She paused. "Actually, I don't. My parents and I are leaving for a cruise this afternoon, a ten-day Caribbean. The limo is picking us up at four this after-noon." She looked at her watch. "So you've got about five hours before I have to leave. Is that long enough?"

"Hey, great," Ed said with enthusiasm. "Which cruise line?"

"Do you have a girl-friend?" She folded her arms across her chest and sat back in the chair.

"There is a special lady in my life, Victoria. Very special in fact. She lives in England. I plan on asking her to marry me. I can honestly tell you I have no idea what she will say. If 'yes', we will marry. If 'no', then I...I don't know."

She nodded her understanding. "This is a questionnaire for boy-friend status, not future husband. I appreciate your honesty."

"You're welcome. Which cruise line?"

"Princess. Give me your card. I'll share it with my parents."

Ed grabbed a card from his wallet and handed it to her. He extended his hand. "Thanks, Victoria; it was a pleasure meeting you. Have a great cruise. If your parents contact me, I will do my utmost to help them in their travels."

She slipped the card in her purse, put on her coat and walked to the door. "You passed the test, Ed. If, when I return, you want to phone me, I'd like that. I'd prefer you give me a quick kiss, but if you insist on shaking hands, so be it."

Ed took her in his arms, held her tight and gave her more than a quick kiss. "I'll phone you."

"Not a word to the girls."

"Not a word. Happy New Year!"

She gave him a quick kiss, and left.

He sat down at the kitchen table, unsure of exactly what was happening. Victoria was really a lovely person, which was obvious. But just as obvious was the fact that something, that 'major event', was troubling her. He shook his head and decided to play things as they arose and not jump to any conclusions. The phone rang.

"Merry Christmas, Season's Greetings, all religions included," he said cheerfully.

"Hi, it's me again," Victoria said. "You may or may not have a cell phone, but I do. I'm halfway home and I wanted to touch on a couple of things. Sitting in my car makes it easier to talk about, at least for me. Don't worry, I'm parked."

"Your dad's Jag?"

"No, my car. It's not a Jag, its German made"

"VW?"

"Try again."

"Hmm. Volvo?"

"That's Swedish."

"Porsche?"

"Correct."

Ed's eyes widened. "You're kidding?"

Victoria laughed. "Of course I'm kidding, it's a BMW." She paused a few seconds to change the subject. "Look I wanted to tell you about that event I mentioned, the one my father is concerned about. It wasn't really major – things happen – but I wanted to explain." She paused again. "So it was like this..."

Ed interrupted. "May I guess? It may make it easier."

"Guess away."

"You broke up recently with a boyfriend after a long-term relationship?"

"Worse."

"Ouch! You were engaged and it ended?"

"He dumped me," she said quietly. "He dumped me by telling me on a birthday card. Can you imagine that; a damn birthday card?"

Ed shut his eyes at the thought. "May I make an honest comment?"

"Sure, why not. Everyone else has opinions, why not my new friend?"

Ed took the risk. "I think your ex-fiancé is an arsehole, er excuse me; asshole. I think anyone that would do that to someone, *anyone*, is an asshole. In fact a complete and utter asshole. I'm sorry to be rude, but there you are."

He could hear her chuckling.

"You'd like my father. He said basically the same thing, just not as blunt. Thanks, but it's still a little tough to accept."

"I have a suggestion. Stupid perhaps, but I think it may help."

"Why not? What else are new friends for?"

He crossed his fingers. "When your friends ask you about it, you tell them that you were engaged to a boyfriend with a wooden leg and you broke it off."

She held the phone away from her, not believing what Ed had said, unsure whether to laugh or cry. She chose both. "You're crazy, do you know that? The girls told me about your play with words, but that's just plain crazy." She wiped her eyes, smearing the makeup running down her cheeks. "Crazy as hell, but I'll try it next time someone wants to console me. Thanks. I owe you."

"I'll make you a deal," Ed replied, thanking his lucky stars he hadn't made and lost a new friend in less than twenty-four hours. "You do a report on the cruise; food, cabins, entertainment, the works, and when you get back that'll be one reason for us to get together for a nice meal. My treat. Make sense?"

"Sure. Is there a second reason – to get together I mean?"

14

"Of course there is." He didn't expand, and she didn't need him to.

She felt good inside. "I think next year will indeed be a happy new year, Ed. I'm going to enjoy the cruise, do a super report for you and look forward to that dinner. Bye, for now."

She hung up.

CHAPTER FOUR

SUNDAY, DEC 29TH, 1985, 8PM

E d pressed the speaker button, wondering who would be visiting. "Merry Christmas, Season's Greetings, all religions included," he said.

"Ed, it's me Pat. Buzz me in."

Ed buzzed her in, opened the door ajar and stepped back. There was no reason for Pat to visit him unannounced. She lived and worked in Ottawa. They were ex-lovers, but she was now engaged to Ed's best friend and Ed was to be the Best Man at their wedding next May. Since she and Roy had become engaged, she was the happiest he had ever known her. She did not sound happy this evening. This meant business. Pat worked for CSIS, and while Ed's full time job was as a travel agent, he worked as a consultant for MI6; Britain's Secret Intelligence Service. But it made no sense that Pat would visit unannounced. He was worried, very worried.

Pat entered his apartment and pointed to the kitchen table. "Let's sit, Ed."

"It's Carolyn, isn't it?" Ed asked certain he was correct.

"I have some bad news, Ed…"

"Oh God almighty," Ed groaned. "What has happened? Please don't tell me…"

Pat spoke quickly and forcefully. "Ed, stop for a minute please. It's bad news, not terrible news." She took a breathe. "Listen to me and don't interrupt."

Ed nodded; only bad news!

Pat spoke with assurance. "Carolyn is in hospital in London. She has been hurt and is expected to fully recover: certainly in plenty of time for the wedding. She will be my Maid of Honor as planned."

Ed took a deep breath, nodding for Pat to continue.

"She has a broken arm and some facial damage. She was in Rome airport Friday when the El Al terminal gate was attacked. She was booked on a TWA flight. They share gates. She was not an intended target. I know that doesn't matter in the big picture, but it is important." She leaned over and touched his hand. "You okay?"

Ed did his best to smile "Yes, much better. I appreciate your coming to tell me yourself, Pat. That means a lot to me."

Pat winked. "What are good friends for, eh?"

"Coffee?" Ed asked.

Pat shook her head. "We don't have time. You're on this evening's 10:15 Air Canada flight to London. The limo is waiting for us downstairs. Go pack. We'll finish the conversation on the way to the airport."

Ed stood and walked quickly to his bedroom. "What about…?"

Pat waved him off. "What about nothing! I have it all arranged. I'm meeting with your boss tomorrow at 8am. Go pack."

Knowing better than to argue with Pat, Ed did as he was told.

CHAPTER FIVE

St.Thomas' Hospital, London, England Monday, December 30th 1985, 1:30pm

E d gently took Carolyn's right hand making sure he did not wake her. He watched her breathe slowly, now knowing how close she came to death. She lay on her back with her left arm in a cast that lay across her chest. The left side of her face was covered in bandage and tape. What limited part of her left eye he could see was black and blue, more black than blue. How one can be happy she is like this, he wondered, but he knew the answer. He sat holding her hand for an hour before she stirred, looked up at him with a feeble smile, and spoke with a squeaky voice.

"What kept you?" She squeezed his hand.

Ed shrugged. "Pretty busy at work. Couldn't just drop everything could I?"

She struggled to sit up and he adjusted the pillows for her.

"I must look a mess," she mumbled, combing her hand through her hair.

"You've looked better, Miss Andrews, but you're always beautiful."

Before she could reply, the door to the private room opened and her mother entered. Her entry reflected her status in the room. She was the mother; Lady Stonebridge; the decision maker on all matters – simply the person in charge. "Good afternoon, Mr. Crowe. You took your time getting here."

"So I've been told, Lady Stonebridge. It's nice to see you again. Better circumstances, perhaps?"

"Indeed, Edwin. Indeed." She shook Ed's hand. "I appreciate your being with us." Taking a deep breath, she took the lead. "We are moving Carolyn to Stonebridge Manor this afternoon. I will look after her at home, plus we will have made a bed available here for a more seriously ill patient. You will join us of course, Mr. Crowe, and you will stay at the Manor as long as you like. Your mother has been invited to join us for New Years, and I am happy to say she has accepted our invitation. Given the circumstances," she continued, looking at Carolyn, "I think we will have a joyous and comforting celebration with an expectation that 1986 will be just a little less exciting than 1985. I shall return." Without further explanation, she left the room closing the door behind her.

"I can see where you get it from," Ed commented.

Carolyn smiled a crooked smile. "Tell me what you know, Ed."

He took her hand. "Well, let me see. What do I know? I know I love you, two times two is four…"

She squeezed his hand as hard as she could. "To the point, Mister. To the point."

Her using his MI6 code name was welcoming, yet it also reminded him that they met through his involvement with MI6; her full time job was as a MI6 operative, with her father, Lord Stonebridge, being the head of MI6. He understood it was time to speak seriously.

"Pat explained as best she could. You were in Vienna working on behalf of the UN looking into Kurt Waldheim's military involvement during the war. You were selected since you speak German fluently and, perhaps ironically, because your father wanted you to be involved is something a bit safer than you have, we have, been involved with lately. Apparently you have some interesting reports to submit, but Pat wouldn't say what." He waited, but got no response except a smile. "So, anyway, you were heading to New York to report to the UN. You were sitting in Rome airport when the attack began, and you were one of the seriously injured. The attackers were Palestinians, but according to Arafat not members of the PLO. Several of the attackers died and several got away. Now Pat said something about your getting a couple of shots away, but when you woke at the hospital in Rome, your gun was nowhere to be found. She seemed to think that was good." He shrugged with a grin. "I guess I don't think like a woman...but then *that* is a good thing. How did I do?"

"Not bad. Apparently it was organized by Abu Nidal who heads up a terrorist Palestinian organization that is not supported by the PLO. This was not his first attack, and likely won't be his last."

"And the gun?" Ed asked.

Carolyn motioned her right hand to wave off the question.

"And the gun?" Ed took her hand.

Carolyn took a deep breath. "The Italian police kept it and made no comment about it in their report. Eventually we'll get it back via the diplomatic pouch."

"Because?"

"Why do you think, smarty pants?" She tried to smile.

"Either you weren't supposed to carry one or more likely, and I hope is the case, you hit one of the attackers."

Carolyn nodded. "Correct on both accounts. I'm not sure if I killed him and the police won't give my father any more details. It's a non-discussion point." She paused, not wanting to consider the possibility of actually having killed someone. "We'll never know."

Ed leaned forward and kissed her forehead. "Well in my humble opinion I'd suggest that you should be thinking along the lines that whether or not you killed him, the chances are you stopped him from killing more people than he did. Well done, Miss Andrews!"

"Will you stay for a few days, Ed, after the New Year I mean? I know you must be busy at work sending all those cold Canadians to warmer climes, but…"

"Of course I will, Miss Andrews. Just don't let me out-stay my invitation, from your mother's perspective that is."

She laughed awkwardly. "You don't know my mother very well, lover boy. She thinks you're the best thing that's happened to me since…"

"Paul Reynolds?" Ed interrupted, mentioning Carolyn's childhood friend to whom she was 'expected' to marry since they were eight years old; the two families being lifelong friends and neighbours. Carolyn had cancelled their relationship having returned from Turkey where she met and fell in love with Ed.

"Sometimes, Edwin William, just sometimes…"

"Sometimes?" Ed grinned.

She squeezed his hand. "Sometimes I love you more that others. Let's leave it at that."

CHAPTER SIX

STONEBRIDGE MANOR, ENGLAND WEDNESDAY, JANUARY 1ST 1986

The two families enjoyed a wonderful New Years.

During her brief visit, Ed's mum took long walks through the grounds of the manor with Lady Stonebridge. The weather was cool and damp, but it did not interrupt their pleasure of walking and getting to know each other better. While their current life-styles were significantly different, their childhoods had been similar. Both were too young to remember much of the war, but they recalled the 'joyous suffering' in the years following. Their fondest recollection was the day in February 1953 when rationing was removed from sweets. There were few sweets to be had, but the message was clear: not only had they won the war, they were now allowed to eat unlimited amounts of chocolate – as soon as it was available. This, as it turned out, was not soon enough.

Lady Stonebridge recalled US soldiers who had unlimited amounts of 'candy', dropping bagfuls off at her school. All the girls loved the soldiers she recalled, laughing, in spite of their dreadful haircuts and funny accents. More sobering was her recollection that when they visited the school with their much appreciated gifts, they arrived in groups of either black, or white soldiers; never mixing. It turned out to be a reflection of America that eventually led to an unfavorable perception of such a great country.

During his days at the manor Ed and Carolyn traveled around the countryside speaking of everything and all things, except what happened to Carolyn and the future of her career. She still suffered a slight hearing loss, but that was predicted for full recovery. Ed spent each night sitting by Carolyn's bed telling her stories of his customer's travels, or reading novels that had no need for killing and maiming. She held his hand and each time he slipped in the words, 'I love you, Carolyn,' she would gently squeeze his hand. After two misses of her catching these remarks, he would quietly slip down the hallway into his own bedroom, knowing she was asleep.

On his final night at the manor he read to Carolyn until 2am when she finally stopped squeezing his hand. He spoke in a whisper. "We'll get the bastards," he said.

To his surprise she opened her good eye. "Yes we will, Ed. Not for me, but for the people they killed." Without further comment or response from Ed, she fell asleep. He was now determined to live up to his promise, knowing full well that she was as committed, if not more so, than he was. He now felt comfortable about Carolyn's state of mind. As her mother had once expressed, she had a seemingly gentle determination that was often not fully understood. It was a determination that didn't waver; Churchillian almost, and that was a good thing.

Before leaving for Heathrow to return to Toronto, Lord Stonebridge, head of MI6, asked Ed to join him in his private office.

Throughout Ed's stay there had been no official discussion regarding the attack at Rome airport and the similar attack at Vienna airport that followed just minutes later. It was not for Ed to ask questions, he was aware of that. Besides he was here as Carolyn's friend not as a consultant with MI6, a role he had been fulfilling for almost two years.

When he entered the upstairs office he was not surprised to see Mr. Cooper, known also as the General, sitting at one of the two chairs directly in front of Lord Stonebridge's desk. It had been Mr. Cooper, Ed's boss at the time, who had recommended and encouraged Ed to take on the MI6 role, a decision Ed was forever to be thankful for. It had resulted in several interesting operations for Ed to be active in, but much more importantly to Ed, it had introduced him to Carolyn. Their lifestyles and backgrounds were significantly different, perhaps a difference that only England could produce. She was the only child of Lord and Lady Stonebridge, Oxford educated, accustomed to the pleasures of being raised and residing at Stonebridge Manor. She held a senior job with the federal government, in reality an MI6 operative. Ed was born and educated in the Kensal Rise area of London, received a secondary school education, and until he moved to Canada as part of his MI6 role, lived with his mother in a charming semi-detached house facing Queen's Park. Carolyn had attended Royal Ascot races wearing an outlandish hat, as was the tradition: he had watched the races on television, wondering how they managed to keep the hats on their heads. Upper class and middle class, as clear as day. But they managed to maintain their love and friendship in spite of their societal differences.

Ed and Mr. Cooper shook hands, exchanged greetings, and then sat facing Lord Stonebridge.

"Tell me, Mr. Crowe," Lord Stonebridge said opening the conversation, "what do you know of a certain Mr. Abu Nidal?"

"I know he was responsible for the recent airport attacks," Ed replied with authority.

"Very clever, Eddie," Mr. Cooper chuckled. "Never heard of him, have you?"

"Carolyn mentioned his name," Ed replied, "but am I correct?"

Lord Stonebridge nodded. "Apparently he is responsible, and in fact has claimed responsibility. He also has a habit of claiming responsibility of any and all terrorist acts committed on western countries. But in this case we believe him. When I say 'we', I mean our own intelligence, the CIA, and most importantly Israel's Mossad. He's Palestinian, but not part of the PLO. He runs his own splinter group that is named after him, the Abu Nidal Organization, which is committed to killing and maiming Jews around the world. He is, as they say, a nasty piece of work."

"And we can't do a thing about him?" Ed asked the question, knowing the answer.

"Not until we find him, Mr. Crowe," Lord Stonebridge answered, "and then you can join the long line of people that want to shoot him."

"Is that a promise?" Ed asked.

"You'll be in line right behind myself and the General," Lord Stonebridge said. "Now go back to Canada, enjoy the snow and skiing, and we'll see you at the wedding in May – if not before." Lord Stonebridge reached into his desk drawer. "Take this with you." He handed Ed a mobile phone. "Have to keep up with technology, don't we now."

The three shook hands and Ed left for the airport.

Ed was going through security when his phone rang in his carry-on bag. The security guard stood back and pointed at the bag.

"It's a phone," Ed said slowly reaching for it.

"Yes, we've heard of those," the man said sarcastically, "even in Southall where I come from."

Ed scrambled to get the phone. "I'm sorry, I didn't mean to..... Crowe's nest," he answered the phone.

"Hey, big guy," Carolyn said. "I just wanted to tell you I love you."

The security guard waited, obviously impatient.

"Tell me again." Ed smiled and handed the phone to the guard who listened.

"Very nice, miss," the guard said. "Can I finish boarding the plane now?" He handed back the phone.

"Love you, kid," Ed said, "I'll phone you when I get home." He clicked off the phone, looking at the guard. "My name is Crowe," he explained.

The guard nodded. "Surprised you can't get home under your own steam." He finished the search of Ed's bag. "You go straight home now." He grinned. "You know, as the crow flies."

Ed smiled as if he'd never heard that before, and boarded the plane.

CHAPTER SEVEN

OAKVILLE, FRIDAY, JANUARY 10ᵀᴴ 1986

Ed looked at his watch, it was three-fifteen. He had met with his last client of the day, and thought it would be a good time to get in touch with Victoria. As he reached for the phone, it rang.

"Ed Crowe here," he answered, setting Victoria's business card aside.

"Got your report," Victoria said with enthusiasm.

"Hey, I was just about to phone you." Ed replied, wishing he had phoned her earlier.

"Yeah, yeah, sure you were."

"I was going to phone you to see if we could get together tomorrow night…Honest."

"No."

"Oh!"

"But tonight is good. You're going to The Queen's Head, right?" He could almost hear the smile in her voice.

"Yeah…but I thought…"

"You go there as usual, and leave the rest to me. Play along. This should be fun. Both Stephanie and Seana are working tonight." She paused. "You are okay with this, are you? I don't want to seem pushy."

"I look forward to both seeing you and playing along. Can I book a supper for the two of us? Somewhere close by?"

"Wonderful, wonderful, Ed. I am so looking forward to this. See you later."

She hung up.

Victoria looked through the side door window at The Queen's Head, keeping out of sight. Holding closed her un-buttoned winter coat, she waited for the right moment. Ed was sitting at the bar chatting to Seana who was pulling a beer. Then Stephanie walked over to say 'hi', while keeping her eyes on her customers. Victoria forced herself not to smile and pushed the door wide open.

She walked directly to her three friends, holding open her coat as she strode, revealing a two-piece light green sequined outfit. It was her favorite.

"Oh, my God," Seana, gasped.

"Whoa!" Stephanie managed, as she almost dropped her tray.

"Evening, ladies," Victoria said with full confidence, "long time." She stood next to Ed, not acknowledging him. She pointed to his beer. "I'll have one of those please, Seana."

Stephanie shook her head, totally confused. "Vicky, you don't drink, and even if you did, a Double Diamond?"

"I've had a single diamond before, so why not a double, eh?"

Seana raised her hand. "Vicky, you okay? If you really want a beer..."

"Yes please," she answered, "one of those things," pointing to Ed's beer again.

Seana started to pull the beer, wondering what had happened to quiet, shy Vicky Kilgour. She put the beer on a beer mat in front of Vicky. "Vicky, this is Ed Crowe," she said quietly, motioning to Ed.

"You may recall we mentioned him to you. He's the friend we travel to the U.S with and share stories."

Ed extended his hand.

Vicky ignored it, but instead put hers arms around him, kissing him full and hard on his lips. Ed shrugged ignorance and then put his arms around her, holding her tight.

Seana held onto the bar her eyes wide open. Stephanie almost fainted.

"Hi, Ed," Vicky said as they separated, "nice to meet you. I used to be engaged to a boyfriend with a wooden leg, but I broke it off."

"Okay, I'm outta here," Stephanie said, shaking her head and returning to her customers. "I think I need a drink," she muttered to herself.

Seana pointed to Vicky and then Ed. "Okay you two, don't go away. I'll be right back." She left to serve others.

Vicky raised her eyebrows and grinned. "That went well."

Ed laughed. "Indeed it did. May I call you Vicky?"

"You can call me Vicky, and you can call me anytime you want."

"I heard that," Seana said, walking back to them. "What gives here?"

Vicky picked up her beer, put it to her lips, pulled a face, returned it to the bar and slid it to Ed. "Happy New Year, Ed."

"Thank God for that," Seana said.

Vicky took the seat offered to her by a fellow customer, and relaxed. "Well, it's like this. You ladies were always telling me about this English 'bloke' – whatever that is - who came to here every Friday night by himself. You said he was an okay guy, so on the last Friday of 1985, while you ladies were probably out partying, I decided to drop down to The Queen's Head to meet him myself." She grinned. "We went over to his place and we kissed a couple of times. The next day, the day I left on the cruise, I dropped over at his place again. I tested him out as a potential boy-friend, he passed, we kissed a couple of more times, and then I left. Oh no, I forgot. On the way home I phoned him to let him know about you-know-who, and now we're new friends." She curtsied slightly. "And tonight he's taking me out for dinner, and I have a special something for him."

Seana pointed to them again. "Don't go away. I'll be back." She left to fill orders as quickly as she could.

"You missed a point or two there," Ed whispered, picking up his beer.

"I know," she winked, "gotta keep them guessing. Where are we eating, new friend?"

"Seven-thirty at the Japanese restaurant just down the street."

"Good, good. It's usually nice and quiet in there and we'll have our own little curtained area. Very romantic."

"What's romantic?" Seana asked.

"Romantic what?" Stephanie added, returning to the bar.

"Ed will explain," Vicky replied. "I have to powder my nose." She left.

"Well?" the ladies asked in unison.

Ed repeated what Vicky had said for Stephanie.

"And what is the 'something special' she has for you this evening, Edwin?" Stephanie asked bluntly.

"A full report on the cruise. You know, as a travel agent, I might be interested in it?"

"Oh, okay," Stephanie nodded.

Seana leaned over the bar. "Ed, here's the deal. We've known Vicky for years. She wouldn't say 'boo' to a goose. She could go forever without starting a conversation. There's nothing wrong with her, she's just plain shy when it comes to mixed company. And then this. Yikes! Great to see, but it is a tad nerve-racking. All we're asking is…"

Ed interrupted. "Not a problem, ladies. I wouldn't do anything to make things worse. The wooden-leg thing was my idea."

"So are you her boy-friend?" Stephanie asked keeping her eyes trained for Victoria's return.

Ed shook his head. "No. I haven't told you, but there is a young lady in England that I intend to ask to marry me. So Vicky and I are friends, good friends, but that's all. She knows about my intensions in Jolly Old."

Seana took a deep breath. "Okay, you'll do until she finds a real boy-friend. Steph?"

"Fine with me. Gotta go. Here she comes." She left to serve her customers.

A totally relaxed Vicky rejoined Ed at the bar. "All okay, folks?"

Seana nodded. "Everything's just fine, Vicky. I liked the old Vicky, and I like the new one even better. Have a nice evening."

Vicky managed effortlessly her selected dish with chopsticks, and lifted her next bite like she was born with chopsticks in her hand.

"They're right, of course, I was always shy at school and I don't really know why. Once I got out with just the girls I felt a lot more comfortable." She popped a shrimp into her mouth. "Nice food."

They were seated in a quiet area of the restaurant and the curtains pulled around the table offered a gentle privacy.

"Nice company." Ed said, just about ready to stab at his food with one chopstick.

"Having said that," Vicky continued enthusiastically, "once I get going talking about the need for life insurance you can't shut me up. I can go on and on about term insurance versus whole life insurance, the benefit of par versus non-par polices, and I just love the guaranteed purchase option available on some policies. And..." Realizing she was going on and on, she stopped talking. "Sorry."

"Don't stop talking because of me, new friend. This meal could take me forever to eat."

"Thanks."

"Oh heck," Ed muttered, and picked up a shrimp with his fingers. "No wonder the Japanese are so slim. It takes so long to eat a decent meal."

Vicky pushed her food tray away and reached into her purse. "Here's the report on the cruise." She handed Ed an envelope.

Ed pulled out the document. "Wow, fifteen pages." He looked at the top page and read aloud. "The Royal Princess – The good and the not-so-good." He set it aside. "The not-so-good?"

"Writing the report on a day by day basis kept me thinking of you, Ed…my new friend. It just made me a bit lonely, that's all. The rest of the cruise was wonderful." She gave him a quick smile. "Don't get me wrong, please. It's just that the last couple of days before I left were so weird. What with me acting so brave at the pub, and then my phoning you the next day… it was so different. But I am so glad I took the risk. The entire experience has helped me think of the future, and more importantly perhaps, forget old wooden leg."

"As it turned out, I had to pop over to England for a few days over the New Year, so I can assure you my new year was quite a bit different than yours. I'll tell you about it some time, but for now, give me a quick verbal update on The Royal Princess."

"Well to start with I had my own cabin, and it had a balcony. Oh was it wonderful….."

Ed sat and listened for thirty minutes while Vicky covered the cruise day by day, almost hour by hour. He enjoyed every minute, mostly because she was so excited about it. Any shyness seemed to have disappeared, and they enjoyed each other's company throughout the remainder of the meal.

"Will you walk me home, Ed," Vicky asked as he helped her on with her coat. "It isn't far."

"It will be my pleasure, young lady," Ed replied. As they stepped onto the sidewalk, she slipped her arm in his.

"You may not believe this, Ed, but I have never been walked home after a date. This is a date, isn't it?"

Ed chuckled. "It most certainly is. Pray tell?"

She took a deep breath of the cold night air. "Well to start with all the boys I went out with on real dates had cars, and who wants to walk when you can drive, right? And then when I got engaged, well we were always driving everywhere. Old wooden leg was car crazy. Probably still is. He's likely dating a female car mechanic."

"Serves him right. I've never seen a car mechanic as good looking as you."

She hugged his arm, and they walked through downtown Oakville, along Lakeshore Rd. into the residential area. What little snow had fallen didn't hinder their stroll, but added to the quietness of their steps. They didn't speak much, each not sure where their friendship was going. The houses were still alight with Christmas decorations, some with larger than life-size Santas and many with deer families enjoying the large front gardens.

She turned and kissed him on the cheek. "This is it," she said.

They stood outside a huge house on the south side of Lakeshore, located directly on Lake Ontario. There were two gates with a U shaped driveway connecting them. Christmas lights were throughout the grounds and around the house. It had a beautifully decorated landscape. The house consisted of a three-story central section with two-story wings on either side. To the right was a three car garage. The lights were on in every room in the home and there were outside lights that lit up the house to reflect its beauty.

"Oh my good Lord," was all Ed could muster.

"That's my bedroom to the left on the second floor. I have direct access to the front driveway. Please walk me to my door, Ed."

She held him closer as he walked her slowly to her door. The doorway to her side of the house was built into a stone-covered archway with seating on both sides.

"Have a seat, Ed. I want to chat for a minute or two."

Ed sat. This was eerily reminiscent of his first visit to Stonebridge Manor, the family home of Carolyn. Vicky squeezed in next to him.

"I wanted to explain, Ed. I was hoping the girls would have, but obviously they didn't. Sorry."

Ed tried to laugh. "Stop saying sorry, Vicky. Your parents have a lovely home. You should be proud of it." He paused. "Having said that, I am a bit gob-smacked."

"I'm not an Oakville Princess, Ed. Sure my parents are doing okay, rich even. But I pay my own way. I don't pay rent; however, I took my parents on the cruise. It was my treat. Besides, and I don't want to sound too proud here, I made more than fifty-thousand dollars last year in commissions. I worked hard for that. Selling life insurance and mutual funds when you're just a 'twenty-something' in many people's eyes is not easy. Okay, I am proud of that. I am a qualified member of the Million Dollar Round Table, and that's not easy."

"I think you're pretty amazing, Vicky. I am so glad we're friends. Good friends."

"Kiss me please, Ed."

"Of course, now I should apologize." He turned, took her in his arms and gently kissed her lips. Then he moved quickly, kissing her cheeks, nose, and neck, returning to her lips with a deep and passionate touch. They reluctantly stopped kissing with her holding on, pressing her head to his chest.

She looked up. "Can we go out tomorrow night, Ed?"

"I don't know, Vicky. I mentioned my lady friend in England…"

"I know, I know. It's not a fair question. But please?" She sat up straight. "Look, here's the deal. You drop by tomorrow evening about seven-thirty. I'll introduce you to my parents, your future clients perhaps, and then we'll…we'll…go to a movie. That's it; we'll go to a movie. Or we'll go for a nice drink and you can give me your thoughts on my report. Just good friends, honest."

"You're a smoothie, you are. Will I need a tuxedo?"

"Of course not, silly. Now give me a good-friend kiss, and I'll see you tomorrow around seven-thirty."

Reluctantly he settled for a good-friend kiss and headed for home.

He got about ten feet away from the porch when she called after him. "Hey, by the way, aren't I missing out on something?"

Ed turned and shrugged. "Another kiss?"

"No not another kiss, cheeky. What about all this British-speak that the girls talk about. Snogging this and how is your father? What about the fruit stuff? Apples and stuff. Don't I rate?"

He walked closer, laughing. "That would be up your apples and pears. That rhymes with stairs."

"Eww, I see," she said with a sly smile and a nod to her door. "How would you like to climb my apples and pears?"

Ed stopped in his tracks. Vicky almost fainted.

"Oh, my God, oh, my God," she gasped, covering her face, "what a thing to say. I am so embarrassed. Oh, my God in heaven. I am so sorry. I wasn't thinking. I…"

Ed walked quickly to her and wrapped his arms around her. "It would be a pleasure to walk up the stairs to your suite sometime, pretty lady. And please stop saying you're sorry."

She looked up to him with a waif-like look. "Please don't tell the girls what I said. Please, please, please. They would never let me forget it. Pleeeease?"

"Maybe."

"Maybe?"

"Give me a real kiss, and it will stay a secret between the two of us."

"Oh, yes," she giggled, reaching up and kissing him as fondly as she could. As they were separating, she licked his lips and gently slid her tongue into his mouth. He held her tight as she tasted him, only reluctantly letting go.

"I'll tell you all about 'how's your father', and 'snogging,' tomorrow, pretty lady. Blimey you're a bird any bloke in Blighty would want a butchers at and be rightly chuffed, yeah?"

"Oh, Ed, I am so looking forward to tomorrow night. I'm sure not sorry I bumped into you."

Ed backed up a few steps, bowed, turned and headed home.

When he arrived at his apartment, he somehow knew there would be a message for him. He pressed the 'message' button before taking off his coat.

It was Vicky.

"Hey, bloke. Nice evening. Tomorrow will be even more fun. G'night, new friend."

He changed, poured himself a glass of red wine and stood looking south out the window. He couldn't actually pick out her house, but could see the area where she lived. It was *the* area to live in Oakville.

"What the hell am I doing," he mumbled, taking a large sip of wine. "Okay, I'll sort this all out tomorrow… for sure."

Feeling better, he went to bed without finishing his wine. Tomorrow was his turn to work Saturday morning and he wanted a clear head for work…and everything else.

CHAPTER EIGHT

SATURDAY, JANUARY 11ᵀᴴ 1986 10:30ᴀᴍ

"Crowe here," Ed said cheerily answering the phone. "How may I make your travel plans better."

"That's a new one," Carolyn said. "You could come visit me if you like."

"Carolyn, Carolyn, how are you? How's your arm, and how's that beautiful face? It's so great to hear from you. I've been meaning to phone, honest."

"Well, let's see," she replied, "my black eye is now a light shade of blue, my arm is still in a cast, and my mother won't stop bothering me and insists I stay in bed twenty-four hours a day."

Ed laughed. "Which, of course, you won't do. Tell me more, tell me more. If the other phone rings I'll have to take it and I'll phone you right back."

The other phone didn't ring and they spoke on the phone for nearly an hour. Carolyn outlined the slow but positive recovery process she was going through, the time frame of getting back to work, and listed the many books she was reading, had read, or was going to read. Ed listened to her, laughed at her jokes, and shared in her struggles to recover. When their conversation was over, after having expressed their love for each other, he was ready for the rest of the day.

Later, as he was leaving the travel agency for the day his phone rang. It was Carolyn.

"Listen I wanted to tell you something, that's a bit difficult to say."

He sat on the edge of his desk. "Okay, now I'm worried," he said.

There was a pause before Carolyn continued. "Lord and Lady Reynolds are coming to dinner tonight, you know the…"

"The parents of the boy you planned on marrying from age eight, yes I know who you mean." He closed his eyes, waiting for the rest of the story.

Carolyn continued. "Well it turns out their son Paul is joining them, er…but not his wife. Apparently they are separated and heading for a very nasty divorce."

"That's too bad."

"Yes, it is, but that's not what I wanted to tell you. When he found out about my 'accident' he sent me some flowers and phoned me a few times."

Ed shook his head. "That was nice of him."

"For God's sake, Ed, help me out here! I can't be rude to him; I've known him all my life. The Reynolds are my parents' best friends. I have to be civilized to him, don't I?"

"Of course you do, Carolyn. It's just…Has he asked you out?"

"For lunch, yes. Tomorrow. We're going out for lunch tomorrow. Look we're just catching up, nothing more. Ed, this doesn't change things between us. I didn't want to tell you, because I know how it sounds. But I feel I must tell you."

He took a deep breath and tried smiling. "I appreciate that. Hey, I drive down to the U.S. with two young ladies and share book readings with them, and I met one of their friends recently. She's going through a tough time after breaking up with her fiancé, so your message just comes at a bad time. I'm reading way too much into it. Why don't I give you a call during the week and you can up-date me on how things went?"

"Thanks, Ed," Carolyn replied, now relaxed. "Phone me Wednesday. Love you."

"I love you, Miss Andrews. I love you very much."

They hung up.

Carolyn smelt the roses Paul Reynolds had sent her. They were lovely.

Ed picked up the phone and dialed Vicky's cell phone.

"Victoria Kilgour speaking." She answered quickly and business like.

Temptation to put the phone down and not start the conversation flirted through his head. He set the thought aside.

"Hi, Vicky. It's Ed. Not trying to be pushy, but could we make it six-thirty tonight?"

She replied with obvious enthusiasm. "Absolutely, bloke. I'll be ready to go at six-thirty. I'll have my dancing shoes on." She chuckled. "Not literally. I don't dance very well."

"Great. See you then."

At exactly six-thirty Ed knocked on the front door of Vicky's parents' home. He heard her quick footsteps on the tile floor. She opened the double doors with extended arms and a beautiful smile.

"Good evening, bloke," she said enthusiastically. She kept her arms wide open for him to walk into them and give her a quick kiss on each cheek, European style. Her shoulder length blond hair was swept up into a French roll kept in place by what looked like a tiara of diamonds. Her light blue dress was tight enough to show off her slim figure without being overly dressy. With her high heels she was only an inch or so shorter than Ed.

"Take off your coat, keep your shoes on and come meet my parents."

She ushered him in, taking his arm and directing him through a large entranceway that was half the size of Ed's apartment and three stories high. The chandelier, if it ever fell, would kill. They arrived at double doors and they stopped before entering.

"You look very nice," Vicky said quietly. "Nice tie," she added, adjusting the knot. "Now my parents can be a bit odd at times, so bear with them. They are looking forward to meeting you, especially my father." She smiled. "Ready?"

Ed shook his head. "Probably not. But before you send this Christian into the lions' den, may I say how lovely you look?"

"You most certainly may." She curtsied.

"You look lovely." He kissed her quickly once more on each cheek.

"I like you," she whispered as she opened both doors, and they moved into a very large, beautifully decorated living room.

At the far end from the entrance was a large wall of windows and glass doors. Beyond them was a lawn, covered with an inch of snow, which led down to Lake Ontario. The room was furnished to allow three separate sections; the section to Ed's left was clearly for card-playing. The central area had the furniture in a semi circular fashion facing the lake. To Ed's right the wall was built around a large wood-burning fireplace, in front of which stood Mr. and Mrs. Kilgour. Ed's immediate reaction was that Vicky's 'bit odd' was a huge understatement.

Mr. Kilgour stood to the right. He was a large man; over six feet tall and built more like an aging athlete than an over-weight middle aged man. He wore a tuxedo with a large bow-tie and wore an eye-patch over his left eye. He looked, to Ed, like someone out of an Inspector Poirot movie.

Mrs. Kilgour, to the left, couldn't have looked different. She wore a long flowing white silk dress. Her hair was casually parted in the centre with a short pony-tail. She looked like a cross between a flapper from the 1920's and a love-child 'Granny dress' wearer of the 1960's. She nodded Ed a welcome and waved him over to join them.

"Mr. Edwin William Crowe," Vicky's father boomed, "welcome to our home. Our Victoria has told us much about you and I have done my own investigation, which I know you are aware of. Come join us for a special treat." Vicky put her arm in Ed's and led him to the special treat.

In front of the Kilgours on a glass-topped coffee table sat a Double Diamond. Ed couldn't help but be impressed. He shook hands with his hosts, thanking them for their generous welcome. Vicky walked quickly to what Ed was later to find out was a butler's pantry, and retuned with a plate of hot sausage rolls. He was duly impressed.

"My favorite food and drink," Ed said helping himself. "I am honored to visit your home."

Mr. Kilgour helped himself to a sausage role. "Do you know the best way to make sausage rolls?" he asked Ed, holding one for all to see.

"With sausage meat?" Ed replied.

"Touché, Edwin," Mr. Kilgour said waving his hand, "but the best way to obtain them is from the frozen-foods department. Neither you nor I could ever make such consistent and tasty sausage rolls, don't you agree?"

Vicky jumped in. "You had better say yes, Ed. Father has a large investment in the company that makes them."

Mrs. Kilgour joined in. "Too much salt in all likelihood," she added, "but quick, easy, and always a hit at a party."

"Ed and I are headed out soon," Vicky said. "You wanted to ask Ed a question, Father?"

"Indeed I do, indeed I do." He pointed to a card table across the room. "There is a file on the table, Edwin, which includes everything I have learned about you. There are no extra copies, and neither my wife nor Victoria have read the contents. Do with the file as you wish. I regret having to feel the need to obtain such information, but recent events and…" he motioned with his arm around the house and garden and shrugged. "One cannot be too certain now days."

"I am intrigued at the idea of seeing what is publicly available about me," Ed answered, but mostly he wanted to know what, if anything, the file reflected on his often last-minute trips on behalf of MI6.

"Having said that," Mr. Kilgour continued, "both my wife and Victoria have seen the CBC clip from their news department as it relates to you interesting trip to Paris last year."

"Very well done," Mrs. Kilgour added. "You should be very proud of both yourself and that very persistent young lady with you."

Vicky quickly spoke wanting to somewhat address the 'honeymoon' issue. "Ah, yes, that young lady is engaged to Ed's best friend."

Before Ed could respond, Mr. Kilgour continued. "Now in my obtaining that news-clip, Edwin, I determined that the CBC was in the process of pulling together a documentary of the Vichy government's activities in regard to their proactive detention and transfer of Jews and others to German concentration camps." He paused and popped a sausage roll into his mouth. "You may be interested to know that additional BBC material was to be an integral part of the documentary. You looked very good, I might add."

Ed nodded his understanding, making a note in his head to phone Pat in Ottawa as soon as he could get to a phone. If anyone could manage the CBC, it would take Pat's superiors at CSIS to start the ball rolling. "That is interesting," Ed managed.

Mr. Kilgour all but grinned. "However I did make it clear to them that, knowing you personally as I do, you would take all and any legal action required to exclude any details other than the news clip itself."

"Er, thank you, sir, I, er..." Ed looked at Vicky for help. She shrugged and smiled.

Mr. Kilgour raised his hand. "Two reasons. First, they no doubt would have emphasized the fact that you and your friend were pretending to be on your honeymoon, and neither of you deserve to be made to look like fools, especially given the success of your activities." He smiled and looked at Vicky. "And secondly, from a purely selfish perspective, I don't want Victoria to have to fend off jokes about dating a 'married' man."

"Oh, Father," Vicky groaned.

Ed interrupted quickly. "Thank you, sir. My friend and I will be forever in your debt. Her recent engagement would surely have been subject to possible ridicule. Again, thank you."

Vicky accepted defeat, but turned to her father. "And, Father, we're not dating, we're just going out."

Mr. Kilgour rubbed his chin. "Hmm…what do you think, Edwin?"

Ed rubbed his chin. "Gee, I thought it was a date; perhaps not. Vicky does have a strong point of view on things."

"Okay, I give up," Vicky responded, "a date it is. Now, Ed, if you'd follow me we'll get this date going."

Ed shook hands with the Kilgours and followed Vicky back toward the front door. "Grab your coat, Edwin William, and we'll go up the apples and pears…to my bedroom."

Ed did as he was told. He picked up the file folder from the desk and followed Vicky up three flights of tile stairs. At the top there were double doors.

Vicky tuned to Ed at the doors. "No naughty ideas please, young man. I have to put on some lipstick and grab my coat and boots."

"It never crossed my mind," Ed lied.

As soon as they entered her bedroom, she closed the doors and threw her arms around him. "Kiss me for God's sake! Hold me and kiss me."

They kissed and held on to each other for some time. She held her head against his body and giggled. "Unzip me, Ed."

"Whoa, Vicky, lets…"

"Unzip me, Ed. Please, and don't argue."

Reaching up, he lowered the zip on the back of her dress and then placed his hand firmly against her back and pulled her close. Her body quivered at his touch and she held him tighter.

"You will notice that there is no clip on my bra. The clip is on the front of my bra." She looked into his eyes. "Just so that you know. Zip me up please."

Ed zipped her up and they separated.

Vicky walked into the powder room and started working on her make-up.

Her bedroom was the size of Ed's apartment with windows on the two sides facing the front and onto Lake Ontario at the rear. The king-size bed was set against the wall facing the entrance. The room was decorated in shades of white with light blue chairs and furniture. It was impressive both in size and décor.

"Blue's your favorite color?" Ed asked.

"Yes it is," Vicky replied, selecting her coat and boots. "But if you're interested, my bra is black."

Ed nodded. "Thank you. That's good to know. Same color as your..."

"Yes."

Ed helped her on with her coat, wrapping his arms around her as she buttoned it up. "You are a very sexy young lady, Miss Vicky. But don't think for a minute you're going to have your way with me."

She unhooked his arms and turned to him with a wide smile. "I'm sure you're right. Now here are the evening's activities. I'll drive, since I don't drink. We're going to a bar of your choosing, and for two hours you're going to tell me all about yourself. Then we're going to a bar of my choosing and for two hours I'll tell you all about myself. Then I'll drive you home. Okay?"

Ed nodded. "Sounds like a date to me."

"Good. Then let's go down the apples and pears to my front door, and let's have a great evening...oops! a great date."

Any feelings of guilt in telling Vicky the 'official' reasons of how and why he had moved to Canada were more than offset by the fact that the story was close enough to the truth and nothing of importance, other than he was a special consultant to MI6, was in the way of sharing his life's story with Vicky.

"So let me see," Vicky said, thinking, "you were a travel agent in England, and now you're a travel agent here in Oakville. You met your friend Pat in Turkey, spent some time with her in Paris, and now she's engaged to your best friend Roy? Have I got that right?"

"Me best mate, yes."

She closed her eyes and nodded, deep in thought. "So at one time Pat was your new friend just like I am now?"

"Sort of yes and sort of no."

"Sort of?"

Ed sat up in his chair and leaned forward. "She works for the government…sort of."

Vicky laughed, shaking her head. "Very clever, I'm sure. But no matter, I 'sort of' believe most of what you've told me, and that's good enough. If my father accepts you knowing what he knows, who am I to ask?"

Ed wanted to move on. "Where were your parents going tonight, dressed as they were?"

"Swimming."

"Swimming? In Lake Ontario?"

"No. In our swimming pool in the basement."

He could see she was enjoying this, but he pressed on. "But they were all dressed up, like they were going to a fancy ball."

She reached over, picked up his hands and kissed them. "I told you they were odd. They dressed like that just for you. My father doesn't have a bad eye, and my mother doesn't live in the past. They were just having fun, knowing full well how difficult it would be for me to explain it all." She kissed his hands again. "But you know what? It doesn't bother me in the least to tell you about them. I like you way too much to let that bother me. Now drink up, and let's move on so I can explain my rather boring Oakville born- and-bred life story."

Ed turned to Vicky as she drove to her choice of show-and-tell location. "Swimming pool in the basement?"

"Doesn't everyone have one?" she asked.

"Er, that would be a definite 'no'."

"Actually it's not a full swimming pool. It's more like an exercise pool. You turn on a motor and then swim into the wave created by a turbine. There are also a hot tub and exercise machines down there. I often have girls-night parties down there; and no you cannot join us sometime."

"Never crossed my mind."

"You tell lies well," she said as they pulled up to park.

Vicky's choice of location was small, dark, and in the basement on a quiet street somewhere in Oakville that Ed had never been to before. Everyone spoke in whispers and Vicky asked for a table in the corner. She ordered him a glass of wine and they didn't speak until the waitress delivered the wine.

"Okay, here's the deal," Vicky said leaning over the small table to Ed. "I'm going to tell you my life story, but with no reference to my rather disastrous engagement." She waited for Ed to nod. "I'll tell you everything, well almost everything; I just don't want to get all tangled up with having to explain what I did when I was with 'him' or with the girls or with my parents. Please bear with me."

Ed leaned forward to reply. "As they say in the entertainment business, you're on; break a leg."

Vicky's head slumped to her chest. "Oh, my God. Am I going to have to put up with your play on words all night?"

"I'm just here to listen, pretty lady."

"So be it," she laughed, "so here I go. Let me start at the end for a bit. You've seen my parents' house, and it's a bit over the top. However we've only lived there for two years and that's since my father made a pile of money in the market over the last five years, mostly dabbling in LBO's – Leveraged Buyouts. My point being that we haven't always lived in as much luxury as we do now."

"Got it," Ed said taking a sip of his wine. "Did I tell you how lovely you look tonight?"

"Yes you did. Now please listen and stop paying me compliments. It confuses me...Although I do like to be confused from time to time." She shuffled in her seat to get comfortable. "I wasn't shy until I started school. I was short, tiny actually, super thin and ended up being called 'Skinny Kilgour'. Not very nice. That hurt."

"Well you've certainly blossomed into something rather lovely since then," Ed said.

She crossed her arms. "Not everywhere obviously, but I'm fine now. No one calls my skinny, so that's an improvement. Then my best friend left town when I was eight and I went into my shy mode again. So on I went through school not exactly Miss Popularity, but academically I did okay." She grinned. "Top of the class actually! Then on to university which was wonderful. No one knew me; I did well and had fun meeting new friends. I've only ever travelled in North America, so if you want to spend a few days in Paris with me pretending to be on our honeymoon, that would be fine...Don't comment, Ed; just a joke."

Ed didn't respond, but listened to Vicky describe the rest of her life story without commenting. He could see she was happy to tell all, and he was more than honored to know that she was willing to share her details with him.

"Sooo that's about it," Vicky said, "except to say that old wooden leg dumping me like a hot potato didn't cheer me up in any fashion."

Ed winked. "Better an empty house then a bad tenant."

"Perfect!" Vicky giggled, leaning over and kissing Ed on his lips. "That is clever. I'll remember that one." She returned the wink. "Besides bumping into you has been very positive. New friend, new perspective, eh? I'll be sure to thank the girls for mentioning you."

"They'll be chuffed." Ed said.

"Chuffed?"

"Happy."

Vicky nodded. "Well I'm chuffed too. So there!"

Ed finished his wine, indicating he didn't want another glass.

Vicky stood. "Okay, bloke, I'll drive you home. Let's go."

The drive to Ed's apartment was only five minutes, but she drove slowly to enjoy the gently falling snow which now lay an inch deep on the sidewalks where few used it. She pulled up in front of his apartment.

Ed leaned over to kiss her, but she held a hand out to stop him. "Aren't you going to invite me up for a coffee or cup of tea?"

"Now that's not being shy is it?" he asked.

"I've given up on shy. I'm taking up being a little pushy. Where do I park?"

Vicky let the way down the hallway to Ed's door. "Move it," she said.

Ed opened the door, hung up their coats and waved her into the apartment with a slight bow.

She didn't move. "What's Brit language for kiss?" She asked.

"Snog."

She wrinkled her nose. "Uggh. Give me a snog anyway. Just keep your hands to myself."

He didn't take the bait, but kissed her gently and escorted her into the sitting area. "Have a seat and I'll make us a nice cuppa tea."

She snuggled into the corner of the chesterfield, tucking her feet under. "Do you usually keep your place this cold?" She asked.

Ed worked on the tea. "I don't usually have a pretty young lady walking around in a short, sleeveless, but lovely dress. Not that I'm complaining mind you. Should I turn up the temperature, or will the tea do the job?"

"I'm fine really," Vicky said, "just an excuse to snuggle up to you. Come over and sit with me while the tea brews."

"Tea doesn't brew," he said sitting close to her, "it steeps. Beer brews."

Silently she sat up and put her feet on his laps. "Would you warm them for me," she whimpered.

Ed rubbed his hands together to warm them, and then ever so gently began rubbing her feet being careful not to damage her panty hose.

"Hold it, hold it," She laughed. "Close you eyes please."

Ed did as he was told. She jumped up, quickly removed her panty hose and sat back down, her feet back on his lap. "There you go." She tucked her dress under her legs. "No peeking," she giggled.

Ed massaged her feet pressing in all the right places. Vicky had to close her eyes and refrain from groaning with pleasure. When he ran his thumb up the back of her left leg to her knee-joint she couldn't stop her body from quivering. "Oh, my God," she groaned. "Have you done this sort of thing before, Ed?"

"Wouldn't you remember if I had?" he replied with a straight face. He then ran his thumb down the back of her right leg.

Her eyes opened wide at the feel of his hands running down her leg. "Oh gosh, not me, not me," she gulped. "I didn't mean me, I meant another female friend. Oh, good Lord, that is so wonderful."

"Nope." Ed said, returning to massage her feet.

Vicky took a deep breath. "You do like me don't you, Ed?"

Ed took his time to ponder the question. "Do you really think I'd be massaging the smelly feet of someone I've only just met if I didn't like them at least a bit?"

"Hey, hey, me feet don't smell," she laughed, swinging to hit his arm.

He gently raised her feet and kissed the end of each big toe. "Of course I like you, Vicky. Let me pour the tea, and we can chat about where we're at."

She tucked her feet under her and watched as he moved to the kitchen, poured the tea and returned with two cups of tea and a small plate of digestive biscuits.

"Here we go," he said handing her a cup of tea, "all important points of discussion should be over a nice cuppa tea."

Vicky took a sip of tea, watching him over the top of her cup. "Okay, so…" she started.

Ed interrupted. "And I'll have you know I'm a MIF person. That's important."

Vicky looked and was confused. "I hope I don't know what that F stands for, Ed."

"First, Vicky, milk in first. When you pour tea, some say it's the lower classes that put their milk in first. That's Brit talk."

"Ed, that is totally unfair. I'm trying to…"

Ed raised his hand and put his tea on the side table. "Vicky, you're right, that was rude. But let me say there are two things that I must keep in mind in this discussion. No, three. First; you are a very, very lovely lady. I think you are beautiful, super sexy, and a tremendous amount of fun to be with. Secondly; you know of my lady friend in England…"

Vicky jumped in. "Ed, for God's sake. You're not engaged are you, and surely you're not turning into a monk or something? Jesus!"

Ed nodded. "Point taken and the answers are no, and no. The third thing is about you, and you must know that. I don't want to, and never would, do anything that would hurt you as you have been hurt recently. The girls have asked me to be nice to you, and implicitly so has your father. I just…"

"Oh, Ed. Maybe you are too damned nice!" She moved closer to him and took his hands in hers. "Look I'm no angel. It's not like I'm a virgin for crying out loud. We did it a lot to start, although not so much recently. Please. Ed, I just want you to treat me like anyone else…well, any young lady that is. Okay?"

Ed nodded and gave her a quick kiss. "Turn around, Vicky." She turned her back to him. He unclipped the top of her dress and slowly, very slowly, unzipped her dress. Holding her dress at her shoulders he began licking and kissing her back all the way down to her panties. "Now, Vicky, pretty lady, we're going into my bedroom and I'm going to remove your dress and then you're going to undress me to my underwear. Okay?"

She nodded. "Oh, yes, please."

They stood, and taking her hand he walked to his bedroom, stopping at the end of his bed. He removed her dress and placed it carefully over the back of a chair. She took off his shirt then sat on the bed and carefully undid his belt, unzipped him and let his pants fall to the floor. Looking up to him with a beautiful smile, she removed his under-pants exposing his full erection. She held it fully in both hands and teasingly licked the top of his cock. "Relax," she whispered and gently took him fully into her mouth. The pleasure was almost unbearable as she licked and kissed him, with Vicky seemingly enjoying it as much as Ed. Slipping off his cock with a kiss, she slid to the floor removed his pants and socks. Keeping her eyes on his, she took him fully in her mouth again as deep and fully as was possible. He reached down and helped her to an upright position. He moved to sit on the bed with her standing in front of him in her black bra and panties.

"Do you like them?" she asked. "I wore them just for you."

"That's not just a black bra," he said, touching it with both hands over her firm nipples, "that's Crowe bait."

As she giggled he unclipped her bra and began kissing, touching and sucking her breasts like a hungry animal. She rolled back her head taking in the pleasure of his unending touch, holding his head to encourage him to never stop. He stopped only briefly to pull her onto the bed, and then continued in his hungry search for her warmth and comfort. He moved down to her stomach kissing, licking, touching.

"Don't stop, please don't stop," she groaned, reaching for his cock. "Touch me, please touch me, Ed."

He moved up quickly to kiss her lips, gently now. "Turn over."

She turned over onto her stomach and he started working on her back with gentle licks and kisses. He gently lifted her bum and she knelt comfortably as he moved into position behind her.

"Oh, Ed, I don't know," she said looking back at him, her face clearly showing concern.

"Relax, Vicky," he said reaching down to hold her small round breasts. He smoothly slipped his hands over her body across her back and into her panties. He held her cheeks and squeezed them nicely, her body moving slowly as he pressed gently.

"Please touch me," she groaned.

He moved one hand to her now wet loving area, and slid a finger into her. She moved slowly with his touch, never wanting his touch to end. He gently turned her onto her back, moving up to kiss and lick her mouth and lips. "Relax, pretty lady," he whispered. She closed her eyes and nodded.

Reaching under her body, he removed her panties in one motion. He slid a pillow under her back and moved down between her legs. She squealed as his tongue entered her, flicking from side to side. Her body shook and her legs kicked against his back as she struggled from reaching orgasm. "I want you in me now, Ed," she cried. "Please, please, now."

Ed moved into position. He looked down at such a beautiful lady. "Don't ask, Vicky. Don't say please."

She nodded knowingly and managed a sly smile. "Fuck me, Ed. Now!"

Ed moved swiftly into her thrusting as solidly, as deeply and as quickly as he could. In only a few minutes they exploded together and he fell into her open arms. They gulped for air, neither wanting to speak first.

"Wow!" she muttered. "Now what?"

"Would you like a digestive?" he asked keeping a straight face.

"Only if it's long and hard like you," she replied.

He stroked her face. "I hope I didn't...you know?"

"Well I expected you to make love like an English gentlemen, not a bloody sex starved Russian soldier, if that's your question."

Ed shook his head. "Look, I'm sorry if I..."

She covered his mouth with her hand. "Shut up for God's sake. We don't need you saying sorry now. Especially when I hope we both just had a wonderful time. I know I did." She kissed him quickly on his lips. "Having said that, I didn't know normal people did the sorts of thing we just did, and you know what, I don't care either."

He stroked her hair. "I hope we are...normal that is."

"Well if we are, *he* wasn't. Can I have that digestive now? The small flat one, that is?"

They sat on the bed munching on their digestives, having pulled up the sheet to keep warm.

"I'd like to tell you something, Ed, and I'd like to tell you now, while we're still in bed. It's personal, but I want to say it anyway."

"And I promise to keep it a secret." Ed said.

"You are only the second person I have ever made love to. When we first met, I wanted it to be that way. Now I've said it. Any comments?"

Ed finished his digestive. "You have lovely breasts, Vicky."

She fell back on the bed, pulling the sheet with her. "Then hold them all night, bloke. We may never do this again."

Ed lay down next to her and held onto her breasts as they fell asleep.

CHAPTER NINE

SUNDAY, JANUARY 12TH 1986

E d woke to find Vicky sitting up in bed with the sheet pulled up covering her body, sipping on a cup of tea. "Your tea's next to you," she said. "And yes, I'm a MIF type person."

Ed picked up his tea and took a long comforting sip. "Thank you, pretty lady. Did you sleep well?"

Vicky nodded. "I did indeed. I did however have a dream."

"Really? A nightmare?"

"Far from it. I dreamed that about three o'clock, I woke up to find you kissing my entire body, especially my breasts."

"Never?" Ed said amazed. "I had the same dream. Further I dreamed that you asked me to make love to you a special way. A lovely way, I might add."

Vicky giggled. "I want to talk to you about that, Ed. Seriously I mean."

"Of course."

"So last night," Vicky continued, "as we began our loving experience, I was a bit nervous when you had me leaning over with you behind me. God, this is difficult!"

Ed put down his cup and reached for her hand. "Last night was new for both of us, Vicky. I know what you mean. But don't feel you have to tell me things you don't want to."

Vicky took a deep breath. "I do want to tell you. I'm sure as heck never going to tell anyone else, ever."

"Then I'm honored."

Vicky kissed his hand in thanks. "When he and I made love and we were 'that way', at times he didn't do what you did at three this morning. He, you know, went higher. It wasn't enjoyable and in fact it hurt. So when you, when we…"

"Enough said, Vicky. I understand, and give you full credit for having the courage to tell anyone." He leaned over and kissed her now flushed cheek. "More importantly I do hope the three o'clock special was up to your expectations."

"Marvelous, Ed. Never better! Now can we clean up, have a slice of toast and I'll get on my way."

"I like it when you give orders, Vicky."

She laughed. "Me? Give orders? Right! But one more thing, Ed. Once we're out of this bed I don't want to talk about our love-making like we have just now. Okay? So if you have anything else to say that private, please say it now."

He thought for a moment. "Two points; you have lovely breasts, if you'll excuse the unintended play on words, and I want to tell you I love you in a very special way."

She dropped the sheet, exposing her breasts. "Kiss them please, Ed." As he leaned over and kissed her breasts, she whispered in his ear. "And I love you, Ed, in a very, very special way."

Fresh tea and a couple of slices of toast were a fine breakfast for the very happy couple. The conversation was a bit awkward, so Ed was unsure of asking, but needed to know more.

56

"Were you planning a honeymoon?" He asked casually.

Vicky replied immediately. "Off to Hawaii in June. Got our passports last September. First time out of North America for both of us."

Ed jumped at the chance. "I need to re-new my passport soon, which office did you go to?"

"Hamilton, for sure. Mississauga is way too busy. There are line-ups to find out which line-up you have to get into." She sipped her tea.

"Where is he now, Vicky?"

She shrugged with a laugh. "I don't know and now, more than I ever thought possible, I don't care. He mailed the birthday card, then left town. Apparently his parents don't know where he lives and neither does his, now, ex-employer."

"What's his name?" Ed asked. "Maybe I can help."

"Give me a piece of paper please."

Ed quickly grabbed paper and pen and passed them to Vicky. She wrote on the paper, turned it over and slid it back to Ed. They both left it at that, and she stood up to leave.

At the door to the hallway, she leaned over and kissed him with a peck on his lips. "Stay in touch. Keep in mind we can go for a coffee and not feel it has to be a date. If I drop down to The Queen's Head some Friday night, it will be to say 'hello' and share a drink, nothing else. And by the way, your file is still in my car."

"Oh, right," Ed said. "Why don't you hold onto it, and if I need to see it, then I'll need to phone you, correct?"

Vicky chuckled. "That's sneaky, young man. Sure, I'll keep it in my bedroom and I promise not to read it. And you know what they say about a promise?"

"A promise made is a debt unpaid..."

Vicky opened the door to leave. "You impress me more and more by the minute, Edwin William. You may not be too, too nice but you are a nice bloke."

She left with a wave and he could here her gentle voice as she walked to down the hallway. "There are strange things done in the midnight sun…"

Ed looked at the clock. It was just past eight. Just past one pm in England and Carolyn was having lunch with her ex-boy friend, ex-almost fiancé, ex-everything. He set the thought aside and phoned Pat at home in Ottawa.

As usual Pat answered the phone quickly.

"Ed, my boy, how are you?" Since getting engaged to Roy Johnson, Ed's best friend, Pat had never been happier.

He didn't want to waste time. "Wonderful, Pat. Can you do me a personal favor?"

"Hmm, is it legal?" she asked.

"I think so. Maybe you can tell me."

"Tell me what you want, Ed. If I can help I will."

Ed crossed his fingers. "Well I met this girl recently…" He outlined the details that were sufficient to provide Pat what she needed, but nothing of his and Vicky's personal relationship.

"So let me understand this, clearly," Pat said after listening to the story, "you want me to determine the passport number of this Philip guy, which you just happen to know was issued out of the Hamilton passport office last September, and then you want me to contact several international security departments to see if he is in their country. And you want to do this because he broke off his engagement to a girl you recently met and happen to feel sorry for. Have I got this right?"

"Right on." Ed said, fingers still crossed.

"He hasn't broken the law, robbed a bank, threatened to hurt someone; just broken off an engagement?"

"Correct."

Pat thought for a moment. "Okay, Ed, I'll look around, starting in the US, but only if you promise me this isn't in any way related to you - how do I say this? – increasing your personal relationship with this new girl friend of yours."

"Pat, she is not a girl friend per se, but more importantly I promise you there are no friendship-enhancement issues here. I wouldn't ask you if it in any way affected our friendship, which is of much greater importance to me."

Pat was impressed. "I'll poke around. Are you working on your Best Man speech yet?"

"As we speak," Ed laughed, "as we speak."

"May I…?" Pat asked

"Of course."

"Is she good looking?"

"Very," Ed replied, knowing there was more to come.

"Tall, short, blond, redhead?"

"Tall, blond, lives in Oakville, has a very good job and very wealthy parents."

"Oh my," Pat smiled, "sounds perfect."

"Alas, her ex doesn't seem to think so."

"Good answer, Ed. I'll get back to you." She hung up.

CHAPTER TEN

MONDAY, JANUARY 13TH
1986
2PM

"That was easy," Pat said, not giving Ed a chance to fully answer the phone.

Ed stood and closed his office door. "I am impressed. What can you tell me?"

"Well the easy thing is that he flew out of Toronto airport November 30th last year and arrived in California five hours later."

Ed closed his eyes and prayed he was wrong. "San Francisco?"

"Bingo. Now I'm impressed."

"It was something she said." Ed muttered.

"Look, can I ask her name? You've got me a bit worried here. For you, not her."

"Kilgour. Vicky Kilgour."

"Good lord," Pat said slowly. "You mean she's the daughter of Peter Kilgour...*the* Peter Kilgour?"

"That's my new friend. What else, Pat?"

"Are you sure you want to know? Of course you do. That was a silly question. He was smart enough to register with our Consulate General, which means he intends to stay there for a while." She paused. "They went to the trouble of taking a photograph of him."

"No doubt for a good reason." Ed said.

"The reason is because the photo on his passport didn't look like him. On his passport photo he had a full head of hair and no diamond stud in his ear."

Ed knew the answer to his question. "His head is shaved now, correct?"

"Yep, and it suits him. Big smile, good teeth."

"So he's…"

"He's what you Brits would call 'light on his loafers'."

"That would be the nicest description I'm afraid." Ed said.

Pat continued. "So listen, I can't tell you any more. Besides I'm sure you now have a lot to think about. If you're the one to pass this on to her, and it will come out eventually…"

"Excuse the pun," Ed interrupted.

"Good to see you've still got a sense of humor, Ed. If you have to tell her, I'd suggest you have a spare hanky and a big shoulder. I simply couldn't imagine…."

Ed rubbed his eyes. "I suppose the good news is that he didn't take off after they were married."

"Not one to correct your English, Ed, but I wouldn't use the words 'good news'. How about; the one positive in all of this…"

Ed felt a little better. "Good thinking. Thanks for this."

"Bye, Ed." She hung up.

CHAPTER ELEVEN

WEDNESDAY 15ᵀᴴ JANUARY 1986 7:30AM

E d ran from shaving to answer the phone. "I hope this isn't for duct cleaning," he said with a false smile.

"My, you're in a feisty mood," Carolyn said. "Should I call you back later?"

Ed swore to himself. "I am so sorry, Carolyn. Please forgive me. I was expecting to chat with you later."

"I see," she said cheekily, "and here I didn't want to wait any longer to speak to my...my...exactly what are you, Ed?"

"The man you love. The man who loves you. The man who misses you so much. The man..."

Carolyn smiled. "Ah, yes I remember now. How could I forget – the man who changed my life in so many ways. How are you, Ed?"

"Actually I'm feeling a little guilty about the way I responded to your telling me that you were going to have lunch with Paul Reynolds. Sorry."

Carolyn laughed a little. "Actually I felt happy that you were a tad put off, but also guilty that I was happy. See what you do to me, Mr. Crowe?"

"Can I ask?"

"I don't know, can you?" He could 'hear' her grin.

"Okay, may I ask?"

Carolyn spoke clearly. "We had a good lunch, you'll never guess where, and he asked me to marry him. Not a bad day, eh? He's the second person to ask me to marry them."

"You are a rotten bugger, Miss Andrews," Ed replied. "I'm guessing he took you to the Sun Inn at Little Kimble – where I originally planned on asking you to marry me – and I only pray that you gave him the same answer as you gave my best friend Roy Johnson who was the first man to ask you to marry him; that you were not in a position to say yes."

"Actually," Carolyn replied very slowly, "I told him….that I would not marry him and that I had another man in my life. So there!"

"I see," Ed said. "So who is this other man?"

Carolyn replied in her posh voice. "That, my friend, is for me to know, and you to find out."

Exactly the reply he was expecting, anything else would have been a disappointment. "That I will consider a challenge, Miss Andrews. If I may, how did he take it?"

Carolyn thought for a few seconds before replying. "I'm not sure I want to talk about it really. Suffice to say he likely didn't actually expect me to accept his offer." She swallowed to control her feelings. "The fact is we were talking about getting married since were eight years old, went through school and university with that in mind, and until some bloke came along everything was just fine and dandy." She paused. "And then he finally asked me to marry him and all I can say is thanks but no thanks. To be honest with you, I feel very bad about the whole process. Sorry to dump on you, but you did ask."

"Well there is a somewhat good side for him isn't there?" Ed asked.

"Really? So tell me the good side of going through a difficult divorce and being told by the person whom he 'has always truly loved,' saying no."

Ed cringed, wishing he hadn't made the comment. "Well if you two were to get back together, wouldn't his ex have more ammunition...sort of?"

"Well let me see," she pondered aloud, "why don't I phone him and tell him that. Maybe I could suggest he sing Monty Python's, *Look on the Bright Side of Life?*"

"Okay, sorry. Bad thinking. But there is a very positive side for me. Why don't we talk about something else?"

Carolyn nodded. "Yes. Why don't we? What happened to that girl you mentioned whose fiancé disappeared?"

Ed cringed. "Way too long a story. Another time perhaps."

"When we next get together perhaps?"

"Hey, when we next get together I don't want to talk about another young lady."

Carolyn lowered her voice. "After perhaps?"

"After what?" Ed grinned.

"Well, like I say; that's for me to know, and you to find out."

"Oh my goodness!"

"I'll leave it at that, lover boy. Keep in touch." They exchanges kisses and hung up.

Ed rushed to get ready for work.

Carolyn went back to reading a report on the various searches in place for Abu Nidal.

CHAPTER TWELVE

FRIDAY, JANUARY 17TH 1986
THE QUEEN'S HEAD.
6:30PM

Standing at the bar on a busy Friday night, Ed felt a jab in his back. "Stick-em up?" Vicky growled in a deep voice.

Ed lifted his arms, bringing attention to himself. "Okay, okay, you can lower them now," Vicky said, trying not to look too embarrassed.

Ed kept his arms in the air and turned to Vicky. "Take what you need, but let me live," he hollered, mostly for the benefit of the other customers.

Vicky decided another approach would work better. She put her extended finger to Ed's stomach. "Okay, drop 'em, mister!"

The grin on Ed's face and the whooping from the other customers had Vicky all but running away, but she held her ground. "I meant your arms. Pleeease."

Ed dropped his arms and the other customers went back to their own entertainment. "Nice to see you, Vicky. Bit too much blush on those cheeks me thinks."

"Very funny, bloke," she replied, waving her hand in front of her face to lose some of the redness. "Can I see you outside for a moment?"

Putting a beer mat on his half finished pint of Double Diamond, he grabbed his jacket and followed her to the side door. There was a small area outside somewhat protected from the weather. Facing each other, they were only inches apart.

Vicky pulled her coat around herself. "Now first I want you to give me a hug. But before you do I read in a magazine today that a hug should last the length of someone singing Happy Birthday. So you hug and I'll hum. Now please."

Ed knew better than to argue and was more than happy to hold her. As they hugged she hummed the slowest rendition Happy Birthday he had ever heard. They separated.

"Thank you," Ed said.

Vicky wasn't going to give up. "Ah, but we have a problem here. This is Canada, a bilingual country…so we must do it in French also."

Ed hugged her again and she hummed again, only slower this time.

Ed smiled as they separated. "I think that was very similar to Marilyn Monroe's birthday greeting to JFK. Rather sexy if I may say so."

"You may," Vicky grinned. "Listen, any news on the 'him' front?"

"Yeah, but not here. Okay?"

Vicky understood. "Okay, ten tomorrow morning. Your bedroom or mine?"

"Whoa…" Ed stammered.

"Okay, Tim Hortons on Lakeshore. I know we may never make love again, but I can try, right? I'm off for an evening with Seana and Steph." She kissed him on both cheeks. "See you tomorrow." With a cheeky wink, she walked to her car.

Ed returned to his beer feeling lonelier than he had been fifteen minutes earlier but more comfortable with their meeting location.

CHAPTER THIRTEEN

SATURDAY, JANUARY 18ᵀᴴ 1986.

E d arrived at the Tim Hortons at exactly ten, and found Vicky sitting at a corner table with two coffees in front of her. Ed gave her a quick hug and they sat facing each other.

"Nice time last night?" Ed asked.

Vicky sipped her coffee. "Very nice. We spent the evening talking about you."

"You're kidding."

She laughed. "Of course I'm kidding. We had a nice time chatting about girls' things and that doesn't include you, or any bloke for that matter."

"Good," Ed said, slipping a piece of folded paper across the table. "I know this may sound weird, but would you go to the ladies' room and recite, out loud, what's on that piece of paper three times, looking into the mirror and speaking louder each time. You're an army general, okay?"

She shrugged. "Sure, why not."

Removing her coat she walked into the ladies'. There was no one else around. She unfolded the piece of paper, read the words to herself, looked into the mirror and spoke:

"There are men in the ranks who will stay in the ranks and I'll tell you why. Because they don't have the ability to get things done."

She took a deep breath and repeated, this time louder:

"There are men in the ranks who will stay in the ranks and I'll tell you why. Because they don't have the ability to get things done."

She smiled, took a deeper breath, and almost shouted:

"There are men in the ranks who will stay in the ranks and I'll tell you why. Because they don't have the ability to get things done!"

"Okay!" she said aloud, and walked back to their table. Standing with her hands on her hips she looked down at Ed. "Okay, soldier, give me that report and give it to me now!"

Ed looked around at the curious looks they were getting. "Have a seat, Vicky."

Vicky sat with her hands still on her hips. "Now, Ed."

Ed took a sip from his coffee. "Yes, ma'am." He leaned forward to speak. "He's in California…San Francisco, actually."

"Really? Why there?" Vicky asked

Ed moved closer. "AC/DC?"

Vicky shook her head. "What do they have to do with it?"

Ed rubbed his forehead. "Not the band. Forget that. He's shaved his head and he has a diamond stud in his ear."

"Oh my God," Vicky gasped covering her mouth with both hands. "You mean he's gone queer?"

Ed looked around smiling at the people that had turned to watch them. "Ssshhh, Vicky. I don't think he's 'gone' queer, as you put it. I think he always was and has now has decided to live the life he wants to, not how other people want him to live his life."

Vicky shook her head. "He was a Toronto cop for crying out loud. Oh my God." She lowered her head and Ed could hear her mumbling, "There are men in the ranks, there are men in the ranks, there are men in the ranks." To Ed's surprise she raised her head and had a broad smile on her face. "Well at least we know now. All I have to do is tell my parents. That won't be easy."

Ed reached over and took her hands in his. "They already know, Vicky. I phoned them just before I came here.

"Oh my. And?"

"They were surprised, but more relieved I think."

Vicky closed her eyes and two small tears slipped down her cheek. Ed reached over and wiped then away with his thumbs. "Don't be too sad, young lady. You've got your entire life ahead of you."

She sniffed to stop crying. "The tears are for Phil. He must have been so unhappy to be living the life he had here. I only wish him the best….There are men in the ranks, eh?"

Ed nodded. "Yes, there are. Why don't we both drive to your place, I'll wait outside while you touch base with your parents, and then we'll drive to Niagara-on-the Lake for lunch and do some post-Christmas shopping? I'll drive."

"You're an okay bloke, Ed. Lunch on me. I'll talk about insurance for ten minutes and then I can claim the expense for tax purposes."

Ed waited for twenty minutes, far longer than he had expected, for Vicky to have a quick visit with her parents to tell them the news. When she left the house she exited from her own private entrance. She walked up to the car with a smile and a file in her hand. "Pop the trunk," she asked. She put file in the trunk and got in the passenger seat with a knowing grin. "That's your file, Ed. I didn't read it and now for sure I don't want to. Drive."

Ed turned left on Lakeshore, biding his time and waiting for an explanation. Vicky didn't speak until they were on the QEW heading west.

"So…" she started, "I told my parents that I was okay with it all, and then guess what my father did?"

Ed thought for a moment about her rather eccentric father. "Gave you a big hug and told you I was a better friend?"

Vicky shook her head. "Next time maybe. No, he phoned Phil's parents to tell them and guess what?" She didn't wait for a response. "They already knew. You were, are, correct. He's living in San Fran with a boyfriend, but he calls him a partner. Phil phoned them last night. His parents were happy for him to phone, but really mad at him for what he did to me."

Ed nodded. "That's nice."

She turned to face Ed. "Yeah, that's nice, but here's the big deal. The fact that you could find that out, well to me that's a little scary. So, your file is in the trunk. I don't want that anywhere near me, young man. I'm afraid I just might read it and find out things about you I don't want to know. What do you say about that?"

Ed shrugged. "Nothing scary about me, pretty lady. Just a regular hard-working travel agent. Want to stop at Tim's for a coffee?"

She jabbed him in his arm. "Oh yeah, what about the time you told the girls that the reason you had your head all bandaged up last year was because you had to deal with three drug bad-guys? What about that then?"

"Maybe a doughnut with the coffee?"

"I'll have a bagel please."

Twenty minutes later they were enjoying their bagels and coffee with Lake Ontario to their left and the Ontario wine district to their right. It was a bright, sunny, cold day.

"So I have a question for you," Vicky said, licking her fingers clean. "When do you plan on asking your very lucky lady friend in England if she will marry you?"

"Next May," he replied.

She finished her coffee. "That is a nice time of year to get engaged. Good for you. I hope it goes well…But what if it doesn't? What if she says no?"

He thought about the question. He had asked himself the same question a hundred times, but had yet come up with an honest answer.

Before he had time to reply he heard her mutter under her breath, "There are men in the ranks…"

"I think I'll join the French Foreign Legion and become one of those 'men in the ranks'."

Vicky laughed. "I suspect not, Mr. Crowe, I suspect not. A new James Bond perhaps, but no man in the ranks."

"We shall see."

"Fair enough, Ed. And by the way I owe you one for helping me out with Phil. And when I say 'one' I mean a sleep."

"Sorry?" Ed asked.

"I mean a sleep-over, big guy. Your place or mine. No rush. If you phone me in May, I'll put two and two together…and perhaps get a three-o'clock special in the deal."

"You are a very cheeky, young lady. I suspect by May you'll have more boyfriends wanting your attention than you will know what to do with. Now let's enjoy a nice tax-deductible lunch and you can tell me all about life insurance."

"Yes, Mr. Potential Customer." She was delighted at the thought of talking insurance.

"And by the way, cheeky young lady, the article on the timing of Happy Birthday was in reference to brushing one's teeth, not hugging blokes."

"Hey, six of one, eh? They're both good for you. You complaining?"

"Never."

"Then we'll keep it as it is. But only in private. I am a lady you know."

Ed nodded. "Every inch a lady."

She kept her lips together and held her tongue….something Ed had not done the previous Saturday night.

After doing little in the way of shopping, they ate at a local restaurant, selecting a table by the window to enjoy people-watching.

Vicky reached for Ed's hand. "Hold out you left hand face up, Ed, I want to show you something."

Ed held out his hand. Vicky laid her left hand under his and gently placed her right hand on the top of his hand. "Now close your eyes and think of nice things. Just relax."

He closed his eyes and relaxed, wondering what she was doing.

She spoke softly, almost in a whisper. "This is called TMII, transformational meditational inter-body in-sighting." She very gently moved her right hand in circles over his hand, their skins barely touching. "Relax and think good thoughts," she whispered, "nice and easy, nice and easy." After several minutes she squeezed his hand between hers and then took them away. "Okay you can open your eyes now," she said.

Ed opened his eyes with a wide smile. "That felt nice. Thanks. Now what?"

"Ah," she said, leaning close to him, "I just read your mind. And what I found out was that our making love last weekend was the best thing you've enjoyed all year. What do you say about that?"

It was easy for Ed to agree, given the suffering that Carolyn had endured, and he didn't want to remind Vicky it was only eighteen days into the year. "I would have to agree, Vicky. You're very clever, I must say. Actually I've heard of TMII before, only under another name – FIBS. The FI stand for Female Initiated!" He winked. "But your insight is correct, and again, I thank you."

"We could always elope, you know," Vicky said, sipping on her very hot cup of tea.

Ed put his cup down, spilling tea as he did. "Excuse me?"

"If she says no in May, we could elope. Get married. Travel the world. What do ya think?" She raised her eyebrows to show off her baby blue eyes. "Could be fun."

He picked up his cup, and keeping his eyes on Vicky, took a long sip. "Well there could be a lot worse things in the world than being married to you, I'm sure," he said.

"Gee thanks. You know how to make a girl feel wanted, don't you?" She wiped away a make-believe tear.

Ed smiled. "*If* she says no and *if* you don't have four or five young men battling for your attention, then maybe we can go out on a date, okay?"

Vicky grinned widely. "Sure, but forget the 'maybe'. We will go out on a date. Now…how much life insurance do you have on your life?"

At Vicky's request Ed drove back to Oakville the scenic way. Staying off the QEW he meandered through Ontario's wine country. Vicky pointed out the workers in the fields collecting the now frozen grapes to be used in the local specialty; Ice Wine. She treated them to coffee at Tim Hortons in the small community of Winona, and asked him to pull over once they were back on the quiet country road. Ed pulled over, turned to Vicky and waited.

"So look, Ed, I have something to say to you. Please do not reply, verbally anyway. I want to make my point. No discussion. No response. Just listen, okay? Nod your head if you agree."

Ed nodded his head.

Vicky continued. "Okay, so here's my point. I want us to make love again, reasonably soon. I want that to happen for two reasons. First, and most importantly, it seems to me if we don't do it again, we'll always consider what happened as a one-night-stand. That is totally not true and not acceptable to either of us, of that I'm sure. Nod if you agree."

Ed nodded.

"Good. Thanks for that. Now secondly I want to do it again because I liked it so much, as I'm sure you did." She smiled. "Especially the three o'clock special. Now I know, and I know that you know, that I haven't had the liveliest love life; especially lately. Now you changed that, and all I'm asking is that it happens at least, and I stress at least, one more time. Nod if you understand, *and* think that I'm not an idiot."

Ed nodded.

She reached over and gently touched hid face. "Good. Thanks again. Drive on, bloke."

Ed drove on, considerably more at ease than he had been before they had pulled over. After a few minutes he began humming Happy Birthday and Vicky felt super happy.

Ed pulled up in front of Vicky's entrance to her parents' house and slipped the gear into neutral. He turned to her and took her hand. "I would like to say something, young lady. Same rules please."

Vicky nodded.

"The other day, after we made love, I told you that I loved you in a very special way. I meant that, Vicky. It wasn't just the occasion. Of course I want us to make love again. But I don't want to get us, or me anyway, to a level that makes it difficult to not make love any more. I don't want to hurt your feelings, and to be blunt, I don't want you to hurt my feelings. This may sound all rather wimpy, but I'd rather look at it as thinking that our relationship is tenuous and that is a good thing. If it were on more solid ground, then I can only foresee the huge possibility of one of us having our feelings hurt big time, and for sure you don't need that again. Nod if you understand, *and* think that I'm not an idiot,"

She nodded.

"Thanks," Ed said. "Now give me a kiss."

She pointed to her mouth, and raised her eyebrows.

Ed laughed. "Yes, of course you can speak."

"Before you give me a good-bye kiss, Ed, here's the deal." She looked at her watch. "It's ten past two. I'm going upstairs – after we kiss good-bye – and I'm going to change my undies into the sexiest undies I have. I'm going to be standing outside your door at three o'clock, in forty minutes. I will not knock, just stand and wait. If you open the door we will make love for the last time, or at least the last time until May. If you don't open the door, I'll go shopping. That can be a lot of fun also. Now give me a kiss, bloke, and be on your way."

They kissed quickly. She slipped quietly out of his car, walked to her door and entered without looking back.

CHAPTER FOURTEEN

SUNDAY, JANUARY 19ᵀᴴ 1986

"You phoned?" Pat asked.

Ed walked with his new mobile phone toward the window, wanting to think through his wording. "Yes. Thanks for getting back. I have an important issue to talk to you about."

For a change, Pat was relaxed. "Can't make it to the wedding?"

"I want to kill Abu Nidal. I want you to help me do that. And no problem with the wedding, I'll be there with bells on."

Pat waited for more, but nothing was forthcoming. "Would you like me to fly down so we can chat about it?" she asked.

"What's to chat about?"

"Do you know where Great Yarmouth is, Ed?"

Ed shook his head, not understanding the question. "Yes, of course I do. It's a great bird watching place. I don't …"

"But did you know that seventy-one years ago today, in 1915, the Germans bombed the town, the first aerial bombing in British history?"

"Are you trying to tell me to bugger-off, Pat?"

"No, Ed, I'm trying to tell you that if the British didn't see a bunch of Zeppelins cross the English Channel during a time of war, it's quite likely that one man can hide from all the spy agencies in the world, if he has plenty of help and support."

Ed thought for a moment. "Where did you come up with that piece of interesting, but useless, data?"

"Ever heard of the Internet?"

"Of course I've heard of it."

"Get on it, Ed. You'll thank me for this recommendation in the years ahead."

"Pat?"

"Yes, Ed."

"About Abu Nidal…"

"Take a seat, Ed. Please."

He looked around wondering if there was a camera in the room. He sat. "Okay, I'm sitting."

"Good. Now listen. If I told you everything I knew about our Mr. Nidal, the battery in your cell phone would run out. Like many in the industry, I'm working on getting him and bringing him to justice – or killing him, whichever comes first. He has lots of enemies including the PLO, in fact especially the PLO. But he also has lots of friends, including Gaddafi. He has master-minded a great number of terrorist attacks, plus has claimed responsibility for some he was not involved in. We will get him; it's just a matter of time." She paused. "Now, Ed, if you think I can make it happen that you're there, ahead of everyone else, to shoot him, then I thank you for your confidence, but suggest you shake your head just a little."

Ed licked his lips like a cat licking its wounds. "Okay, I'm sorry…"

Pat quickly interrupted. "Don't apologize for a moment, Ed. I seem to recall being told that *you'd be there* right behind Lord Stonebridge and the General. We'll I'll be right behind you making sure your aim is good; or at least better than your first shooting experience." She was referring to his less than perfect aim at shooting the Libyan soldier who had killed a female police officer from the Libyan Embassy in London in 1984.

He laughed, relaxed now. "Thanks. You made your point."

There was a pause that got Ed thinking. It seemed Pat wanted to say something, but was reluctant to do so.

"What is it, Pat? What's going on?"

"Having said all of the above..." she started.

"Please, Pat. This means a lot to me."

"Well....there is a report that while we don't know where Abu Nidal is at this time, one of the shooters that got away from Rome airport is, how do I say this, running out of friends?"

"I want in, Pat. I want in."

"No promises, Mister," Pat said, now using his code name and making the discussion official.

"Done! Thanks, Boss." It was now a working situation and as much as possible, emotions had to be set aside.

"By the way, how did the discussion go with your non-girlfriend girlfriend?"

"Very well, thanks. She was impressed. Took me out for lunch. We talked about life insurance."

"Very romantic, I'm sure," Pat said, not believing him in the least.

"So what's next, Boss?"

"I'm visiting my parents this weekend; I'll see you at The Queen's Head, Friday at 6."

"I'll be there!"

"Like that's a surprise," she added.

"Hey, what about..." Ed asked quickly.

"I'll wear a different shade of lipstick."

He smiled, turned off his phone, and pumped the air with his fist. "I'm coming; ready or not," he said aloud, repeating the words he had used a thousand times playing hide-and-seek as a child.

CHAPTER FIFTEEN

THE QUEEN'S HEAD
FRIDAY, JANUARY 24TH. 1986
6:45PM

P at joined Ed at a table in one of the corners, far from the bar where she had expected him to be standing. She sat with her back to the rest of the tables and motioned to the bag at his feet.

"Plenty of clean underwear?" she asked.

"No dirty underwear."

Pat laughed. "Very funny. You look relaxed."

"You look very nice tonight." Ed kept a straight face.

In fact he hadn't immediately recognized her when she had entered the pub. Her short brown hair was replaced with a long blonde wig, her breasts had been pushed up and were overflowing her low cut top, and the four inch heels made her look considerably taller than her five feet. Her skirt was tight, very tight.

She leaned forward and whispered, "The name's Ann."

"Hi, Ann," Ed nodded. "Nice to see you again." He waved over their waitress Stephanie and ordered two beers. Pat pulled a face, but knew better than to order her regular winter drink; Caesar, with lots of ice.

When Ed and Pat had worked together on his first operation, *Operation Niagara*, they had regular drinks at The Queen's Head. Her name was Pat Wilson then, not her real name, and officially she had been killed in a bomb explosion in her apartment along with an *unknown male*. For the bad guys, the unknown male was Ed. To the rest of the world it was simply an unknown male. A change of lipstick shade wouldn't have done it, but this change of appearance was a winner. She got lots of looks from the men in the pub, but clearly no one recognized her. Ed had to take a second look when he first saw her, and they had been lovers in the past. All history now, but no regrets on either side.

Stephanie returned with their beers. She nodded to the bar. "There's someone to see you, Edwin."

Ed looked up and Pat turned to look. Vicky was standing at the bar with a big smile and waving an envelope. Ed stood and motioned he would join her at the bar. "Excuse me, Ann," he winked, "that's my insurance agent."

Pat raised her eyebrows but kept her thoughts to herself.

The bar area was very busy. Ed gave Vicky a quick hug, and motioned for them to move to the vestibule where they could speak without having to speak extra loud to hear each other.

"Hi, bloke," Vicky said. "Long time no see." She gave a wide smile and held it.

"Look about last Saturday," Ed mumbled. "I wanted to open the door, but...you know... I, er..."

"No matter," Vicky said, now feigning hurt feelings, "I had to be put in my place sometime in my life."

"Vicky, please. I..."

She raised her hand put a finger to his lips. "I'm kidding, Ed. I think you made the right decision for both of us."

Ed nodded his thanks. "How was the shopping?" he asked gingerly.

Vicky waited until Ed's friends Bill and Ann were behind her heading into the pub. "Well it wasn't an orgasmic experience if that's what you're asking." She spoke louder than was necessary, and then went back to a wide grin.

Bill and Ann quickly entered the pub. Ed closed his eyes not sure how to respond. He didn't need to. Bill poked his head out of the door. "He is English, you know. That might explain things." he ducked back in.

"You owe me big time," Ed laughed shaking his head.

"Yes, I know," she chuckled, "and I know how to pay off, don't I?" She handed him an envelope. "Here's the quote for your life insurance. Have a look, and if you're interested…"

Ed interrupted. "Look I have to leave town for a while. Can I give you a call when I get back?"

"Of course." She nodded toward the bar. "Travelling with that good looking blonde, are you?"

Ed shook his head. "No, she's a work associate."

Vicky closed one eye and gave a suspicious look.

"Only one blonde in my life," Ed smiled, giving her a quick kiss on her cheek. "I'll get back to you as soon as I'm back in town."

Vicky nodded. "Promise?"

Ed crossed his heart. "Cross my heart and hope to die."

"Then sign the application," she said pointing to the envelope.

Ed put the envelope in his back pocket. "Bad choice of words. I'll phone you as soon as…"

Vicky gave him a quick hug and kiss. "Be careful in your travels, bloke."

She turned and left.

"Your life insurance agent, my behind," Pat remarked as Ed sat and took a well deserved sip of his beer.

Ed shrugged. "That's who she is."

Pat leaned forward. "That young lady is Victoria Kilgour. You can't fool me. Remember I looked up her passport information for you."

"That's correct," Ed said with a wide grin, "but she is also my life insurance agent. Got a quote in my pocket."

Pat waved her hand to end the conversation. "Let's talk business, Mister."

"I'm all ears."

"Do I need to talk to your boss?" Pat asked.

"No, I'm on a week's vacation."

"Very nice," Pat said, raising her eyebrows "Isn't it a bad time of year for a travel agent to be taking time off?"

"Priorities," Ed replied.

Pat looked at her watch. "You're on the nine-twenty flight to London. I booked you in first class. You owe the difference from business class. I'll charge it to your credit card."

Ed nodded.

"You'll be met at Heathrow and then you're heading on to Damascus in Syria. I don't know how they plan on getting you there. You'll need a visa, and your London contact will have it for you. What do you know about Syria?"

Ed shrugged. "Not much. Arab, Muslim – mostly Sunni. Problems with Kurds. Leader not a nice person."

Pat gave him an envelope. "Syria 101. Read it, remember it, and then eat it."

Ed gave her a look.

Pat laughed. "Okay, just destroy it. I've always wanted to say that."

"Anything else?"

"Carolyn..."

Ed opened his arms, gesturing for more.

"The scar on her face is still very obvious, as is the bend in her left arm."

"And?"

"She will be very self conscious about her face."

"I understand that. I..."

"No you don't, Ed. You may think you do, but you don't."

"Okay, help me out then."

"When you see her, you give her the European kiss, once on each cheek. Then you never mention it or her arm."

"Okay."

"Okay's not okay. Tell me you promise to do as I say."

"Pat, for God's sake…"

"Promise!" she said louder. Then she leaned forward. "And it's Ann."

Ed bowed his head to apologize. "I promise, Ann. I promise."

"Then let's go," Pat said, pushing away her unfinished beer. "Let's get you to London."

CHAPTER SIXTEEN

SATURDAY, JANUARY 25TH, 1986 HEATHROW AIRPORT, LONDON.

E d shook hands with Lord Stonebridge, Mr. Cooper, and Carolyn. No-one spoke at length, just mumbled greetings. Lord Stonebridge led them to a room marked 'Airport Security'. It was windowless and not inviting, no chairs or tables, just a grey silence. The scar on Carolyn's face was noticeable, as was her left eye that had been black but was now green for an inch around it. Getting better Ed thought.

Lord Stonebridge looked at Ed, motioned with his eyes toward Carolyn and back to Ed. He didn't need another hint. Ed walked to Carolyn, held her gently by the upper arms, and kissed her twice cheek to cheek. At each touch he whispered "I love you, Miss Andrews."

"Sorry, did you say something, Eddie?" Mr. Cooper asked with a slight smile.

Ed responded quickly. "I was just telling Miss Andrews that the shade of green gives her a close resemblance to the Wicked Witch of the West from The Wizard of Oz."

"Very romantic, I'm sure," Mr. Cooper said.

Carolyn held back a tear. "Can we get to the matter at hand please, gentlemen?"

Lord Stonebridge nodded and took charge. He handed Ed an envelope. "Here is your visa for Syria, Mr. Crowe. The goal of this operation, Operation Spring, is, in no particular order, to capture and return to Rome for prosecution, or to kill, our man in Syria. Our man is Abid Hafiz. As we all know he was a shooter at Rome Airport and somehow managed to escape." He handed a photo to Ed. "This is a rather grainy photo of him taken from the security cameras at Rome airport. He's Palestinian, Muslim, young, takes drugs, or did for the shooting, and no doubt he would rather kill or be killed than 'surrender' to any level of authority."

Ed looked at the photo that showed a young man, surely no older than himself. The photo showed him in the process of throwing a grenade. Because of the short distance it needed to travel, it only had to be thrown underhand. It was difficult for Ed to not speculate if it was the grenade that had hurt Carolyn, but he did not raise the question. It didn't matter; the man had to die.

Ed looked up from the photo. "So we kill him then?"

Lord Stonebridge took back the photo. "The British Intelligence Service is not in the active business of killing people, Mr. Crowe. Surely you know that?"

"Of course he does," Mr. Cooper responded, putting his hands on Ed's shoulder, "of course he does. He asked the question just in case push comes to shove. Isn't that so, Eddie?"

Ed nodded. "If push comes to shove! Exactly." He took a deep breath and turned to Lord Stonebridge. "Who is lead, sir?"

Carolyn's eyed opened wide. This was a question she was concerned about asking her father, but it had to be asked.

Lord Stonebridge rubbed his chin. "Hmm," he pondered. "I hoped, Mr. Crowe, that you wouldn't be concerned that I would select Miss Andrews, because..."

"No, sir," Ed interrupted. "I would be concerned that you would not select Miss Andrews because..." He didn't finish the sentence.

"Then it is decided," Lord Stonebridge said quickly, "Miss Andrews is lead operator for Operation Spring."

"Thank you, sir," Carolyn said, knowing how difficult it would be for her father when her mother found out what was about to happen.

"The plane leaves in an hour and twenty," Lord Stonebridge responded. "You'll be met by your contact at Damascus airport. Let's go get a cup of tea."

Carolyn and Ed walked several steps behind Lord Stonebridge and Mr. Cooper, managing to hold hands briefly.

Carolyn squeezed his hand. "You're okay with me...?"

"Absolutely."

She stopped and turned to him. "Why so positive?"

"Well you're Oxford University, and I'm just lowly Aylestone Secondary Modern, Kensal Rise, right?"

"BS," Carolyn replied. "Come on, let's hear it."

"Well how about you're older than I am, and that enhanced maturity will mean a lot, yes?"

"Double BS," she laughed. "Twenty three-days! I just wanted to be a Virgo and not an airy-fairy Libra. Out with it!"

He leaned forward. "Because you'll have to do the paper-work explaining why push came to shove." He grinned and gently pulling her, moved to catch up with their leaders. "Let's get some tea," he said. "May be the last good cup of tea we get to sip on for a while."

CHAPTER SEVENTEEN

SATURDAY, JANUARY 25TH, 1986, 5:30PM DAMASCUS INTERNATIONAL AIRPORT, SYRIA

"I wasn't expecting snow," Ed said as Glen Surbey led them to the limo.

"It'll be gone by tomorrow," the CIA representative replied, loading their bags into the trunk of the limo. The three of them jumped into the warmth of the vehicle as it sped off to downtown Damascus, a forty-five minute drive. Surbey was tall and athletically thin, almost un-American Ed thought. His hair was neatly combed and all in place. Very American, Ed thought.

The security clearance at the airport was surprisingly quick and simple. There was a definite friendly welcoming atmosphere to it all, and Ed and Carolyn were through customs and security in minutes. It was a great deal easier than Ed had experienced in entering Ankara airport in Turkey, less than two years ago. That trip had resulted in both Ed meeting Carolyn, and his becoming involved with MI6. A trip of a lifetime, and one that had changed his life permanently.

Surbey dropped them off at the Cham Palace Hotel, handing Carolyn a business card and two room keys. "SOP," he said to Carolyn, who, unlike Ed, knew what the reference was.

As they entered the hotel, Carolyn gave one of the keys to Ed. It was for room 222. She waved the second key for Ed to see: room 221. They walked up to their rooms and Carolyn motioned for Ed to join her in her room, which he was happy to do.

She took a quick look around. "Two rooms across from each other for safety, one facing the front of the hotel the other facing the back, second floor so escape is possible. The room has been scanned for bugs, and under the mattress in each room is a handgun." She reached under her mattress and pulled out a Smith & Wesson 9mm pistol. "SOP." She grinned slightly, like a boss training the new hand.

"Hey, who are we working for?" Ed asked, surprised at the process. "And what does SOP stand for?"

"Standard Operating Procedure," Carolyn answered with just a touch of smugness. "Hands across the sea and all! Not sure I like our Mr. Surbey, but we have no choice do we. Go unpack and I'll buy you dinner if I may?"

Ed relaxed. "You most certainly may. Be ready in fifteen."

Less than fifteen minutes later, Carolyn knocked on Ed's door and entered before he could get to it.

"Same lock," she explained with a grin.

Ed raised his eyebrows. "So mine can open yours?"

Carolyn nodded. "But you wouldn't enter a lady's boudoir without waiting, would you?"

"Never!" Ed said. "So this is just an acceptable level of sex discrimination is it?"

"Yes."

"Oh, okay. Just so as I know."

Carolyn looked around the room, noticing the mattress had been disturbed. She sat on the sofa. "Can we chat?"

"Yes, Guv," he replied, taking a seat facing Carolyn.

"Please don't call me Guv'nor, Ed. I'm not your superior, besides it's personal."

Ed moved over quickly and took her hand. "Yes, dear."

She slipped her hand away gently. "It's not that personal, and please don't call me dear."

Ed nodded. "Yes, Miss Andrews."

She always loved it when he called her Miss Andrews, and he knew it, but she let it pass this time. She took his hand and held it on her lap. "When you joined us for New Year's, you were so kind to me – reading to me every night so gently. Well I want you to know that meant a lot to me. I cried each night after this happened," she said touching her face, "until you flew over and read to me. I know I'm a big girl, and I know surgery will mostly hide this scar. But having a friend like you help me through it all was wonderful, and I want you to know that." She leaned forward and kissed him gently.

He returned the kiss, touching his lips to the scar ever so gently. "Nothing would have kept me away, Carolyn. Nothing."

She stood indicating that conversation was over. "And I suppose you were put off we didn't make love?"

Ed shrugged raising his hands in answer. "Never crossed my mind," he lied.

"Really?"

"Business is business, right? Just like this trip."

Carolyn walked to the door, locked it and turned. "Make love to me please, Ed."

"Now? We're on an operation. Isn't that…"

She crossed her arms over her chest. "Do I have to beg, Ed?"

"Oh, no," he said, walking to her loosening his shirt buttons. "I'll do the begging, Miss Andrews."

"I love it when you call me that," she said, taking off her suit jacket. "Not slow and careful this time, Mr. Crowe. I want us to make wild passionate love and be dressed for dinner in ten minutes."

Ed did as he was told.

CHAPTER EIGHTEEN

SUNDAY, JANUARY, 26TH.
1986.
6:30AM

" Surbey will be here at seven sharp," Carolyn said as they enjoyed their breakfast in the hotel's dining room. There were only two other guests in the room, two men eating quietly at a corner table.

"That would be SOP would it?" Ed asked.

"Very good," Carolyn smiled. "You're catching on quickly."

"So what don't you like about him?" Ed asked, nodding to the entrance where Surbey would enter.

She gently shook her head. "Don't know. It's just a feeling. Feminine instinct perhaps."

Ed shrugged, not sure where that would lead. He moved on and toasted her with his cup, his very small cup, of tea. "At the risk of repeating myself, Carolyn, and before we move into operational processes, I want to thank you again for a lovely evening, starting with the pre-dinner – shall I say *welcome* – and the wonderful meal including the quick history of Syria."

"You knew more than I suspected," Carolyn said. "I'm very impressed."

Ed decided not to mention the material Pat had given him for the flight over. "Just your normal secondary school curriculum," he said proudly.

"Very good. So what s the capital of Somalia, Mr. know-it-all?"

Ed thought hard. "We didn't take Africa before I left school at fifteen to get a job to help bring money into the household to pay for the basics of life."

Carolyn shook her head. "You so full of... Here's our guest," she motioned toward the door as Glen Surbey walked into the dining room.

Surbey nodded to them, asked if he could join them, and sat before he received an answer. "Nice evening, I trust?"

Ed and Carolyn nodded.

Surbey turned to Carolyn. "We may have met before. I was in Langley the same time as you were a few years ago. You were learning, I was teaching."

Carolyn nodded. "I am impressed. You look rather young to teach."

"Nothing special. I teach firearms, specializing in hand guns." He turned to Ed. "And you're a new Canadian?"

"Oakville, Ontario, just outside..."

"Toronto," Surbey interrupted. "I've been there. Also visited Ottawa, Winnipeg, and Vancouver." He grinned. "I can also spell and pronounce Saskatchewan correctly." He grinned even more. "Good day, eh."

Ed reached over and shook his hand. "I think we'll get along."

"When you gentlemen are ready..." Carolyn said subtly.

"Right," Surbey said. "Let's get to it. The man we're after, Abid Hafiz, is in the Old City. That is good and bad. It is a small area surrounded with a wall so not so easy to get in and out of discreetly. It has seven gates, each of which is guarded by us or a friend." Ed took the friend reference to mean the Israeli Mossad. "That's the good news.

The bad news is that there are seven churches and two mosques in the Old City, and we sure as hell aren't going to chase him into a place of God to capture him."

Ed wanted to ask why not, but didn't. Carolyn did.

"Why not for Christ's sake?" Surbey exploded. "Why do…"

"Is that a play on words?" Ed asked. "For Christ's sake."

Surbey looked at Ed and then at Carolyn, apparently unable to speak.

"It's in his nature," Carolyn explained. "You'll get used to it."

Surbey shook his head and scratched his chin. "I'm not so sure I will." He paused. "Now where was I?"

"In a church or a mosque," Ed said helpfully.

Surbey closed his eyes, spread his hands on the table and tried to smile. "I see I'm going to enjoy this arrangement." He spoke with just a touch of sarcasm.

"So he's in the Old City and we have to catch him with his pants down, so to speak," Carolyn said.

"Yes, so to speak." Surbey agreed.

Ed snapped his fingers. "I have an idea."

"I dread to think," Surbey muttered.

"Is our man married?" Ed asked.

Surbey responded carefully. "Yes. Wife and kids in Palestine. But I hope you don't think…"

"He doesn't," Carolyn responded.

Ed waved the comments off. "He's a man, right? A guy? A bloke?" His eyes widened. "He needs friendship, right? A bit of company, a bit of 'how's your father' perhaps? Maybe we can help him out here?"

"I don't like where this is going," Surbey cautioned.

"Keep going, Mister," Carolyn said, now using Ed's operational name.

"God help us," Surbey mumbled. "Keep going then."

Ed turned to Surbey. "One question before I sort it all out in my mind. Do you have any local Syrian operatives? I mean Sunni Syrians, not Christians?"

Surbey nodded. "Yes, we do. Or seeing where you're going with this, perhaps I should say; yes, I'm afraid we do."

Carolyn ordered a pot of coffee, and only after it was delivered and poured did they listen to and discuss the pros and cons of Ed's idea. The discussion was a mixture of politics, religious understanding, with a solid background of history, both local and national. Surbey liked it the least, but knew it would happen in any event; and he wanted some level of involvement to keep it under control. He didn't know of Ed and Carolyn's relationship; however he was well aware of where and how Carolyn got the scar on her face. Besides, if it was successful, he wanted part of the limelight.

After the plan had been agreed upon Surbey left seemingly feeling put-upon. They had agreed to meet later that day after each had checked with their superiors. Carolyn waited for a moment and turned to Ed.

"Do you get that feeling?" she asked.

"Not at all," he replied. "Typical American as far as I can tell. So when do we phone for approval?"

"We don't." Carolyn answered.

Ed let his head drop. He was expecting that answer. He rested his elbow on the table and rubbed his chin. "Hmm. If I may…"

"If you think," Carolyn interrupted, "that I'm going to ask permission…." She let it end.

Ed leaned forward and spoke in a whisper. "What if he wasn't your father?"

"But he is!"

"Yes, of course he is," he conceded in an understanding fashion. "But, on the other hand, you're okay for me, the person that loves you, to accept the plan?"

Carolyn grinned. "It was your bloody plan, Mr. Crowe."

"Yeah, I know," Ed groaned, "But I wasn't thinking ahead. I just….oh shit!"

"You'll be there to protect me, Ed. As they say in Australia – no worries mate!"

They drank their coffee with Carolyn obviously concerned about where they were heading. Ed didn't want to interrupt her thoughts. This was her first assignment as lead operator. He didn't want his personal concerns to get in the way of her thoughts. "I have an idea," she finally said, and not waiting for him to respond she continued. "Today we will discover Damascus, relax, and enjoy each other's company."

Ed smiled his un-needed approval.

"Tomorrow morning we will go our own way. You will find the appropriate hotel and room with Surbey's help, and I will drop in at the British Embassy. I'll touch base, introduce myself, and make sure there is nothing going on 'officially' that our plan would in any way hinder."

Ed nodded but was uncertain what her real goal was. *Let her lead,* he said to himself.

"Can I take you out tonight on a date?" he asked.

Carolyn chuckled. "On a date?"

"I'll make arrangements for dinner at a nice restaurant. I'll pick you up at your hotel room at, say, seven-thirty, and we'll have an evening together. No business, no departmental chit chat, no spying or spooking. Just a wonderful meal and enjoy each other's company."

Carolyn leaned back in her seat grinning, while being careful of the scar on her face. "That is a date," she agreed.

CHAPTER NINETEEN

WEDNESDAY, JANUARY 29TH 1986 2PM CHAM PALACE HOTEL

E d tapped on the door and walked from the bathroom into the main area of room 201. The tap was only out of respect. Carolyn sat cross legged on the bed facing the door to the hallway. Dressed in a full niqab, only her eyes were visible. She quickly removed the headpiece and took a deep breath.

"This plan isn't working," she grumbled, "and here I am sitting in a hotel room looking like a bundle of clothes in a laundry." She was obviously not happy.

Ed offered her a glass of water. "Give it time," he said, trying to encourage her, but also feeling his plan was failing badly.

"So far," Carolyn continued, taking a drink, "I've had four of Surbey's men visit me, and only two others. Not a good result." She shook her head. "And one of his associates even tried to bribe me into having sex with him. What a waste of time and energy."

Ed held up his camera. "With the photos we have of the other two men, we can be sure they won't say too much of their experience in this room."

The plan was simple. When a 'real' client entered the room, the agreed upon money would be left on a side table and Carolyn would stand by the side of the bed and open the niqab revealing her in underwear and a diaphanous silk negligee. When the client moved towards her, Carolyn would turn and Ed would burst into the room, camera in hand, taking several photos of the man and Carolyn. Having maintained her face covering, she was not identifiable, but the client was. Each of the men had begged forgiveness. It was then that one of Surbey's associates would enter the room and make it clear that to save the 'client' from total family disgrace they had to act as if they did have sex with 'the English lady in a niqab', and tell their friends accordingly. It was not perfect, but seemed to make sense as Ed had described the plan on Sunday.

"Let's give it until tomorrow night," Ed suggested, gesturing that they had limited choice.

Carolyn was about to reply when they felt more than heard steps on the wooded floor of the hallway. Carolyn got back on the bed and covered her face. Ed moved quickly but quietly into the bathroom. He pulled the door too, and sat silently on the bathtub. He relied on sounds from the room, not direct vision. *If I can see him, then....*

The door opened and within a second Carolyn recognized Abid Hafiz from the photo. To her surprise he was nervous and closed the door behind him slowly, not even thinking to lock the door. The key didn't work in any event, but he could not know that.

Hafiz was less than six feet tall with dark curly hair that was longer than normal for an Arab. He obviously hadn't shaved in several days, but overall he appeared well kept. His eyes were set deep, and he looked tired, very tired. He reached into his robes and extracted a sum of money which he placed on the table as directed by Carolyn. She slide off the bed, removed her facial covering, reached into her niqab and smoothly and quickly withdrew her gun and pointed it directly at Hafiz's face.

"Tahmil!" she shouted in Arabic.

Ed burst into the room and pointing his gun at Hafiz's crotch, he shouted, "Down!"

To their surprise Hafiz gave no resistance, which disappointed Ed. He had convinced himself it would be appropriate to kill Hafiz if needed, and Ed didn't require a lot of circumstance to create need. Hafiz put his hands on his head and fell to his knees. He looked at Carolyn as if wishing she would pull the trigger.

"Search him," Carolyn said, moving to one side of Hafiz. If she pulled the trigger, there would be no concern of hitting Ed. Ed put his gun aside and patted Hafiz as best he could with him in the kneeling position. Carolyn motioned for him to stand, which he did.

"Finish," she ordered, looking at Ed.

With some reluctance Ed patted Hafiz below the waist, maintaining as much honor for himself and their prisoner as he could. Ed motioned to indicate all was safe.

To Ed's surprise, Carolyn spoke in Arabic to Hafiz but in a halting manner as if she had practiced it for some time.

Hafiz shook his head, pleading, "No! no! no!" He spoke with a strong accent.

Carolyn Nodded. "Yes, yes, yes. Rome airport!" she said raising her voice and pointing at the scar on her face.

Ed looked at Carolyn, shrugging in ignorance.

"I told him to take off his robes," she said.

Ed cringed at the thought of what she was asking. To be seen naked by a woman other than one's wife was a great dishonor in the Arab world. He shook his head. "You can't do that, Carolyn." He spoke quietly.

"Yes, I can."

"Okay, you can, but you shouldn't."

Hafiz was now visibly shaking and silently praying. Carolyn motioned to him and he fell to his knees, burying his head on the bed.

"I want to embarrass him," Carolyn admitted. "He killed and injured people. A little embarrassment won't kill him."

Ed pulled Hafiz up from the bed and gesturing him to open his mouth, Ed put his gun into Hafiz's mouth turning the barrel to his left cheek.

"What are you doing?" Carolyn asked, not believing what she was seeing.

"You want him revenge? He'll never forget a bullet through his cheek. Tit for tat, so to speak."

"Perhaps 'what's good for the goose is good for the gander' is a better expression given the circumstances," Carolyn retorted, now visibly relaxing.

"Do I pull the trigger?" Ed asked, while Hafiz looked miserably at Carolyn, somehow understanding that she would decide on his fate.

"Piss on him," Carolyn said, giving up.

"I hope you don't mean literally?" Ed responded letting go of Hafiz and letting him fall back to his place on the bed. He had to smile since they both knew that when Ed got nervous, he had what he liked to call a 'weak-bladder' problem.

Carolyn was now tired of the entire process "Just phone Surbey and let's get out of here". They had their man. How he was transferred to Italy would be someone else's problem.

When Surbey entered the room, gun in hand, Hafiz was, once more, in a praying position, and both Ed and Carolyn had their guns trained on him. They almost felt sorry for him...almost.

"Got him!" Surbey shouted. As soon as he spoke Hafiz jumped up and moved toward him.

In a second Surbey raised his gun and shot Hafiz twice in the chest, knocking him backwards onto the bed. There was a deathly silence of just a few seconds as Ed and Carolyn took in what had happened.

"What the fuck was that?" Ed screamed, reaching down feeling for a pulse in Hafiz's neck. There wasn't one to be felt. "Why the Christ did you kill him?" Ed shouted, not managing to control himself.

Carolyn took a step backwards, letting Ed speak on their behalf. She burned the picture of what had happened into her brain. This made no sense. She cleared her mind as best she could and listened.

Surbey spoke quite calmly "He went for me. I had to protect myself."

"Protect yourself? You killed the bastard," Ed shouted. He turned to Carolyn, looking for support. She just looked at him, saying nothing.

Surbey continued speaking, softly to counteract Ed. He reached for Ed and Carolyn's guns. "Look, the message was clear. We wanted him dead or alive. He's dead."

Carolyn nodded. "He's dead all right. What happens to his body?"

"I'll look after it," Surbey replied. "It will be just one more dead body found in Damascus. Everyone will suspect the police killed him. Say a bad word about President al-Assad, and you're as good as dead in this country." He took a deep breath. "Go back to your hotel and make arrangements to go home. You've done what you came here to do."

Carolyn nodded. Wrapping the niqab around her she moved towards the door to the hallway, taking Ed's arm as she did. He followed in disbelief.

They took a taxi back to their hotel, not saying a word to each other. When they got to their rooms, Carolyn looked at her watch. "It's two-thirty now," she said. "Pack, leave your bag in the room and meet me downstairs for a drink at three, Mister."

Carolyn use of his operational name brought Ed back to reality. "Three o'clock, Miss" he confirmed using her operational name.

They each entered their respective rooms.

When Ed entered the dining room at exactly three, Carolyn was sitting at the far end of the room at a table for two facing him. Ed looked around. There were no other guests. He sat across from

Carolyn, who was now dressed in a blue sleeveless summer dress with a silk scarf over her shoulders to maintain local custom. On the table in front of her was a small silver evening bag and in the centre of the table was an open bottle of red wine.

"You're mad at me, right?" Carolyn asked, keeping her eyes on Ed and the entrance behind him. She was unusually nervous.

"No, not mad," Ed said, pouring the wine. "More pissed-off than mad I would say."

"Okay I apologize for that, Ed, but not as it relates to Mister, okay?"

Her message was clear. What was going on, the way she was acting, was strictly business related, not personal. Ed nodded, acknowledging the message and took a sip of the wine.

"Uggh, what is that?" he managed without spitting the wine back into his glass.

Carolyn managed a smile. "Non-alcoholic local variety," she said. "I think I'll pass." She paused to settle their minds. "Now, Mister," she continued calmly, moving her hand to the evening bag, "when and if I say 'go', I want you to drop to the floor on your left side. Don't wait to look around and please do not move until I say so. Understood?"

Ed nodded. Against his better judgment he refilled his glass and silently toasted her. "Nice weather we're having," he mumbled, wanting to look as if they were carrying on a conversation without distracting Carolyn. At the same time he adjusted his body and feet ready to move if he got the word.

"So as I was saying," Ed continued, "the weather's not bad. I love you. Have since I met you in Ankara. Still plan on asking you to marry me the day after Roy and Pat's wedding." He paused. "Now what else can I tell you, that you don't already..."

"Go!" Carolyn shouted.

Ed threw himself to the floor keeping his eyes on Carolyn as he fell. The fall seem to take forever as he watched Carolyn stand, raise a gun in her right hand, point it to the entrance behind Ed and fire three quick shots. He hit the floor, losing site of Carolyn as he lay as still and motionless as he could. Under the table he could see Carolyn's legs and prayed to whoever was listening they didn't collapse; they didn't.

"Come on up, Ed," Carolyn asked calmly, stepping to one side of the table and looking down at him. "Good job, Mister. I like a man that can take orders."

Ed stood and brushed himself off. "And I love a woman who can give them," he muttered. Taking a breath, he turned.

Just inside the entrance to the dining room, a man lay stretched on the floor, blood still oozing into his clothes. He was obviously dead and if he wasn't, Ed didn't care. Beside him was an UZI sub-machine gun. No one else was in sight, with the only sounds coming from the kitchen area where the staff was in a state of panic. They walked toward the body to make sure.

Ed gasped. "But that's…"

"Exactly," Carolyn said. "Follow me." She led them out the back door of the hotel into a busy backstreet filled with stalls of food of all descriptions and buyers, mostly women in traditional dress, arguing the price of the goods. In a weird way it reminded Ed of Petticoat Lane on a busy Saturday. But Ed had never witnessed a shooting on his many visits to Petticoat Lane, and likely never would.

Carolyn walked them quickly to a busier street and waved down a taxi. As she got in, she handed the driver a piece of paper. "British Embassy," she stated. The taxi took off with a start, heading into the always busy Damascus traffic.

Ed motioned to the piece of paper, shrugging a question.

"Address of the British Embassy in Arabic," she answered.

Ed motioned to the evening bag she was carrying carefully on her lap. Carolyn opened it just enough to show the .25 Beretta she had used.

"Jane Bond," Ed whispered.

Carolyn took his hand in hers and Ed could feel she was still shaking from what had happened. "I'll explain at the embassy," she whispered.

Ed held her hand tightly and smiled his understanding.

Carolyn handed the silver evening bag to the receptionist at the British Embassy. "Thanks for the loan," she said.

The receptionist opened the bag. "Been fired," she stated, smelling the gunpowder. "I'll never be able to take it on a date again without thinking of you, Miss Andrews. Thank you."

"Just don't tell your mother, Lori" Carolyn chuckled.

Lori laughed "God forbid. She's madder than a hatter because I'm in Syria, Damascus even. Not where a Watford girl is supposed to be working."

Carolyn introduced Ed to Lori Quinn. Lori held up the bag with the gun in it. "Did you..?"

Ed nodded. "Dead as a doornail."

"You're not extracting the Michael, are you?" Lori asked smiling.

"No he's not, I'm afraid." Carolyn answered. "Look, Lori, can you get us a private room for ten minutes and then ask the ambassador to join us?"

Lori jumped to assist. "Of course I can. Follow me." She led them down a hallway to an office marked 'Private – No Entry'.

"It's our get-away-from-it-all room," Lori explained. "Used to be a smoking room. Thank God that's all ended. I'll ask Ambassador Wood to join you in fifteen minutes. I think he's going to want to hear all the details." She turned as she was leaving. "I'll look after the 'goods'."

Surbey watched as the hotel staff cleaned up the blood from the dining room floor. The body was gone. In the morning it would be just another citizen gunned down by the secret police. He rolled off a considerable number of Syrian pounds and handed them out to all the staff. He put his finger to his lips and winked. It would be their secret. They each smiled and nodded. It would be their secret – money talks.

Carolyn sat across the boardroom table from Ed and spread her hands on the table, partly to settle her nerves but mainly to give the message she was ready to explain.

"Still pissed-off at me?" she asked.

Ed shook his head. "No, I'm now pissed-off at myself for being pissed-off with you. I should have known you knew what you were doing and couldn't explain everything to me. Sorry."

"Accepted."

"What were you doing? Why couldn't you trust me?"

"Oh, I could trust you, Mr. Crowe." For the first time in a long time, she laughed. "I could trust you to love me so much you wouldn't have acted as you did. You would have tried to be the regular you, but it wouldn't have worked. You'd have never convinced Surbey." She paused. "Besides I wasn't sure I was on the right track until I visited the embassy, and then today..." She closed here eyes and took a breath. "And then today..."

Ed raised his hand. "Okay, Sherlock, let me see what I can conjure up in all of this and you fill in the gaps."

She waved him on. "Please proceed, Dr. Watson."

"Okay, first I think you're a lovely, smart, tricky, sneaky, sensitive lady, and I love you."

"Good start," Carolyn said, "but to the point."

Ed outlined what he had captured. "First, you didn't like Surbey from the beginning – female instinct perhaps. Whatever. It was enough to have you come here to the embassy to do some checking up on things and that obviously led you to believe you, *we*, needed another gun, one that could be carried discreetly. For some reason you expected something to happen quite quickly, hence the meeting in the dining room, with you appropriately seated. Then in walked one of the two men that visited you in the hotel bedroom who was not an associate, at least not a CIA associate, of Surbey's. You recognized him, saw the UZi and shot him. And I might mention those were three very quick, very accurate shots." He took a deep breath. "Beyond that, I don't know what led you to do what you did, but I'm certainly proud and thankful for what you did do."

"Not bad," Carolyn admitted. "Pretty good actually."

"We'll discuss why you couldn't trust me in more detail later," Ed shook a friendly finger at her. "But what led you to take a disliking to Surbey? What happened at the embassy on Monday, and what happened today to convince you it was about to blow up?"

"The first question is a difficult one," Carolyn responded carefully. "He just seemed, I'm not sure what the word is, let's say dodgy, when he looked at me. Sort of a blank look more than anything. So…"

"Hold it now," Ed said, reading between the lines. "What you mean is the way he *didn't* look at you, don't you? Not like the innocent Englishman that met you in the British Embassy in Ankara, who immediately thought you were beautiful and most charming."

Carolyn blushed, and her chuckling couldn't hide her embarrassment. "Maybe you're right, but whatever, it seemed strange. And then he seemed so thin, gaunt-like. Very un-American, that's all."

"Oh, my God," Ed exclaimed. "Not only did you think he was a homosexual, a bit light in his loafers perhaps, you also thought he was suffering from AIDS? Bloody hell!"

"The word is 'gay', Mr. Crowe. Get with the times please."

"As you say, Miss Political Correctness. What did you find out here at the embassy about our Mr. Surbey?"

"After a few phone calls, we determined he is from Minneapolis and married with two children."

"Hmmm…"

"He has been in Damascus three years, starting with a one year assignment with two voluntary one year add-ons. In fact he hasn't been back to the US since he got here."

"Wouldn't that ring bells?"

Carolyn nodded. "It did for us. Further, Lori has seen him a few times at inter-operational meetings and she has noticed a loss of weight on him."

"So far, nothing factual to suggest something was afoot, Sherlock."

"Very true," Carolyn agreed. Her eyes widened. "But then…"

Ed waved her on. "But then?"

"You may recall that when we first met him, he said he may have met me in the US while I was there for joint training, especially in the weapons department where he was a trainer." She paused. "Well…"

"Well what for crying out loud?"

"On a hunch, a lucky hunch, but a hunch anyway, I took the gun he had given me and tested it downstairs in the firing range. And guess what?"

"You got a bull's eye?"

"No such thing. The bullets were blanks. I only fired one, but the rest were blanks, of that I'm sure."

"Oh, shit."

"Please don't swear, Ed. It doesn't become you." She gave him a quick grin. "Naturally I assumed your gun was filled with blanks. Now why would he do that? Obviously he wanted to control our kill capacity. But why?"

"To state the obvious," Ed interrupted, "he didn't want us to shoot who we thought were bad guys, because they may be his good guys."

"Exactly."

"And you became worried today when he took our guns, on the premise that the assignment was over, and he would very quickly realize you knew the bullets were blanks, would assume I knew the bullets were blanks and he wanted us dead."

"Just another two bodies would be found tomorrow morning; on the assumption the secret police had done it."

Ed shook his head in wonderment of it all. "Now what do we do?"

"First thing we do is ask Lori to bring in a nice pot of hot tea."

"And some biscuits?"

Carolyn walked to the door. "And some biscuits."

CHAPTER TWENTY

Lori wheeled in a tray of tea and biscuits just as Ambassador Howard Wood entered the room. "Glad you've made yourself at home," he commented, looking at the tray. "Always time for tea."

To everyone's surprise the ambassador acted as mother and poured. He sat at the head of the table. "Used to smoke, you know," he said almost wistfully. "This room smelled like a Turkish sweat room on a Saturday night. Horrible." He looked at Ed. "You've been to Turkey haven't you, Mr. Crowe?"

"Yes, sir. I…"

The ambassador interrupted. "In fact I just got off the phone with Sir Michael Watson in Ankara. You've met him, Mr. Crowe, correct?"

"Yes, sir" Ed said quickly. Michael Watson was the British Ambassador in Ankara and Ed had met him on his first trip out of England, and that meeting had resulted in Ed's involvement as a consultant with MI6.

Ambassador Wood turned to Carolyn. "Who did you kill, Miss Andrews, and where did it happen?"

Carolyn felt silly with her answer. "At the Cham Palace Hotel… but I'm afraid I don't know who he is, sir. It all…"

Holding up his hand, he looked at Lori. "Find out what you can about any deaths today, especially this one. If it makes sense, go to the hotel and recover the belongings of our guests."

Ed and Carolyn gave their keys to Lori. "Our bags are packed in the rooms and ready to go," Carolyn told her.

"Flights, sir?" Lori asked.

Ambassador thought for a moment. "Get Mr. Crowe on a flight to Toronto tomorrow morning, in-direct. Via South America or something. Get Miss Andrews on a flight to London tomorrow, preferably early and preferably to Gatwick."

Lori left the room.

Ed raised his hand. "Via South America, sir? I don't mean to complain, but…"

"Ambassador Watson asked me to do that," he laughed. "Don't worry Miss Quinn was in on the joke." He loosened his tie. "Now, Miss Andrews, please start at the beginning and tell me everything that happened that resulted in a death."

"Yes, sir," Carolyn replied bravely. But she could not stop the tears that slowly ran down her cheeks. Ed leaned over to touch her hand and give her encouragement, but it was too much.

Carolyn broke down in tears, sobbing harder than he had ever seen her cry. Ed turned to the ambassador for help who was already at the open door calling for Miss Quinn. Within seconds Lori was back in the room, with a large blanket in one hand and waving the two men out of the room with the other. Ed quickly followed the ambassador out of the room, closing the door behind them.

"It was just a matter of time," Ambassador Wood said, keeping his voice down. "Don't worry, Mr. Crowe, Lori has psychological training and has been through this before."

"But I thought…"

"That she's a receptionist. Of course you did. That's just where she sits. It's her gun Miss Andrews used, and she knows how to handle it. There may be one small problem though."

"Problem?" Ed groaned.

"She graduated from Cambridge" he chuckled, "and you know how they get along with those Oxford types?"

Actually Ed didn't know, and in this instance he didn't care. He nodded knowingly to end the conversation.

The ambassador led Ed upstairs and walked him to the front of the building and stood looking out a large window, pointing to the streets below.

"Damascus is the world's oldest continuously inhabited city." Wood said thoughtfully. "Thousand's of years in existence. Yet in 1982 when the military turned on its own people, we stood here and watched them mow down tens, if not hundreds, of citizens. I'll never forget that, and neither will the staff that worked here at that time. It was then that we brought in Miss Quinn. She was, and is, invaluable. Have faith, Mr. Crowe. Miss Andrews will never be the same, but she will eventually accept that what life brings us is often not what we learned in school," he shook his head, "and certainly not what we learned at university."

"I thought that the so-called 1982 Hamas Massacre was actually in Hamas." Ed said carefully. "At least that is what I read in a very brief history of Syria."

Ambassador Wood nodded his head slightly. "And so it was," he agreed. "But alas it wasn't limited to Hamas. There have been many uprisings in the world of Islam in Syria; 1982 was just the latest. The basic issue - problem - choose your word, was that that President Assad is an Alawite, which is a branch of Shia Islam, while the uprising in Hamas was driven by the Muslim Brotherhood which is Sunni. The majority of Muslims in Syria are Sunni. However both the political and, more importantly, military power rests with members of the Shia sect. Things are, thank goodness, quiet now," he shrugged, "but you never know."

An hour later Ed, Carolyn, and Ambassador Wood were back in the room, Lori had left to find out what was happening at the hotel and to recover the bags. Carolyn looked wonderful, of that Ed was sure, and was now in full control of her emotions. A small amount of make-up helped do the trick and she gave Ed a quick wink before she proceeded.

"From the beginning then," Carolyn started. "And if I miss anything, my associate and good friend will no doubt identify any detail I skip."

Ed nodded, doing a bad job of hiding his total respect and admiration of his 'associate and good friend'. He particularly liked the way Carolyn didn't apologize for her setback, no doubt a strong suggestion from Lori.

Ambassador Wood waved her on, while topping up their now tepid tea. It was the message he wanted to get at, not the tea.

"And here we are," Carolyn said summing up the operation to date. "We got our man, but not in the way we intended. Plus another, as yet unidentified man is dead. But for sure there is a problem for the CIA with Surbey's actions."

"May we live in interesting times," the ambassador muttered. He turned to Ed. "Any details missed?" he asked.

"Two comments," Ed responded. "One a fact, the other an assumption. First Miss Andrews shot him three times at a fair distance and each bullet hit the man in the chest. I make this remark just to point out that it was not like a shoot-out at the OK Corral with bullets flying everywhere."

"Noted," the ambassador said.

"And secondly, and Miss Andrews and I have not discussed this, but I think when Hafiz moved toward Surbey it was towards a savior, not an enemy."

Ambassador Wood's eyes opened wide in surprise and he turned to Carolyn for a response.

Carolyn thought for a moment, reliving the event. "Well as I said, sir, we were on either side of Hafiz and when he turned he had mostly his back to me. But I would definitely say it did not seem to be any form of a vicious attack."

"Let's take a break," the ambassador said leaving the room. "I'll be back in a quarter of an hour with more tea and some food."

It was half an hour before Ambassador Wood returned. When he did, he was joined by Lori Quinn, a large tray of tea and sandwiches, and Ed and Carolyn's luggage.

During that time Ed and Carolyn had spoken only about their operation in Turkey, laughing about the time they went bird watching just outside of Ankara where Carolyn 'captured' her first four birds. The operation had gone well for the most part with the PKK freeing the British and American hostages after a large sum of money had exchanged hands.

Once they had served themselves and eaten the sandwiches, Ambassador Wood resumed the discussions.

"Miss Quinn will up-date us on where she's at, and then I have two questions for Miss Andrews before I submit my report, by fax, to London." He looked at Carolyn.

"Yes, I understand," Carolyn said. The message was clear. With a shooting involved it would be only a matter of time before the head of MI6, known historically as 'C', would be advised of the events of the circumstances. Lori was the only one in the room that was not aware that 'C' was Carolyn's father.

Lori updated them in short sentences. "No body. No shooting. Dining room is half full. Nice looking buffet. No apparent activity in your rooms. Bags recovered." She waited for questions and getting none, continued. "Ed flies to Toronto via Amsterdam. 8am flight. Carolyn flies to directly London with SAS. Leaves whatever time is convenient."

"Special Air Services," Ed chuckled. "Wow, does Carolyn rate."

Lori grinned. "Nothing like that. The plane is available. Carolyn will have to report to London as soon as she returns. Save the taxpayers some money."

"Well done, Miss Quinn," the ambassador said. "Perhaps next time I have to fly to London…"

"Yes, sir. I'll make a note of that"

Ambassador Wood took out a pen and note book and flipped a couple of pages. "Now Miss Andrews, if I may? Before I ask my two questions, an opinion from both of you. You, Miss Andrews, knew, or suspected, that your CIA guns were loaded with blanks. Now when you held those guns on Hafiz, and in particular when Mr. Crowe put the barrel of his gun into Hafiz's mouth..."

"Oh good lord," Lori exclaimed. "You wouldn't have would you?"

Ed shrugged. "Probably not."

"To continue," the ambassador interrupted. "Can I assume that Hafiz did not act as if he knew there were blanks?"

"Absolutely not," Carolyn said, pointing to her left cheek. "He thought it might happen."

Ambassador Wood continued. "Good. That suggests only Surbey was aware. Now my first question, Miss Andrews. Since you knew, suspected, the bullets were blanks, what was your fall-back if Hafiz did in fact know?"

"In the pocket of my niqab, I had Lori's Beretta; safety off. I was a second away from retrieving it if needed."

"And she is a good shot," Ed added, wanting to support his leader.

The ambassador nodded, and looked at his notes. "Secondly, Miss Andrews, and this is a bit more, shall we say, ticklish? Why did you not tell Mr. Crowe of your concerns, about the bullets, and about the Beretta?"

"Ah," Carolyn mumbled.

Ed closed his eyes, not wanting to hear the answer.

"Well, it's like this..." Carolyn stumbled.

"Because Ed is in love with Carolyn," Lori interrupted, speaking loud enough to take over the conversation. "She was worried he would let his feelings get in the way. So as lead operator she had to make a difficult, personal decision...sir."

Ambassador Wood put down his pen and looked around the room. All three nodded; Lori with confidence, Carolyn with a gulp, and Ed with a smile.

"That will not be part of my report," the ambassador stated firmly. He looked sideways at Lori. "Perhaps, Miss Lonely Hearts, you could work with me to get our combined report together and faxed as soon as possible?"

Lori walked to open the door for the ambassador, whistling 'Love Is In The Air.' Ambassador Wood made no comment and kept a straight face.

"She's a cheeky one," Carolyn said.

"Cambridge grad," Ed responded.

"There you go then!" Carolyn grinned.

They changed chairs, sitting across from each other, holding hands, but in a position to let go at the sound of the door opening.

"So should we start thinking about the wedding?" Ed asked.

Carolyn looked at him funny. "Don't you want to know the details of why I didn't tell you my suspicions?"

"Nope! Lori explained it well, so why tell the story twice?"

"Hey, just a minute," Carolyn said. "I never said anything of the sort to Lori. She just put two and two together...and got four."

"These Cambridge grads are pretty smart, I'd say. Perhaps smarter than..."

Carolyn squeezed his hand digging in her fingernails. "Now listen, young man, you start suggesting that Cambridge is a better..."

Ed pulled away his hands and held them up in surrender. "I'm just saying..."

"Don't!"

"To the wedding then?" Ed asked.

"To the wedding," Carolyn agreed, re-taking his hands in hers.

The door opened without a knock forty-five minutes later. They managed to separate their hands just in time.

"Interrupting are we?" Lori asked.

"No," Ed responded, "we're just talking about a wedding."

Lori's eyes lit up. "You're getting married! Like wow."

Ambassador Wood stood behind her with a fax in his hand.

Ed jumped up. "Good Lord," he stammered. "Us getting married? Heavens no." He turned to Carolyn. "Isn't that funny, Carolyn?"

Carolyn responded coolly. "Very funny. Ha, ha, ha," she managed.

"As I was saying," Ambassador Wood interrupted. "There has been a change of plans."

"Good," Carolyn said, as Ed sat down.

"What do I know?" the ambassador asked, less than enthusiastically. He sat to settle the matter. "Your plans have changed, Mr. Crowe."

"Oh no." Ed groaned. "I am flying to Toronto via South America? Tell me it isn't so."

"It isn't so," Lori said with a cheeky grin.

The ambassador shook his head slightly. "You're on the same flight as Miss Andrews to England. Only it isn't tomorrow morning, it's tonight. As soon as we get you to the airport."

Carolyn's head sank to her chest. "God help me," she whispered. Then with a quick turn to Ed, she grinned. "Better yet. God help us!"

Ed turned to Ambassador Wood. "You mentioned England, sir. Previously you mentioned London. Could it be that we will be flown to a small airport south of Aylesbury, and when we arrive there will be a limo to drive us to our location: Stonebridge Manor, perhaps?"

Ambassador Wood nodded. "I do believe..."

"Bingo!" Lori threw in.

"We used to call 'housey, housey'," the ambassador said thoughtfully.

"I'll order the car to the front door, Mr. Ambassador," Lori said. "Perhaps we should..."

"Yes, we should indeed," he agreed leaving the room for Ed and Carolyn to talk.

Ed stood and put his hand to his heart. "*Once more unto the breach, dear friends, once more...*"

"*Or close the wall up with our English dead*," Carolyn finished, moving to get their bags.

They kissed quickly and walked to the front door of the embassy.

CHAPTER TWENTY ONE

The converted Land Rover left the compound of the embassy, turned left at the gates and headed toward the airport. Ambassador Wood sat in the front with the driver, while in the back Ed, Carolyn, and Lori bounced around on the makeshift seats.

"Do you always travel first class?" Carolyn shouted to the ambassador.

"Pays to be inconspicuous," he responded, turning to face them as he spoke. He handed Carolyn an envelope. "This is a copy of our report to London. If we made any errors, please correct them as you see fit. However, I think it's rather accurate."

Carolyn reluctantly opened the report and started reading.

"They haven't hanged any one in Britain since August 1964," Lori said casually, "did you know that?"

Ed shook his head. "Is there a message here?"

Lori continued. "Well the interesting thing is the fact that it wasn't one person that was hanged, it was two. Imagine that, eh.? Same crime of course."

Carolyn looked up from the report. "Do you think it hurts, being hanged that is?"

"Good question," Lori pondered. "We discussed that in university once."

"Cambridge; that figures," Carolyn replied.

Lori waved off the comment. "So tell me, Ed, which university did you go to?"

"University of Life," he quickly answered.

"Ahh, I see. A working man. So let me re-phrase the question; where did you gain your formal education from, Ed?"

Carolyn interrupted. "From where did you gain….is the correct wording."

"Point taken. Ed?"

"Aylestone Avenue Secondary Modern School, Queen's Park, in London."

"Hmm. GCE's?"

"None."

"Really?" Lori remarked showing real surprise. "I am impressed."

"You don't *require* a good education to be intelligent," Carolyn commented, without looking up from the report.

"Exactly what my father says," Lori replied.

"And what does your father do?" Ed asked.

"He works for British Railways," Lori sat a little straighter. "On the trains that is.

Carolyn looked up from reading. "He must be very proud of you?"

Lori was caught of guard. "Yes, he is. And so is mum."

"My father died some time ago," Ed added. "Carolyn's father is a civil servant."

Lori smiled her thanks.

Ambassador Wood turned to Lori. "Carolyn's father is Lord Stonebridge, head of British Intelligence."

"Holy shit!" Lori gasped, putting her hand to her mouth.

"Is that a Cambridge expression?" Carolyn chirped in.

"Never heard it at Aylestone," Ed added quickly.

Lori sat staring, still with her mouth covered. She sheepishly removed it. "Sir, you should have…"

"I just did, Miss Quinn," he replied.

Carolyn folded the report into the envelope. "See, there are times when it's best not to tell everyone everything!"

"Bingo!" Lori laughed.

"Housey, housey," Ambassador Wood added, sitting quietly in the front seat.

The VC 10 took off from Damascus airport with a SAS crew of five and Carolyn and Ed as their guests. The crew knew better than to ask who Carolyn and Ed were, and why they needed a priority and protected flight to England. Ed wanted to ask about whether any of the crew had been involved in The Falklands War, since it was commonly known that the SAS played an important role in the war and in particular the successful raid on Pebble Island. He decided against asking.

Ed and Carolyn sat along a side of the plane which was designed for military purpose, certainly not for comfort. He wondered if they would have to parachute out of the plane as he had seen so often on television. The thought almost made him sick to the stomach. Carolyn sat next to him, writing her report on the back of Ambassador Wood's report.

"Can I help?" Ed asked.

Carolyn pointed to her tongue which showed slightly from her mouth.

"You want me to ask for tea?" Ed gasped.

Carolyn smiled and nodded.

Ed rolled his eyes, unbuckled, mumbled something Carolyn could not make out and made his way unsteadily toward the front of the plane. He returned a few minutes later with two thermoses and a container of digestive biscuits.

"You have a choice of tea and biscuits, or biscuits and tea," he said sitting.

"Oh, tea and biscuits, please," Carolyn said with enthusiasm. "Isn't this romantic? Me and the man I love being flown special class to England's green and pleasant."

"It's rained for five days," Ed replied, pouring the tea.

"Hence the green," she bubbled, sipping her tea.

"How's the report?"

She shrugged. "Not too bad. One error. Let me finish my input, I'll let you add what you want to add and we'll both sign it. Okay?"

Ed nodded. "You okay?"

"I'm fine."

"You really okay?"

"Ed, I'm fine. Honest. I killed a man. I'm not particularly proud of that, but I'm sure glad that we got him before he got us."

"We?"

"Yes. We. Us. Our team." She smiled. "Look to be serious I'd rather you had shot him. But…"

Ed laughed. "You're kidding? Why me?"

"Because, young man, your mother would never find out that you killed someone. *My* mother *may* find out. And God Almighty will hear about it if she does! And for my father! Well, he'll never hear the end of it."

"I hear you. Finish your report. I'll keep your tea topped up."

Carolyn went back to her report writing. Ed watched her write, still amazed that they were lovers let alone friends in class-based England. Then, out of the blue, a thought crossed his mind.

"Actually," he said, thoughtfully, "it would be good if you mother finds out you popped him off."

Carolyn looked up. "Really? How's that work?"

"Well, it seems to me that your mother may realize that, well…you know?"

"No, I don't know."

Ed grinned, and took a risk. "That well, you aren't…sort of…you're more…you know?"

Carolyn closed her eyes, now understanding his mutterings. "You mean she'll think I'm more 'Neasden', and less 'to the Manor born', as it were?"

Now Ed really pushed his luck. "Perhaps more 'Kilburn' even?"

"I see," Carolyn responded slowly. "Now let me think this through to capture your twisted imagination. *If* my mother finds out I popped a man off, as you put it, and *if* some bloke from Kensal Rise, not far from Kilburn that is, were to ask me to marry him, and *if*, and I repeat *if*, I were to say yes; you think my mother would feel better about my saying 'yes' simply because I popped this man off? Is that your point here, Mr. Crowe? Mr. Crowe from Kensal Rise that is!"

"Hmmm…sort of."

Carolyn put down the report and put her hands on her lap. "You know, Mr. Crowe, when I was at Oxford, I met a bloke from Kilburn," she lied, "and a very nice bloke he was. Actually we went out on a couple of dates. On one of these dates, he…"

"I don't want to hear," Ed said, putting his hands over his ears. "I'm sorry."

Carolyn waited for him to uncover his ears. "On one of these dates, the last date in fact, he dumped me for a girl from Liverpool. I met her once. I could hardly understand a word she said, her accent was so strong. They ended up marrying and he is now a Member of Parliament." She smiled. "Now my mother would not mind if I were lucky enough to marry a Member of Parliament, don't you think?"

Ed got on his knees in front of Carolyn feigning horror. "I'm sorry, I was just being a smart arse, please forgive me."

It was at that moment that the SAS officer walked up to talk to them. "Are you proposing?" he asked with a broad smile.

Ed's head sank to his chest. He was unable to think of anything to say or do. He didn't move.

"No, Captain," Carolyn said nicely, "he's just begging for forgiveness. He does it all the time."

The officer nodded his understanding. "We'll be landing in half an hour. Maybe by then he'll be…?"

Carolyn nodded. The officer left. Ed sat down.

"How did you know he's a Captain?" Ed asked to change the subject.

"When I was at Oxford…"

Ed immediately covered his ears and started singing: *And did those feet in ancient times…*

Carolyn went back to her report.

Carolyn finished her report just as they landed, and Ed passed on reviewing her comments. If he found an error, which seemed unlikely, he probably wouldn't raise the issue anyway. They sat back and held hands as the huge plane landed on a Second World War airstrip, with the pilot hitting the brakes as soon as he could. It was not the smoothest of landings, but no one was going to complain. They thanked the crew, grabbed their bags, and jumping quickly through a downpour scampered into the waiting limo.

To their surprise Lady Stonebridge was not at the door of Stonebridge Manor when they arrived. As they ran up the steps to avoid the rain Mr. Cooper opened the door, and closed it as quickly as he could once they were inside.

"Sunny tomorrow," Mr. Cooper said, hopefully.

"Literally or figuratively," Ed asked.

The General shrugged and led them up the stairs to Lord Stonebridge's office.

As they entered the office Lord Stonebridge was on the phone. He waved them in. His conversation into the phone was limited, "Yes, yes. Yes, I know. Yes, of course I will," and finally, "I'll keep in touch. Goodbye."

Lord Stonebridge ordered some tea, moved papers away from the centre of his desk, and spread his hands openly on the top of his desk.

"Welcome back," he said genuinely, "it is very good to see you both. I take it you have read Ambassador Wood's report?"

Carolyn nodded, quickly opened the envelope and passed on the combined reports. "I've written mine on the back, sir," she said.

"To save money," Ed added, not receiving the response he had expected.

Lord Stonebridge started by reading Carolyn's report. The silence was only broken when the tea cart was wheeled in. Ed jumped up to act as mother and poured tea for everyone. Carolyn gave him a quick wink as he handed her cup to her. Ed sat and they waited.

"So it seems the major variance," Lord Stonebridge said, as he folded the report, "is that you think Surbey is a homosexual, and Wood's report doesn't reflect that."

"Yes, sir," Carolyn replied.

Lord Stonebridge rubbed his chin. "Intuition is a wonderful thing sometimes. Sometimes, that is."

"I thought…" Carolyn started, but was waved down.

Stonebridge continues. "You were correct, intuitively if I may, that Surbey was not acting as he should; was not approaching the matter professionally. Well done, Miss Andrews."

Ed smiled, knowing there was more to come.

"As it turns out," Mr. Cooper said calmly, "assuming the CIA has it correct, and I think we must, Surbey is addicted to cocaine in a most dependent and serious fashion. They have been worried about him for some months now and have been working with his wife who is in a terrible state."

"I feel really bad…" Carolyn muttered.

"No need," Lord Stonebridge interrupted. "You weren't sent to Damascus to have to work around a problem CIA operative. But in doing so, you accomplished the task and indeed had to take other serious measures, and the killing of a human being is very serious, in order to complete your assignment." He raised his cup of tea to acknowledge the success.

Ed hesitated for just a second as he realized they were acknowledging the deaths of two terrorists with cups of tea. It seemed to lack the enthusiasm of a 007 movie, but he felt good about what was happening and, more importantly, he could see a glow of relief in Carolyn's face.

Lord Stonebridge lowered his cup of tea. "But we think things have gone from bad to worse," he said sadly. "CIA operative Glenn Surbey has gone AWOL and we suspect, in fact we are sure, that he has gone over to the other side, so to speak." He took a deep breath. "We, and I mean the CIA, think he has joined the ANO."

"Oh, Jesus," Ed groaned. "We could have killed him too if we had known."

Carolyn couldn't help but gag. "Killed him too!" she shouted. "Who do you think we are, the bloody IRA?"

Stonebridge and the General waited for an answer, but Ed knew better than to upset Carolyn any further.

Mr. Cooper helped. "I suspect what Eddie was meaning to say was that if we had done *our* job properly before we sent you to Damascus, then you would not have been put at risk as you were, and the assignment goals would have been better understood. Is that correct, Eddie?"

Carolyn stood and poured herself a second cup of tea and put it on the cart without drinking it. "Could I ask that you give Mr. Crowe and me a minute, please?"

Lord Stonebridge and the General were out of the office in less than fifteen seconds.

Carolyn walked to Ed, took his hands in hers and asked him to stand. As he stood she put his arms around her. "Sorry for jumping at you. Just hold me for a minute, okay?"

Ed did as he was told.

A minute later Carolyn opened the door and all four took their seats. "Thank you for that, gentlemen," she said. "Bit of team-building was in order. So where do we go from here? I assume you brought Mr. Crowe to England, and not home to Canada, for a reason?"

"Right on the mark, Miss Andrews," Lord Stonebridge concurred, rubbing his hands together, "right on the mark."

Without thinking, almost by nature, Lord Stonebridge ordered more tea, and Carolyn pushed the tea cart out of the office for pick-up and re-fuelling. SOP? Ed wondered. The process did get Ed thinking if they would soon be determining who might die next – over a fresh pot of tea. He briefly closed his eyes and hoped his mother never found out what he was up to.

The tea was poured, the milk and sugar added and seats re-taken. Lord Stonebridge resumed his role.

"What we have here," he started, "is a unique opportunity to help our friends across the pond. The US that is," he added, looking at Ed. "They are extremely concerned that Surbey has, and will again, assist the ANO in their terrorist and murdering ways. They, the CIA, are now convinced that he was involved in the shootings at Vienna and Rome airports, and killed Hafiz to put an end to any information coming forth about Surbey's involvement. So while he is no longer a double agent, he has skills, knowledge, and information that could seriously damage the US's international relations, especially in the Middle East, and therefore our international relations also."

"A modern Kim Philby, then?" Ed asked innocently.

Mr. Cooper cringed at the name. Lord Stonebridge visibly shuddered. Carolyn looked to the ceiling for guidance.

"Perhaps a perfect comparison, in a round-about way," Lord Stonebridge said quietly. "Since the actions of Philby and his lot caused a major deterioration in relations between ourselves and the US, we now have an opportunity to make amends."

"Cover the scars, as it were," Carolyn touched her face.

"Well put," Mr. Cooper agreed.

"I assume we -they- don't want Surbey dead?" Ed asked.

"Absolutely not," Lord Stonebridge answered, now standing and turning to look out of the huge stained glass window behind his desk. "If they wanted him dead, they wouldn't be asking for our help. That is certain." He turned back to the room. "Just as we would have liked to have killed Philby in the '60s, there are plenty of CIA agents, at all levels I might add, that would like Surbey dead. Dead and gone."

"Would you have liked Philby dead in the '60s?" Ed asked.

Lord Stonebridge shrugged. "I was but a simple civil servant doing as I was told. Working nine to five, trying to scratch out a living for my small family."

Ed stood and looked around the room in a slow deliberate fashion. Looking up at the oak ceiling, down at the Turkish carpet, and around the room at the oak paneling and family paintings. With not a word, he sat back down.

Lord Stonebridge tilted his head in acceptance of the living he was 'scratching his pennies' for. "Oh, I'd had killed him in a moment," he said bluntly. "Perhaps not during the war when the USSR was on our side, but after the war…well that was a different matter wasn't it." It wasn't offered as a question, but as a statement of fact.

"So the continuing goal of the assignment," Mr. Cooper added, "is to find and bring back Mr. Surbey to London for handing over to the CIA Special Services that deal in this sort of matter. We will be getting you some cocaine that has an additional attraction; that being a very powerful sleep additive. If he uses this batch he will be asleep in an hour. You'll likely think he is dead, but rest assured he won't be."

"The risk, however," Lord Stonebridge stressed, "is once he comes out of the induced sleep, he'll be on a high like he's never felt and, by all accounts, stronger than an ox. So pack your handguns just in case." He paused. "And use them if need be. That's an order. Capiche?"

Carolyn and Ed nodded their understanding.

"I do have an important question," Ed said, raising his hand. "Do we ever get to eat? I'm famished."

Lord Stonebridge looked at his watch. "Lady Stonebridge has invited us all out for dinner tonight at a local pub. We leave in half an hour. Let's meet tomorrow at 6am and be ready to leave for the airport by 7."

"Do you know which pub," Carolyn asked nervously.

"The Swan, at Little Kimble," Lord Stonebridge answered. "Nice pub. Out of the way."

Carolyn rolled her eyes, not able to look at Ed. This was the pub where Ed had planned on asking Carolyn to marry him before he changed the date to coincide with Pat and Roy's wedding.

"Do you think Lady Stonebridge would allow me to buy the first round?" Ed asked, not looking at Carolyn.

Lord Stonebridge nodded with a chuckle. "I'm sure she wouldn't mind at all. Remember, she is from Neasden."

Ed sidled up to Carolyn. "Maybe I should change my timing and ask you..."

"Don't you dare! I'd never forgive you."

"But what would you say?" Ed asked.

Carolyn gave him a sweet smile. "That, my dear, is for me to know, and for you *not* to find out."

Ed carried the tray of drinks from the bar at The Swan to the table. Before he set the tray down he gave a small bow.

"Imagine this," he said proudly, "me buying drinks for a Lord, a Lady, a General, and the charming daughter of the Lord and Lady." He put the tray down and distributed the drinks.

"Tell me, Mr. Crowe," Lady Stonebridge asked as she held up her G and T, "how would you describe my 'charming daughter' to your mother?"

"Mother!" Carolyn said sharply. "Don't embarrass our guest."

Ed was happy to respond. "What I would say, Lady Stonebridge is that Carolyn is *the* most charming, most intelligent, most generous, most understanding..."

"Okay, Ed," Carolyn whispered.

"..and the most beautiful person I have ever met." Ed finished with a toast to Carolyn, with a mixture of agreement and embarrassment from around the table.

Lord Stonebridge raised his glass of red wine. "To our Mr. Crowe from Kensal Rise." All agreed.

Carolyn raised her glass of red wine. "To *my* Mr. Crowe from Kensal Rise." Ed felt his face flush which was an unusual event, but his pride at Carolyn's toast made it well worth while.

Lady Stonebridge silenced them with a gentle wave of her hand. "I understand our special guest and my charming daughter are leaving early in the morning, so let's please order our meal and enjoy the evening."

Everyone knew it was an order not a request, and they were all happy to oblige.

CHAPTER TWENTY TWO

FRIDAY, JANUARY 30THTH 1986, STONEBRIDGE MANOR, ENGLAND

I t was still dark when they all gathered in Lord Stonebridge's office at the agreed-upon time. The good news was the office had central heating. The remainder of the manor didn't, certainly not the guest bedroom Ed had slept in. He rushed to get showered in semi-hot water, he shivered while he shaved, and he rushed to put on some winter clothes. But he entered the office without a comment or shiver. A casual walk to the window, where the radiator giving off its life-saving heat was located, and a comment on the warming weather forecast was enough to bring him back to normal. He never thought he would look forward to returning to a Canadian winter, but at that moment he did.

The mandatory trolley of tea was wheeled in and Carolyn played mother and poured for the four of them. It was hot and welcome. When all were settled in, Lord Stonebridge assumed his role.

"So the plan is to bring Surbey back to London, using the VC10 that brought you here and will return you to Damascus this morning. Do not work with any other department or agency; especially the CIA, and report only directly to myself or the General. Use the cocaine I will get you only if you have to and if you do, get him to the SAS people as soon as you can. They've seen this stuff before. In fact your contact on the plane is Sergeant John McAleese. A name you may have heard of."

Ed snapped his fingers. "Iranian Embassy, London, 1980! He was first in the window on the SAS ending of the siege. I saw it all on the telly with my mother."

The General nodded. "That's the man. Tough as nails. As Scottish as his name. In fact he has the cocaine and will show you how to administer it. Don't be afraid to use his knowledge for this assignment. But keep in mind he cannot, must not, play an active part. We cannot have our soldiers carrying out missions in a foreign country. That's called war. Use him carefully. He knows his limitations on activity."

"He has weapons for us?" Carolyn asked.

Lord Stonebridge nodded. "And this time the ammunition is real, so please be careful."

Mr. Cooper looked at his watch. "Let's have a quick top-up, and I'll get you both to the airport."

Carolyn finished her tea. "One further question, sir. I assume, er, Lady..."

"Lady Stonebridge knows nothing of what happened in Damascus," Mr. Cooper said quickly, "and let's all hope..."

"Let us *pray* she never finds out," Lord Stonebridge interrupted with feeling.

It was a short drive to the airport, passing through the village of Halton. There had been a small snow fall during the night and the snow on the village houses and shops looked most scenic. More so, Ed thought, because the car had a decent inside heater. He had insisted on Carolyn sitting in the front with Mr. Cooper; she was the leader of the operation. Besides if she had sat in the back with him, he'd have wanted to hold her hand, and that was clearly not the proper thing to do. But sitting directly behind her allowed him to savor her perfume. He closed his eyes and let his mind slip back to his meeting her in Ankara. So much had happened since he had met her less than two years ago. His daydreaming stopped quickly as the car pulled up beside the VC 10, and Carolyn jumped out to lead the way. He was now comfortably warm and happy to follow.

Within twenty minutes they were bumping down the runway, more grass than cement, and the plane lumbered into the air over the snow dusted fields and villages of England. But there was no warmth in this plane. They sat in the seats they had flown over in. They weren't built for comfort, which was a stark reminder of the days ahead. Comfort would not be the word of the day.

"You okay?" Carolyn asked.

"Never better," Ed replied smartly. "Never better."

At twenty thousand feet the plane leveled off, and down the centre of the plane walked their SAS contact; Sergeant John McAleese. He was of medium height, but built solidly and looked ready for action in his camouflage uniform.

"Call me Mac," the Scot said, shaking their hands. "I'm here to make sure you get back alive, so dinna do anything I tell yer not to, yeah?"

They nodded, acknowledging he wasn't about to waste any time on formalities. He handed each of them a Browning hand gun from his waistband. "This is a single action pistol," he explained, not waiting for any comment, "which means it has to be cocked before the first shot can be fired. Because of this you will carry it cocked and ready to go. They have been adjusted to accommodate the release of the safety and the first shot almost instantly, so be careful." He turned to Carolyn. "Now you've killed twice before, so you know the process." He turned to Ed.

"Excuse me!" Carolyn interrupted. "I have not killed twice thank you very much!"

McAleese took a seat next to Carolyn. "Yes yer have, miss. At the Rome airport shooting you killed one of the attackers. The bullet that killed one of them was from your gun, and no-one else used it. Correct?"

Carolyn closed her eyes and lowered her head. One killing was bad enough…now twice a killer. She couldn't look up.

"Look, Miss Andrews," McAleese continued, "yer killed him before he killed you and probably others. He was a terrorist – a killer. He dinna have a wife and two bairns waiting for him in a semi-detached somewhere. He dinna give a damn about yer, and would likely have been proud to have killed yer first. Are you with me here?"

Ed responded to give Carolyn some time to think. "I've killed a man, Mac. But what's your message?"

"The same as I just made, Ed. The people we're dealing with, *you're* dealing with, are not nice people. They think and live differently than we do. They're not the first bunch to kill in their God's name, hell we've done that ourselves. But the point is they will kill you if they think they need to, so you must be ready to do the same."

"Kill or be killed?" Carolyn muttered, clearing her throat.

"Aye, I'm afraid it's that easy," McAleese acknowledged. "Now down to business. I've booked two rooms at the Biet Akbik Hotel in Damascus. It's quite lovely. It's also old and allows some level of protection from the general public. The rooms are next to each on the third floor, facing the front. I want yer to both to sleep in one room, switching rooms each night. Obviously I dinna mean for yer to sleep *with* each other, in fact I want only one asleep at a time. The sleeper, let's call him 'A' will sleep on the floor by the side of the bed furthest away from the door to the hallway. The second, 'B', will sit in a chair as far away from the bed as possible, in a corner facing the door to the hallway. So it will be three hours sleep each, and then one hour sleep each. Total four hours each sleep each night. Okay so far?"

Ed sat open mouthed, not daring to ask questions. Carolyn was now smiling totally impressed with their handler. "What if…?" she started.

"Yer have to see a man about a dog?" McAleese asked.

She nodded.

"Then yer do what you have to do, and yes you flush the toilet. But," and he raised a hand, "if ye're 'A' you don't go back to the sleeping position for at least a minute. Stay in the bathroom, gun in hand."

"Makes sense," Ed nodded.

McAleese continued. "So I want yer both to wear underwear all night. No distractions."

"Even small ones," Carolyn asked, looking at Ed.

"That's the spirit," McAleese added. "Now most important. If ye're 'A' and the door flies open during the night – and yer can rest assured it won't be room service – I want yer to start shooting toward the door before you raise your head. So sleep in a position that allows yer to raise your gun, rest it on the bed for accuracy, and start shooting. With me, yeah?"

They nodded.

"If you're 'B', I want yer to shoot first at the person in the room, and then pump several bullets through the doorway at the second person; and there will be a second person. Then shoot the first person again, even of yer think they're dead. If they are dead, it dinna matter. If they're not, then it matters. The guns have thirteen rounds. Don't be afraid to use them all if need be, but I'd prefer you use ten rounds and keep the remaining three, just in case. If it happens, hopefully the attacker will have entered the other bed room first. This will give yer a few moments warning. So be sure to make up the bed in the second as if someone is sleeping in it. Questions?"

Ed looked at Carolyn who shrugged, obviously not sure what to ask. Ed had to ask. "What are the chances that someone will try and kill us like that? I thought we were here to catch, or kill, him!"

McAleese smiled. "I practiced climbing over buildings and jumping through windows a thousand times; and I only did it for real once. But when it happened, it was just a part of my life. I didn't enjoy killing the man I killed…but I'm here to tell yer about it, aren't I?"

Carolyn nodded. "One question. How do we make sure 'B' doesn't fall asleep? This could go on for days."

McAleese grinned. "Aye there's a fine question. First yer keep the door to the bathroom slightly ajar for light. Secondly, I'd suggest 'B' does something to keep the brain going. I'd propose writing a book, or a least an outline of a book. Third, there's a spare bedroom at the embassy if one of you needs to catch up."

"Callie the Cat," Ed said enthusiastically. "When I'm 'B', I'm going to write a book about my friend's cat. That's Roy Johnson," he continued, looking at Carolyn with a cheeky grin. "You know the bloke that asked you to marry him?"

Carolyn rolled her eyes. "Of course I remember, and I might have said yes if it was a few years ago. But now…well I'm not sure I'll ever say yes to anyone."

Ed knew when he was losing, so he said no more.

McAleese stood. "Well I'll leave yer two to discuss matters." He looked at his watch. "We land in three hours. I'll be back in a while to tell yer about our special cocktail of cocaine. Maybe get some sleep." He walked to the front of the plane.

"I've an idea," Carolyn said enthusiastically.

"Here? Now?" Ed asked. "Maybe they'd hear us?"

Carolyn waved away his comments. "When I'm 'B', I'll follow on with your book about 'Callie the Cat'. A joint venture perhaps?"

"Puuurrfect," he responded. "The cat's meow even."

Carolyn groaned. "Do you ever give up?"

"Never with you, Carolyn. Never with you."

"That's good," she smiled. "Now get some sleep. It's going to be a busy week."

Ed adjusted his body to lie on the seat and resting his head on Carolyn's lap. "I'll sleep in the presence of an angel," he whispered, closing his eyes.

Carolyn looked down at him waiting for further comment. To her surprise Ed fell asleep in a couple of minutes. She made a mental note herself to tell him that he could not now state they had 'slept together' on the plane to Damascus. She closed her eyes to get some rest. Almost immediately, she too fell asleep.

"Wakey, wakey girls and boys," McAleese shouted loudly. Carolyn and Ed stumbled awake, sitting up straight while trying not to look embarrassed. "Good to see teamwork," McAleese continued handing each of them a cup of tea.

Carolyn adjusted her hair and sipped on her tea.

Ed gulped the hot tea down in a couple of gulps. "Thought there might be a shot of whiskey in it," he said grinning.

"Maybe on the way home," McAleese muttered, "but only if we, that is yer, have a successful trip."

"We will, Mr. McAleese," Carolyn said with conviction. "We work well together in spite of our lack of experience."

McAleese laughed aloud. "I dinna wish to be rude, Miss, but three dead bad guys and a suicide in our favour, inna so bad!" Until then, they were not aware of his knowledge of Ed's experience in Libya, where a 'bad man' had committed suicide with his own bayonet in front of Ed rather than allowing Ed to shoot him for a second time, this time to kill him.

Carolyn wrinkled her face at his description of the events. "I certainly hadn't thought of things in that light. It makes us sound rather nasty."

McAleese shrugged, "Ye're here, and they're not. Yer point is?"

"No point, sir" Carolyn said sheepishly. "Nice cup of tea."

"You're welcome. And it's Mac please. I'm not that much older than yer to be called sir."

Ed raised his cup in salute. "Cheers, Mac. And onto the drugs!"

"Exactly," McAleese nodded. "I assume neither of yer use cocaine?"

Carolyn choked on her tea, spilling some on herself.

"I'll take that as a no," McAleese said turning at Ed.

Ed shook his head. "I've never graduated past beer and wine I'm glad to say."

McAleese nodded reaching into his pocket. "Well if yer smart enough to get out of London and go to Canada, yer should be smart enough not to screw yer brains up on drugs." He held up two small glass bottles, both containing white powder. "This one, the one containing the most substance, is cocaine. The other is 100% Triazolam."

"Yes of course, Triazolam," Ed said smugly.

Carolyn laughed. "Don't worry, Mac, he's never heard of it before. A couple of beers and a glass of wine are all that Ed needs to fall asleep."

McAleese continued. "If you get the opportunity, or need, to use this on Surbey, just combine the two bottles which should be enough to satisfy any addict. The cocaine is pure, so no concern regarding a bad batch." He looked at them separately to make his point. "But beware. When he wakes up from this sleep he'll be a raving mess. He'll be like a raving bull and won't know what he's doing, and wouldn't care if he did. And before you ask he'll be asleep, like the dead so to speak, for about four hours. No more than five. He will need to be tied down, if nothing else for his own sake."

Carolyn didn't like the idea at all. "How long…"

"About an hour," McAleese interrupted, "and then he'll very quickly collapse into a deep coma for about another three hours. Then he'll wake up with a hangover from hell and, like I said, with little recollection of what occurred."

"Then this should be our last tool in the process?" Ed asked.

"Absolutely. I've seen it used once and it was no fun," McAleese offered, his face reflecting his comments.

Carolyn gulped before asking. "What happened? To the man I mean."

He took time before answering. "He jumped from a second floor building, landed on a metal fence and lost a leg at the knee in the process." He paused, "The worst part was that he started to run on one leg and wouldn't give up."

"Only got about one foot, I suppose," Ed quipped.

"Oh, shit!" Carolyn exclaimed, covering her mouth to stop from bringing back the tea.

McAleese looked at Ed and then turned to Carolyn. "He's a friend by choice is he?"

Carolyn nodded, almost reluctantly.

McAleese shrugged. "I guess opposites do attract."

Ed grinned, winking at Carolyn.

McAleese stood. "I'll leave you to think things through. We arrive shortly, and you'll be on your own to make your way to the hotel and work you magic. I'll leave shortly after you and will always be close to the two of you, but you won't see or recognize me."

"No kilt then?" Ed asked, trying to calm the atmosphere.

"Not this time," McAleese replied and walked to the forward of the plane.

Carolyn sat shaking her head. "I hope he was exaggerating."

Ed winked, "Sort of, ya know…pulling our leg!"

"You are sick, Mr. Crowe, bloody sick," she gasped, but then couldn't help but chuckle. "Pulling our leg…Yuchh!"

After the slow process of proceeding through customs, Ed and Carolyn got a taxi to their hotel. The hotel was small with just five floors and beautifully decorated throughout the entrance and large lobby area. As organized by McAleese the rooms in their names were 306 and 308, and faced the front onto a small but busy street. Room 306 was in Carolyn's name and was closest to the elevator. They quickly decided that room 308 is where they would sleep for the first night on the assumption that if anything as dramatic as what they were planning for did happen, then room 306 would be the first room to be attacked. After dropping off Carolyn's bags in 306 they both entered room 308.

Ed held Carolyn's arm as they entered and pulling a face whispered. "Come into my parlor said the spider to the fly."

Carolyn raised a hand. "The correct wording is 'Will you walk into my parlor…'."

Ed feigned a tear. "Ah! The benefit of an Oxford education. I am so embarrassed."

Carolyn held out her arms. "You'll get by. Now give me a hug and a kiss. Keeping in mind," she continued as Ed hugged her, "that this will be the extent of our loving for a while."

"I'll take what I can get," Ed replied, starting to kiss her face and lips.

They were interrupted by the phone ringing. Ed picked it up and grunted more than spoke, "Hello."

"Glad to see you selected the correct room," McAleese said. "Good thinking. I'll keep in touch from time to time. Close the curtains please."

Ed closed the curtains, and then for several more minutes they held each other not speaking except to confirm their love for each other. With a final hug they separated.

Carolyn spoke first. "Okay, let's unpack in our rooms and I'll be back in twenty minutes to sort out the sleeping arrangements." She smiled. "I'll leave my curtains open for a while to make sure our guardian angel sees me safe…and alone. When I get back we can get something to eat?"

"Yes, Miss," Ed said, now using her operational name.

The work now had to begin and their personal relationship was set aside.

CHAPTER TWENTY THREE

MONDAY, FEBRUARY 3RD, 1986 8:15AM BIET AKBIC HOTEL DAMASCUS.

E d put down his writing pad and pen. "This isn't working," he said quietly. "There are people walking the halls, and we're kidding ourselves that Surbey is about to come blasting into the room to kill us. It doesn't make sense. If we have to go through another three more days of this, I'll be concerned we won't be ready to react. We'll be too relaxed...if we aren't already. What do you think, Miss?"

Carolyn was lying on the floor as outlined by Mac, and had not had a good night's sleep...again. "Keep talking, Mister. Tell me what's in your head." She raised the gun above her head and resting her hand on the bed, aimed the gun at the door. She knew Ed was correct. They had to stay alert.

"Okay, let's go over where we are," Ed said, raising his gun to the door; if only to be in the same mindset as Carolyn. "We've had a coffee in every café within six blocks of here. In addition to getting high on that much bloody coffee, we've asked everyone and anyone if they've seen a tall thin blond American, who looks sickly and, unbeknownst to him, needs medical attention. Nothing! Nada! Zippo! Not a bloody thing."

Carolyn interrupted. "Please don't swear, Ed. It doesn't become you."

"Sorry."

"Apology accepted. Please continue, Mister."

"So we can assume he knows we're looking for him. He has to know why, so he has to either keep under cover until we give up...or come get us. Since he hasn't..."

The knock on the room door changed everything. Ed raised his gun higher to the door, and Carolyn gripped her gun and adjusted it slightly to make sure it was aimed correctly. She had to fight her natural inclination to peek over the bed.

They waited, holding their breath.

"It's me. Surbey." He knocked again. "Listen, I know you're in there. If I wanted to hurt you, you'd be dead already." He paused, giving them time to think. He knocked again, only louder. "Unlock the door and let me in for Christ's sake."

Ed looked to Carolyn for direction. She was the lead.

Slowly Carolyn lifted her head above the bed, put her fingers to her mouth, shook her head, then pointed to Ed. He understood and nodded.

Carolyn looked to the door. "What do you want?" she asked as casually as she could.

"No. What do you want?" Surbey replied.

As he spoke, Carolyn pointed to Ed and motioned him to act.

"Stand back from the door." Carolyn said loudly and clearly.

As she spoke Ed quickly grabbed the door key from the side table and as smoothly as he could slid the key under the door. He stayed on the far side of the door, knowing intuitively not to cross in front of the door a second time. Carolyn ordered for him to move to the wall at right angle to the door. He moved quickly, and pressing his back to the wall he raised his gun to eye level and pointed it toward the door.

Carolyn took a deep breath, moved to the end of the bed to separate herself as far as possible from Ed's location and spoke as calmly as she could. "Come in carefully with your hands above your head. If there's another person with you, you're both dead."

The key turned in the lock and slowly the door opened. Surbey's hands came in first and as he entered the room he raised his hands above his head. Without waiting to be told he pushed the door closed with his foot and taking a small step backward, he stood with his back against the door. He kept his head still, looking around the room with his eyes. "Well done," he said. "Ya done good."

He was wearing a thin pair of pants and a thin white tee shirt. He was not dressed for the weather; he was dressed to make it easy for all to see he was unarmed. His face was thin to being skull-like and the gauntness of his body was difficult to look at.

"Turn and face the door," Carolyn said, rising to stand up.

Surbey nodded, and very carefully turned.

Carolyn motioned to Ed who carefully put his gun under the pillow on the bed, moved to Surbey and quickly patted him down repulsed at having to touch such an obviously sick man. The only article on Surbey was a package of cigarettes in his shirt pocket. "Bad habit," Ed quipped and returned and picked up his gun.

"Well done boys and girls," Surbey said without moving. "You've been trained very well."

"Why are you here?" Carolyn asked, unable to think of a more relevant question.

"No, why are you here?" Surbey replied, looking sideways at Carolyn. "Why have you been looking for me throughout downtown Damascus? And at great risks to yourselves I might add."

Carolyn motioned for Ed to respond. She needed to think.

Ed spoke slowly trying to ensure what he said made sense. "We're worried about your health," Ed said. "We're here to take you to Britain. Good health care, and free," was all he could muster.

Surbey's body shook with laughter. "Good health care!" he shouted. "I'm dying for Christ's sake. Nothing can save me, least of all your damned National Health Service. I'm waiting to die. I sure as hell don't want to wait in an over-crowded poorly run British excuse for a hospital."

Carolyn raised her hand for Ed to stop that conversation. She counted to thirty before she spoke, "Are you dying of AIDS, Mr. Surbey?"

"Yes, I am," he snapped back, "but it's not what you think it is."

Carolyn nodded her understanding. "I suspect, Mr. Surbey, that you contracted the disease through a dirty needle in your use of cocaine." She paused before continuing. "Are you addicted to cocaine?"

He shook his head. "No I am not addicted, but let me make this clear. Cocaine is the only help I get in living this life that has screwed me, and I want to die in peace and comfort. Is that asking so much?"

"By turning traitor against your own country?" Ed asked.

"Don't you dare say that," Surbey screamed, turning and leaning toward Ed in a fit of rage. "I'm no fucking traitor!" He backed off as both Ed and Carolyn now had their guns aimed at his head. He leaned back against the door. "I'm not a traitor," he repeated, quietly this time. He bowed his head, eyes closed.

Ed didn't need the look from Carolyn to know that he had gone too far, too quickly. He mouthed his apologies to her and they waited.

"You don't understand," Surbey muttered, barely above a whisper.

"Try us?" Carolyn said. "In fact, let's do this, Mr. Surbey. Why don't you let us handcuff your wrists and ankles, then you can sit on the bed and tell us what we don't know? I should add that we have both killed in the past, so we will not hesitate to kill you." She paused. "Indeed, I killed the man you sent to kill us. Perhaps your explaining that would be a good start?"

Surbey nodded. "Sure, let's do that."

Ed collected the handcuffs they were planning to use when Surbey was high on cocaine, putting them tightly on his hands and then added the leg cuffs to his ankles as he sat on the bed. Carolyn kept her gun trained on his head as they moved carefully about the room. Ed and Carolyn sat on chairs at ninety degrees from each other to ensure any shooting would not put the other at danger. Carolyn motioned for him to speak.

"To start with," Surbey said, looking at Carolyn, "I did not send that man to kill you. If he had fired the machine-gun it would have jammed. I fixed it to jam, and adjusted it after I picked it up. He would have tried to kill you with his bare hands but you killed him first, so it worked out okay. Three fine shots by the way."

Carolyn almost choked as she covered her mouth to stop herself from gagging. "What?" she gasped.

Ed kept his eyes on Surbey and took control of the conversation. "Why would we believe that?" he asked calmly. "You shot Abid Hafiz in front of us, and now you're telling us you sent another man to his death. Surely you knew we would kill him? We may not be the CIA, but we're not stupid."

Surbey shrugged. "He's not worth talking about." He turned again to Carolyn. "While you were being shot at the airport in Rome last December, that man was killing and wounding people, with great enthusiasm I might add, at Vienna airport at the same time, so don't waste your time feeling sorry for him."

"Why would he do that?" Ed asked, endeavoring to give Carolyn time to recover and take the lead.

"The simple answer," Surbey replied, "is that he's a Palestinian. The longer answer is that when the Jewish State was approved by the United Nations in 1947, the fighting between Arabs and Jews in 1948 resulted in his family losing their farm and land. The land was taken over by the Israeli Army and now forms part of the State of Israel." He shrugged. "We wouldn't be happy if that happened to us, would we?"

"Whose side are you on?" Carolyn asked, now feeling comfortable enough to take back control of this totally un-planned situation.

Surbey was ready for the question, and turned to Carolyn to make his point. "I'm on the side of innocent people who are caught up in the politics of war. Sure I feel sorry for the Palestinians. The partition of Palestine was a mistake. Obviously it was a mistake. Britain didn't even vote in favor of it at the United Nations. It predictably resulted in the 1948 Arab-Israeli War, and there hasn't been any level of real peace since then. But these on-going political and military actions aren't going to be resolved by the killing and maiming of people such as you."

Carolyn couldn't help but agree. "I understand and appreciate what you're saying – although I would add that Britain abstained…"

Surbey interrupted. "They didn't vote in favor. That's what I said."

Carolyn nodded with a smile. "I just wanted my associate to know the facts. He's too young to know these things."

"Thank you ma'am," Ed said, with a nod of appreciation. Carolyn was twenty-three days older than he was. He would address her comment in private later.

Any tension in the room was now gone, which allowed Carolyn to get the facts of the matter that brought them to this situation. "The CIA, your employer as it were, is of the opinion that you have changed sides and to be honest you have given them every opportunity to believe that to be true. However, today you seem to be somewhere in…in…I don't know…in the middle maybe. You've given yourself up. You must know we have to repatriate you – to Britain that is – so why are you here?"

Surbey inhaled deeply and started the explanation that he so much wanted someone to hear and, more importantly, understand. "I am dying of AIDS. Weeks, not months. It is important that you - - everyone - understand that I contracted this deadly disease through a needle. I am not homosexual, and it is extremely important for my wife and family to know that. Neither am I proud to admit that I use cocaine, but I want you to assure me that you will pass this information on to my family. The agency will not do that. I know they believe that I contracted the disease through…you know what I mean."

Carolyn nodded her understanding, but decided not to make any promises she could not, in her own mind, guarantee.

Surbey waited for a verbal response and then continued when it was clear there wasn't one coming.

"I've messed things up with the agency. They think I'm some sort of rebel; a traitor for God's sake! I'm not a traitor. I'm a loyal American one-hundred percent. My goal is to prove who I am in a way the agency would never allow, not even the CIA. My final act will prove to everyone, especially my wife, that they were wrong in their judgment. It will be for God to judge me."

"Final act?" Ed asked.

"I plan on killing Abu Nidal and as many of his henchmen as I can take with us."

Carolyn waited for him to continue. He didn't. "Us?" she demanded.

Surbey laughed. "Not us, not here. Nidal and myself. I plan on killing him and others in the same way as he has killed; and he has killed many. He was sentenced to death in absentia by the PLO after he tried to assassinate Mahmoud Abbas. He is a crazy man who needs to die. And I need your help to do it."

Carolyn raised her eyebrows and almost laughed, but didn't. She could see he was being honest. Ed looked at her with a shrug and just a tiny knowing smile. She was the lead, and he wouldn't want it any other way.

"Mr. Surbey," she began, "we are here to take you back to Britain from where you will be turned over to the CIA, at the highest level I might add. We don't want some gun-toting agent to shoot you, the 'traitor', while you were 'trying to escape'."

"Certainly not in Britain," Ed added.

Surbey turned to Ed and almost spat his response. "There's nothing God-damned special about Britain when it comes to safety. There have been more riots in jolly old fucking England in the last few years than in the US, in fact probably in any other western country. Does 'Brixton riots' sound familiar? So don't be so fucking smug!"

Ed responded immediately. "At least those hurt in the riots could go to hospital and get help – at no charge." He calmed down and took a deep breath. "Besides, no one was killed."

Surbey turned to Carolyn. "I apologize for my language. Now are you going to help me?"

"I doubt it," she replied, "but exactly what would you have us do?"

"Nothing special," he answered with a shrug, "I just need you to get me some Semtex, and leave the rest to me. Hear me out before you respond. Please?"

Carolyn waved him on.

"Yes, I have access to the local members of the ANO, and yes, they believe I will work for them in a minor way. However, they do not trust me entirely so I have to be careful; very careful. And yes, I told them you were coming here on your first visit, and they know you are here now. Most of what they know is from me, but they have at least one other source to information. I sometimes wonder if what I am telling them is more confirmation of what they already know. This makes my situation even more tenuous, since I can't be in the position of giving them false information. What I tell them must coincide with any other data they may be collecting. If it doesn't, then I'm dead and nothing useful will have resulted from my miserable circumstance here. More importantly, my wife will always think of me as a traitor... and worse."

Carolyn put her hand to her mouth to think. Surbey waited.

Ed decided to help out the situation. "Our orders, sir, are to take you back to Britain, or kill you 'if need be'. You're asking a great deal of my associate to let you go free in order to attempt a killing of people - certainly bad guys – and yet you stated your concern was the killing of people. You want to do exactly what you state is the wrong solution to what is a very complex situation."

Surbey smiled his understanding. "My concern is for the *innocent* people that die. I have no sympathy for soldiers of any country, of any status. You join an army, you must expect there is always a risk that you have to fight, and possibly die. It's the nature of the beast. But the killing of innocent people, whether it's the IRA, the US during the Viet Nam War or the British Bomber Command in the Second World War is wrong. That is not war. That is a form of terrorism, plain and simple."

"And how will killing Abu Nidal help toward world peace?" Ed asked.

"Don't be a smart ass, mister," Surbey replied angrily. "With him dead most everyone will be happy, especially the PLO. Their own leadership is hugely concerned that the world now believes that all Palestinians are criminals. They have enough on their hands without rogue members taking the role of executioner of all the people he doesn't like."

Ed turned to Carolyn for her response.

"That is true," she agreed. "In fact their deputy chief said as much in direct response to the Rome and Vienna airport attacks." She gently stroked her facial scars as she remembered her own experience. "What if we decline your request, Mr. Surbey then what do you do?"

"Well I am dying, that is a fact of life. So I won't make it easy for you to get me to Britain." He looked toward the window. "Maybe I'll take a run and jump through the window right now. Would that make you happy?"

Ed instantly moved between Surbey and the window and raised hi gun.

"Let's calm down please," Carolyn interjected, motioning Ed back to his spot.

Surbey smiled. "Sure, let's do that. Maybe you'd let me have a smoke?"

Carolyn nodded, and with his handcuffed hands Surbey removed the cigarette package from his shirt pocket, removed a cigarette and put it between his lips. His smile turned into a grin.

"Oh shit," Carolyn groaned, realizing what had happened. "No matches!"

Surbey held the cigarette filter between his front teeth, carefully snipped off the tobacco portion of the cigarette and tossed it away. "Potassium Cyanide," he grinned. "Be dead in two minutes."

Carolyn's shoulders slumped and she lowered her gun. "What a stupid mistake on my part."

"If you bite down on that," Ed said, as calmly as he could, "your wife will forever think of you as a traitor...or worse."

Surbey shook his head. "No she won't, because Miss Andrews would make sure she knew the truth about my plans...if not the actual cause of death. Isn't that correct, Miss Andrews?"

"Probably," Carolyn nodded. "No sense in causing pain to an innocent person. Isn't that correct, Mr. Surbey?"

Surbey nodded his thanks. "Absolutely. Well said. And thank you."

Ed tried to keep the communication level and on-going. "What we have here is a failure to communicate," he said bravely. "Surely no-one wants you to die today, Mr. Surbey, and possibly, just possibly, we could work out an arrangement that is satisfactory to all."

Carolyn turned to him. "Really? And how might that happen, Mr. Crowe?" There was no humor in her voice.

"Ah, there's the rub," Ed replied. "A rising tide lifts all boats. That's what I say."

Surbey turned to Carolyn. "Is he always like this?" he asked, laughing aloud. Before the question was out of his mouth, Ed lunged at him slamming his entire body into Surbey's back as hard as he could. Surbey gasped wildly swallowing the cyanide pill in a second.

"Shit!" Surbey screamed. "Fucking shit."

Carolyn grabbed and raised her gun. "Exactly, Mr. Surbey. That's where you'll find it."

Ed moved to stand in front of the window. "Sorry about that." He spoke calmly. "Now why don't we keep the conversation going?"

"Fuck you," Surbey replied, still gasping for air.

Carolyn assumed her lead role, and turned to Surbey. "Tell me exactly what your plans are; assuming, that is, the pill you swallowed is standard CIA and will not disintegrate in you stomach."

Surbey caught his breath, and turned to Ed. "Do you know who first said 'A rising tide…,' smart ass?"

Ed lied and shook his head.

"John F. Kennedy; our greatest ever president. That's who. No damn Shakespeare this time. And don't you forget it."

Ed decided not to raise the Bay of Pigs affair, and let the comment stand. He stood and walked to the phone. "Maybe I should order some tea?"

Surbey groaned in disbelief. "At least make it coffee for Christ's sake."

Ed ordered coffee for three with a bow to Surbey. "Discretion is a better part of valor."

"Thank you, Ed," Carolyn smiled. "That was good thinking."

Ed bowed to Carolyn. "Some are born great, others achieve greatness, and some have…"

Carolyn interrupted loudly. "Ed, shut up!"

"Et tu, Brute," Ed mumbled, standing back.

Surbey shook his head motioning to Ed. "I'll do just about anything to get away from him."

"You're likely not the first to say that," Carolyn nodded. "Now your plan please, Mr. Surbey."

"Before I explain my plan," Surbey started, "you need to know where I'm at currently with the Abu Nidal Organization."

Carolyn motioned for him to proceed.

"Well to start with, they know who I am and what I do. I attend some of their less important meetings, most of which are pulled together very quickly and last no more than ten, maybe fifteen minutes. If they think someone has betrayed them they will kill them on the spot. I have seen three members killed, one was only a boy who made the unthinkable error of talking to a young Jewish girl. That was on direct orders from Nidal himself. In my opinion he is maniacal. These are not nice people."

"The understatement of the year, perhaps?" Ed said.

Surbey ignored the comment. "Now in three days Abu Nidal is coming to Damascus. He will be meeting, unofficially of course, with government people, perhaps President Assad himself. He will be looking for money and military weapons. It is not likely that he will get what he wants, but the government will not want to make an enemy of him. He will be in and out of the city in a matter of hours. Now the only good news in all of this is that he will attend a local organizational meeting before he meets with the government. That is where I will kill him; and everyone else at the meeting of course."

"Of course," Carolyn said curtly. "What are a few dead people here or there?"

There was a knock on the door. Ed quickly opened it as little as he could, took the tray of coffee without comment and placed it on the side table. He took orders and poured.

"So how can you be assured you will be invited to the meeting?" Ed asked.

Using both hands, Surbey took a long sip of the strong and very hot coffee. "They make good coffee here," he said.

"The invitation?" Carolyn asked.

Surbey replied with a grin. "I will be invited because that very day I will kill an enemy of the ANO." He turned to Ed. "And that will be you."

Ed slowly took a sip of his coffee, keeping his eyes on Surbey. "I'm sure it will be a pleasure working with you," he said.

Carolyn raised her hand to stop the conversation. "Expand please?"

Surbey continued. "The two of you will be walking into the British Embassy…" he began.

Fifteen minutes later Surbey sat back as Carolyn and Ed reviewed the proposed plan silently to themselves. He was more satisfied each minute that passed before either of them spoke.

Ed led the way. "And all *we* need do is get you some Semtex…and additionally I have the pleasure of being 'attacked' by an American hero; as the story will ultimately reveal." He raised both eyes as a question. "Will this plan have a name?" he asked as an afterthought.

"Operation Crowe Bait," Carolyn replied immediately.

"Exactly!" Surbey laughed aloud: "Operation Crowe Bait it is."

Ed bowed in recognition. "Charmed I'm sure. What do we do next?"

Surbey pointed to the fan in the ceiling. "The first thing we do is get your associate in here to work on the details."

"Excuse me?" Carolyn said, looking at the fan. It was only then that she noticed a small dark spot on the fan's connection to the ceiling. "Damn!" she muttered, taking a deep breath before she continued. "When you're ready, Mac, why don't you join us?"

Ed did his best to calm matters. "SOP right? Standard operating procedures."

"Yeah, right," Surbey laughed. "The check's in the mail and I'll love you in the morning."

Carolyn closed her eyes, keeping her comments to herself. She felt betrayed by her own people. She couldn't believe her own father would approve of her; *them*; being spied upon. She sat and waited.

Five minutes later there was a knock on the door. Ed quickly walked over and opened it.

"Hi, Mac," Ed motioned him into the room.

Mac and Surbey introduced themselves and shook hands with the handcuffs rattling nicely. Carolyn nodded to Ed who grabbed the keys and removed the shackles on Surbey, who thanked him with a smile.

"You should know," Mac said, turning to Carolyn, "that I don't work for MI6; I work for Special Air Services. What I do, I do of my own accord. Personally I hope you don't mention the special effects." He pointed to the fan. "That was my decision and mine alone. I'm here to help and protect you both, not to be Mr. Nice Guy – as you Americans say." He nodded to Surbey. Ed was surprised how Mac spoke with less of his Scottish accent when addressing a formal issue.

Carolyn spoke firmly "We'll talk about that later. What do you think of Mr. Surbey's plan?"

"Well I wudnae accept any plan that resulted in the death of one of our own. Once yer died, ye're died" He shrugged, looking at Surbey. "But if yer reck it's the oonly way..I widnae git in the ways."

"Can you get the Semtex?" Surbey asked.

"Aye. As much as yer need."

Carolyn turned to Ed and Mac. "Can you give Mr. Surbey and me five minutes please?"

They nodded their understanding and left the room.

"Mr. Surbey, I need to…"

"Please call me Glen."

Carolyn nodded. "Okay, Glen, I need to talk to you about your plan. I simply cannot accept it."

"Well it seems to me, Miss Andrews, may I call you Carolyn?"

"No, please don't."

"Well it seems to me, Miss Andrews that it is not up to you to accept or decline it. It is my plan, and the CIA does not need approval from MI6 to do anything. The assistance from SAS is a direct contact, and I can safely assume the SAS never requires approval from MI6." He paused for effect. "My plan will work whether or not you and Mr. Crowe assist in the process. And assuming you do assist, then at least your report to your senior staff will look considerably more effective than would be the case of reporting you had no input into the entire matter. Your initial goal of returning me to Britain dead or alive will not be accomplished. But even if it is accomplished, I can assure you I will not be alive. So either way I will be dead, and nothing will be gained by my death." He shrugged. "Except, of course, your having accomplished your rather meaningless operational goal."

"And what about your wife and children? Where do they come into the not-so-pretty-picture of your *meaningful* death?"

"Ah," Surbey smiled. "That's where you can play an important role."

"Oh, really?"

"Yes, really."

"Pray tell."

"My bosses will believe what you tell them about my death and, all things being equal, I will be remembered as an accomplished agent, and in fact one that even did things his own way. Not a regular occurrence in my field of work, I might add. But my wife will only accept what she hears from you, or at least someone like you. Someone who was there, that spoke to me and knows all the details of my current medical circumstances. She will not be proud that I am... was...a drug addict, but she would prefer to know the brutal truth and that I was not infected through sexual contact, and most certainly not with a man." He softened his tone as he continued. "I hope you would be good enough to do that for me, for my wife, and in the long run for my two children."

"I most certainly will not," Carolyn replied, pointing to the microphone on the fan. But she nodded and crossed her heart. "I will," she mouthed.

Surbey thanked her with a brief bow and thumbs up. He motioned to move closer to which Carolyn reluctantly agreed. When he was within reach he suddenly gave her a warm and friendly hug. "Thank you," he whispered.

Ed entered the room as they hugged. Realizing he had entered the room they quickly and confusingly separated. Ed froze, was at a total lose of words and turned to leave. It was only Mac standing immediately behind him that stopped him.

Unaware of the events just seconds before, Mac spoke to Surbey. "Wha' nags at me is the concern that you feel your advice to them is jus' confirmation. I dinna like tha'. Tell us more."

Surbey managed to respond without looking directly at Ed or Carolyn. He replied with his eyes and energy on Mac. "It was just a few small things," he said, thinking back. "For example when I mentioned these two were here a few weeks ago; it was if they all ready knew you were here. And when I mentioned one was carrying a Canadian passport, they shrugged like that was normal – which it ain't. Just the way they looked and motioned to each other at the meeting made me leery."

"And?" Mac asked.

"Most recently I was totally surprised when I mentioned you were here to take me back. They knew that for sure. The way one young man grinned made that obvious. He seemed…let me think…he seemed happy to hear my input."

Ed jumped in. "Confirmation of a personal input?"

Surbey thought for a moment. "Could be." He paused. "Look I've gotta go. Is our plan in place?"

"I'll get the Semtex to you," Mac said.

"*Your* plan is in place," Carolyn added quickly.

Surbey accepted her response, nodded to the group and left the room. No handshakes, no fond farewells: he just left the room.

"Shit!" Ed said.

"Double poop," Carolyn responded.

Mac shrugged in ignorance. "Okay I dinna follow ya thinkin'. Perhaps it's ya English brains that confuse me?""

Carolyn took a deep breath to steady her nerves. "We need to re-think our actions after the shooting. If Ed and I are correct in our assumptions, then a different world of problems arises." She turned to Ed. "Correct?"

"One hundred percent, Miss." It was all business now.

Carolyn drew them close and spoke quietly. "Here's what we are thinking, Mac. You'll understand if we are wrong and mess up, we'll all be in deep do-do."

"That's deep shit," Ed added with a cheeky grin.

Mac nodded. "Been there, done tha'."

Carolyn outlined their concerns from the information provided by Surbey, with Ed nodding his agreement as she spoke. Mac listened and now understood the implications of them being wrong, and the more serious implications of them being correct, but doing nothing to address them.

"So what are your revised plans?" Mac asked.

Ed grinned. "That's where you come in. Right, Miss?" Carolyn nodded

"Aye, thought as much," Mac chuckled. "Scotland saving the day agin!"

CHAPTER TWENTY-FOUR

Monday, February 3RD 1986 3PM

E d carried the cups of coffee over to the corner table where Carolyn sat. She was obviously uncomfortable, chewing on her lips and tapping her fingers nervously on the table. Ed knew better than to banter about their up-coming activities. He placed the coffee on the table and drew up his chair. He waited several minutes before he spoke.

"We have to do it, Miss," he said quietly as he sipped on the way-too-strong coffee.

Carolyn smiled an apology. "Not Tim Hortons, is it?"

Ed shook his head. "No it's not Tim Hortons. It's not nineteen-eighty four. And it's not Ankara where we met less than two years ago." He raised his coffee in a toast. "We seem to have aged somewhat."

"Regrets?"

He leaned forward. "Lots! But none that won't wear off when we finish our operation here and head home."

"You to Canada, and me to God knows where."

"Yep. That's one regret that won't wash off easy. But as they say, life's not fair."

Carolyn stood and nodded to the busy streets of Damascus. "Well *they* can mind their own bloody business. Let's go for a long walk."

Ed stood to join her. "And let's hum *Jerusalem,* and when we get to the best part, we'll sing it out loud."

"*In England's green and pleasant land,*" Carolyn sang aloud. "Let's go!"

They headed down the streets and alleyways of Damascus, weaving in and out of the citizens who were busy doing their shopping. Smiling and humming together they were happier than they had been for some time; just waiting to sing out loud the best part.

CHAPTER TWENTY-FIVE

THURSDAY, FEBRUARY 6TH 1986 10:00AM DAMASCUS. OUTSIDE THE BRITISH EMBASSY

E d stood up straight with his head held high as he and Carolyn walked toward the entrance gate of the British Embassy. Neither had slept well during the past three nights and it showed on both their faces. Carolyn was particularly on edge. She was the lead in the operation and the decisions she had made got them to where they were at this moment weighed heavy. She had not contacted London, and had not returned her father's phone call from the night before. If she had maintained any food in her stomach she would throw-up on the spot, but like Ed she had barely eaten since their joyful walk through Damascus several days earlier. It had been a short-lived walk of confidence and they had barely spoken to each other since. She wanted it all to be over with – and then it happened.

His tall frame, dressed in an Arab's robes, stepped out from the crowded street. He raised his arm directly at Ed's heart and fired the gun. As Ed fell back with blood gushing onto his chest and shirt, Surbey turned the gun on Carolyn. He pointed in at her face, held it for a second, and then dropped the gun. Turning, he ran back into the now screaming and cowering crowd, raised his arm in victory, and quickly disappeared.

Carolyn dropped to her knees and covered Ed's chest with her hand. She shouted to the crowd "Help me! Someone please help me!" Not willing to become involved, they all took a step back and shook their heads. Some of the women covered their faces, turned and walked away.

The embassy door swung open and Mac came running out. He was wearing his SAS uniform, but his jacket was missing, his tie was undone, and his shirt sleeves were turned up and what looked like a fresh coffee stain was on his shirt front. "Let me in there, let me in there," he shouted.

"He's English," Carolyn screamed as Mac ran toward them. He was down the three steps in a second and as he gently pushed Carolyn aside, he picked up Ed and ran back into the embassy. As he crossed the doorway, three security guards appeared from the back of the embassy and holding their rifles in front of them stood stone-faced toward the crowd. One helped a now weeping Carolyn into the embassy. The remaining guards picked up the hand gun and stood their ground, threatening no-one. The crowd gradually moved away. Just another killing in Damascus, only this time it was an unwanted foreigner.

Several minutes later three Syrian army jeeps drove through the crowds and stopped in front of the embassy. The embassy guards didn't move and the soldiers knew there was nothing they could do: the embassy was British property. The jeeps sat for several minutes then turned and drove away.

Inside the embassy Ed lay motionless on the beautifully tiled floor of the rotunda. Blood had soaked his shirt and was now oozing onto the marble tiles.

Ambassador Wood, Carolyn, a lady neither Ed nor Carolyn knew, and Mac looked down at him, each shaking their head. They stood in silence, except the lady took photos of Ed lying in blood on the floor. Lori Quinn ran down the grand staircase from her office on the second floor. She held her gun in her right hand, keeping it pointed to the floor. "I heard shooting…Oh, my God!" she gasped as she took in the complete picture.

"What do you think?" Carolyn asked quietly.

"Dead as a doornail," Mac replied, crossing himself.

Ambassador Wood simply shook his head.

Lori put her left hand to her mouth in horror as she walked slowly toward Ed's body. "What happened?" she asked, struggling to speak.

Sitting up straight from the waist like the Frankenstein monster, Ed turned to Carolyn. "Went as planned, Miss."

"Yes, it did," Carolyn replied quietly nodding her head.

Ambassador Wood raised his hand. "Perhaps, Miss Andrews, you could explain in some detail where this is all headed. Your phone call this morning needs further explanation. And this, ladies and gentlemen," he added pointing to the lady standing to one side, "is my Director of Communications Jo-Ann Gisel."

Gisel turned to Carolyn. "Please respond to the ambassador's request, Miss Andrews with an explanation as detailed as possible. I am extremely concerned about what is going on here."

Carolyn nodded, and then turned to Ed. "Please clean up that cow blood as best you can. We have to be out of the country as quickly as possible."

Ed did as he was told.

Carolyn turned to Ambassador Wood. "I'm afraid, sir, I have made some most unusual decisions since we last met, and I pray they were the right ones. You will recall, sir, Mr. Crowe and I were sent here to capture and return to the UK, or kill, a CIA agent; Mr. Glen Surbey."

She nervously licked her lips. "Well the plans changed rapidly, and let me explain the circumstances as quickly and as completely as I can."

Carolyn outlined the events in some detail regarding their search for Surbey and the lack of results, until he had approached them in their hotel room. Ambassador Wood and Lori Quinn listened in silence, not moving a muscle.

Jo-Ann Gisel took notes, asking several questions for complete details.

Carolyn turned to Ambassador Wood. "So the point, sir, is that Mr. Surbey is now on his way to the meeting where, in about forty minutes, he will attend a meeting of the ANO, at which Abu Nidal will be in attendance." She took a breath. "His plan, and I stress *his* plan, is to commit suicide with a bomb attached to his body and kill everyone in the room, with emphasis on killing Nidal."

"No, no, no," Lori screamed, raising her gun to point it directly at Carolyn's head. "Where is the meeting?" she shouted waving the gun, "where the Christ is the meeting?"

Ed moved to stand between Lori and Carolyn. "We don't know. He wouldn't tell us." He moved toward her, holding out his hand, but she shook him off.

Lori spoke directly at Ed. "Tell me, or you're dead."

Ambassador Wood turned to Lori, raising both of his hands in peace. "Lori, Miss Quinn, what is the matter here? If we don't know where the meeting is, what can we do? And, Lori, why does it matter to you? Please tell me."

Tears ran down her face as she tried to answer. "My boyfriend... Mohamed...they only want their land back from the Jews... Oh, my God, please help me."

Her head dropped to her chest.

A quarter of a mile away, Surbey, entered the restaurant running and pumping his arm in the air. "He is dead!" he screamed in Arabic. The twelve men looked up at him from their sitting positions, some smiling, some curious. Abu Nidal at the far end of the room shook his head nervously.

Surbey reached into his pocket and pressed the button.

Ed took a quick look at his watch and closed his eyes.

In the distance there was an explosion. While they could not confirm it, they intuitively knew what had just occurred.

Carolyn spoke first. "We lied about the timing, Lori. I'm sorry."

Lori dropped the gun; fell to her knees covering her face with her hands, which were now shaking uncontrollably.

Mac took a step toward her, kicked away the gun and three seconds later he had handcuffs around both her wrists. He waited a few seconds before he spoke. There was no trace of his Scottish accent. "Miss Quinn, I am arresting you on a citizen's arrest under Section 24A of the Police and Evidence Act of nineteen-seventy-four. I am charging you with, pointing a loaded gun at a civilian, breaking your oath of allegiance to The Queen and Country, and Treason." Lori shook her head, but didn't speak. Mac continued. "You should say nothing until you have a solicitor representing you, and that will have to be delayed until you return to the U.K, which will be in about four hours." He turned to Ed and Carolyn. "That goes for you two also. The plane is waiting. This embassy is now under enhanced surveillance. Ed, you will have to be taken to the plane in a coffin and while the coffin will be removed in England, you will stay on the plane for the continuing flight to Toronto. I will stay in Damascus and find out further details of the explosion. I will report back through my commanding officer, and he will pass on the details of my report to MI6."

Jo-Ann Gisel took control. "Thank you, Sergeant. Ambassador Wood and I will report directly to Lord Stonebridge as soon as the plane is out of Syrian air-space." She paused. "And may God help us all."

"Whoever's God." Carolyn added.

They separated, moving to different areas of the embassy. The blood stain was left to dry.

CHAPTER TWENTY-SIX

THURSDAY, FEBRUARY 6ᵀᴴ 1986 1:15 PM

The Lockheed TriStar KC1 roared and thundered down the main air-strip of Damascus International Airport. Its maximum capacity was a crew of four and one-hundred-eighty-seven passengers. Today it held a crew of two and three passengers.

Ed looked down at the historical city of Damascus and the expansive desert to the east. He wanted to go home. As stupid as it sounded, he wanted to go to The Queen's Head tomorrow night and have a couple of beers and enjoy his friends' company. He wondered if Vicky might drop in unexpectedly – but he doubted that.

Carolyn sat fifty feet away in row twenty-eight writing her report using the food tray as a table, valiantly attempting to make the best of the events that had taken place since they had left England just a few days ago. It was not easy. She was not aware of the contents of Ambassador's verbal report to her father, which made it more difficult to decide how much detail to include. She had to tell the truth, which went without saying, but it was a report that would reflect seriously on both her and her father. It was her father she was worried about.

Lori Quinn was handcuffed and shackled several rows ahead of Carolyn. She hadn't spoken a word since being arrested, and that was to become her new approach to life. Her lover was dead. She would never love again. Her father was an MP. It was her father that she was worried about. Her actions would devastate him, and he might never speak to her again.

The co-pilot turned to the captain as the plane climbed, reaching ten-thousand feet in four minutes. "Who are these people?"

The captain shook his head. "I have no idea. But Sergeant McAleese made it quite clear we were to fly to Halton airport outside of London, drop off the two females, and then fly the male onto Toronto – no questions asked. We get the co-ordinates from Heathrow control as we pass south of London." He chuckled and winked at the co-pilot. "But hold onto you hat. The landing strip is barely long enough for us to land. And if we had any more weight, we'd never take off again. The strip is short and it's grass. Second World War vintage."

Twenty minutes later the plane was a forty-three thousand feet, its maximum flying level. Ed walked to the door of the flight deck and knocked. "Would you gentlemen like a cup of tea?"

The door was opened by the co-pilot. "Milk and sugar in both, please."

"Done," Ed nodded. "It'll be hot, and MIF."

The co-pilot closed the door. "He doesn't sound very Canadian to me. Sounds like a Londoner."

"You could try French," the captain replied cheerily.

"Yeah, right! My favorite language. I do wonder why the lady is cuffed and shackled."

"Don't know, can't ask."

"Maybe something to do with the bombing earlier today? I heard more than ten people died." He sat down in his seat and together they turned on the autopilot. It used less fuel and was smoother at high altitudes.

Twenty minutes later Ed knocked again and delivered their tea. "May I ask a question?" he said.

"Ask away," the captain replied.

"Why does the RAF have a plane that looks like it could carry hundreds of people? In pretty nice fashion to boot."

"Good question," the captain answered. "But the answer is simple. In a couple of months this ex British Airways baby that flew thousands of passengers millions of miles will be an air-to-air tanker, which, in English, means we will be able to re-fuel two fighter jets in the air – at the same time. Saves time and money. We learned during the Falkland's War the benefit of air re-fueling. Would have been nice to have had it then, but soon it will be the norm."

Ed nodded. "Thanks, that's interesting. I'll just go back and see if the two ladies would like a cuppa."

"Friends?" the co-pilot asked.

"Never met them before," Ed replied. "Be interesting to know why one's in chains, eh?" He left the flight deck.

"Would you like a cup of tea?" he asked Lori who was sitting with her head down.

She shook her head, and then looked up. "I should have killed you and the bitch behind me when I had a chance. Bastards!"

"Milk? Sugar?" Ed asked nicely.

"Fuck off," Lori spat out.

He understood. "Let me know if you change your mind. It's a long flight."

Carolyn looked up as he arrived. She nodded. "The usual please… Unless you can add a shot of vodka?"

Ed motioned to her report. "How's it going?"

"You want me to swear?"

"I'll get your tea, Carolyn." He turned to leave, then changed his mind and knelt next to her. "While I don't understand everything you did or said back there, we did accomplish our goal, as gory as it turned out to be."

She shook her head. "Mission accomplished, yeah?"

Ed shrugged. He wasn't going to add anything that Carolyn would consider positive. "I'll get your tea, Miss."

As he walked away down the centre aisle, Carolyn almost started crying, but she held it back. She didn't want him to hear her cry again, and she certainly didn't want Lori, a Cambridge graduate, hear her cry. She sucked it up and went back to her report.

CHAPTER TWENTY-SEVEN

THURSDAY, FEBRUARY 6TH 1986 HALTON AIRSTRIP NORTH-WEST OF LONDON 5:45 PM

T he plane barely missed the tops of the horse chestnut trees as it landed. The brakes were applied immediately, normal only for an emergency landing. It bounced along the airstrip, finally coming to a stop. The engines were turned to idle, but not turned off.

The forward door was opened quickly and a jeep with stairs attached pulled up to the door. Within minutes the local police escorted Loti Quinn off the plane. She didn't speak or make a fuss.

The coffin was carried off gently; giving the appearance there was a body inside.

Carolyn stood at the door, looked at Ed and gently shook her head. "I don't know what to say, Ed."

"You did better than you think, Carolyn. You made decisions that were tough to make and I, for one, retrospectively think they were the right decisions. Shall I phone you tomorrow?"

Carolyn waved off the question. "Give me a couple of days. I'll phone you."

To both of their surprise they reached out and shook hands. She forced a smile, turned, and left the plane.

Twenty minutes later, with the help of the ground crew to turn the plane around, it took off and headed west for Canada.

Ed sat for twenty minutes looking down on the 'pleasant land' he loved so much. But he knew what he had to do: he walked to the kitchen area to make a fresh pot of tea.

CHAPTER TWENTY-EIGHT

FRIDAY, FEBRUARY 7ᵀᴴ 1986
THE QUEEN'S HEAD
7P.M.

H e finished his second pint of Double Diamond standing
by the bar. He hadn't yet recovered from yesterday's flight
home. They had run into a wicked jet stream, which he learned more
about than he wanted to. The northern jet stream moves from west to
east, so flying west meant they were heading into the massive wind
blasts. The stream was three miles thick, so there was no easy way to
avoid it. Being an RAF plane and not a commercial flight the pilot was
more than reluctant to request clearance to fly over US air space. Ed
doubted he would ever enjoy flying again.

Seana was working the bar and way too busy to spend any time
catching up with Ed. It was a Friday night in the winter darkness.
Some of the older customers were keeping warm in Florida or Arizona,
but the warmth and friendliness of their local allowed those not lucky
enough to head south to enjoy a start to the weekend. He decided he
would have one more pint. He was walking home, so nothing to worry
about drinking and driving.

He couldn't help but reflect on the events of the past week as he sipped his third pint. He felt no remorse, but couldn't convince himself that the suicide bombing was the right thing to happen. The CBC, CNN, and ITV had covered it as just another bombing in Damascus. All he had learned from the television reports was that eleven people had died, and one was rumored to be an American citizen. The biggest news was the freezing temperatures in London and across the U.K., which was affecting all rail travel and resulted in hundreds of accidents on the roads. If only it was that 'cold' outside here he wished.

He turned to face the restaurant area. As usual it was full with a twenty-minute waiting time. Great food did that. In the corner to the left there were four ladies enjoying a meal. Ed waved at one facing him. She waved back. It was Josie, the owner of the Queen's Head. She had opened the pub some twenty years ago and it was now managed by her two sons. Returning to his pint he wondered what he would cook for himself tonight. He didn't like to eat alone in a restaurant, even in his local.

He felt a tap on his back. It was Josie with her wide smile and charming Scottish accent. "How are ya, Ed?" she asked.

"Fine, Josie, fine. Never better."

"Well, ya look terrible. Are ya working too hard?"

"Been on the road for a while," he replied, nodding his understanding.

"Well I know ya willna join me and my lady friends, so I'm going to order some chicken wings for you to take home. And git a good night's sleep." She smiled. "A tha's an order."

Ed thanked her with a hug and she returned to her table via the kitchen area. The wings were delivered, on the house, ten minutes later. He finished his pint, waved thanks to Josie and headed for home – feeling a great deal better.

CHAPTER TWENTY-NINE

WEDNESDAY, FEBRUARY 12ᵀᴴ 1986 5:30 P.M.

E d picked up the phone, expecting one of his regular customers to be asking for a last minute cruise or a flight to Florida to escape the snow and cold. "Crowe here. Come fly with me." There was a slight pause.

"Ed, it's me, Carolyn."

He stood up, walked around his desk and pushed the door closed. "Hi, Carolyn. Been a while."

"Yes I know. Sorry. Can you speak?"

"Feel free. There's only me and my boss left in the office, and she's on a conference call."

"I wanted to up-date you on what's happened since last week. I was going to call you later at home, but it's late here and I need a good night's sleep." There was a slight pause. "I hate to admit it but I saw my doctor today and he's prescribed a sleeping pill. Mother is waiting for me to finish this call then she's going to watch me take it. She doesn't plan on leaving my room until I'm dead to the world."

Poor choice of words Ed thought. "I hear you, Carolyn. Sleep does seem to be a bit of a luxury lately."

"You want the bad news or the not so bad news first?"

"Can we start with the response to your report? How was it received, what did your...what did Lord Stonebridge say? I haven't heard a thing about the bombing since last week, and that was just a passing news release on CNN."

Carolyn took a deep breath. "Well my father is still talking to me, if that's what you're asking. Officially I got a telling-off in no uncertain terms. By the way, there was a photo of your 'dead' body in the English speaking newspaper, The Syrian Daily. Jo-Ann Gisel wanted the world to know your death was part of the killing spree, not just the ADO people."

Ed shook his head at the thought. "And what else did your father say?"

"He didn't say it, but I think he's pleased with the limited success."

Ed sat up in his chair. "I'm listening."

"Well..." There was a long pause.

"For Christ's sake, Carolyn!"

"Abu Nidal isn't dead. He was in the room, but survived."

Ed closed his eyes and his head fell to his chest. He moved the phone away from his mouth and covered the mouth-piece. "Fuck!" he shouted. "Fuck! Fuck! Fuck!" He calmly returned the phone to his mouth. "Okay. Go on."

"I heard that," Carolyn said quietly.

"Sorry. I know you don't like people to swear. I apologize."

"I think I'm beyond that now, Ed. Let me fill you in. From what we've learned from our sources – read CIA – there were twelve people in the room when the bomb exploded. Eleven died, including, it seems, the young man Lori was passing information onto. Nidal was hurt, no doubt about that. His people took him to a local doctor who fixed him up. Then they killed the fucking doctor. Can you believe that? He fixed him up, and then...Oh shit." She started to cry.

"Hold on, Carolyn. Please hold on." He waited a few moments. "Do you want to finish this tomorrow?"

"No bloody way." She wiped her eyes. "I said *it seems* Lori's friend died in the bombing, but it turns out he had been shot before the bombing. The assumption is that Nidal had him killed when he found out he was in touch with her. He's been known to do this sort of thing before."

"Where is Nidal now? Do we know?"

"It seems likely that he's made his way to Libya as a guest of Gaddafi. Bird's of a feather perhaps."

"What about the dead?"

"Well if there's any good news in this entire miserable process, that is it. The dead consisted of the major leadership of the ADO in Damascus, and therefore Syria. President Assad is glad to be rid of them and Nidal. Arafat is saddened to hear that he survived. Not exactly what we had in mind."

"But some good news, Carolyn. Let's not forget that. Let *you* not forget that."

"Yeah, right."

"You'll agree with me one day soon. By the way whatever happened to our luggage?"

"Mac had it delivered to me. Your stuff has been washed and will be air-expressed tomorrow."

Ed grinned. "You washed my dirty underwear?"

"I said it had been washed. I don't do underwear."

"What about my book, 'Callie the Cat'?"

"Your book?"

"Well I started it, I named it, and I've written most of it. Doesn't that make it mine?"

Carolyn thought for a second. "Have you ever heard the expression, possession is nine tenths of the law? Besides it's my turn to write, correcting your poor English as I write."

"Poor English? Me? Never."

Carolyn sniffed and raised her head. "My Callie doesn't go around speaking like a Cockney with nothing on her mind but finding a Tom to…to…to reproduce with."

Ed let her comment pass. "Anything else? Before you get a good night's sleep, that is?"

"Sort of, but it's strictly un-official."

"Mum's the word, Carolyn."

"I spoke to Surbey's wife today. And before you tell me that you heard me say that I would not do that, listen to me. I said that so you and Mac would hear me say that, since that was the official response. In any event, it was not an easy conversation but it did offer her some comfort. It's a strange world where knowing someone you loved was a drug addict is more comforting than knowing they loved in another fashion."

Ed didn't find that strange in the least, but held his comment. "What was the official word from the CIA?"

"Collateral damage! What an expression. In other words he happened to be in the room when the explosion occurred. It's amazing where political correctness is leading us these days."

Ed couldn't believe what he was hearing. "So you told her he was a suicide bomber?"

"Absolutely. That's what he wanted her to think of him; as a dying killer of terrorists."

"Brave lady."

"Yes, she is."

"Actually I meant you, Carolyn."

There was a long pause in the conversation before either spoke. Ed was waiting to be blasted by a very tired Carolyn, and Carolyn had to think through Ed's comments. Ed waited her out.

She chose her words carefully. "I'm sure it's the worst message I'll ever have to relay to anyone, or at least I certainly hope it is."

Ed decided to take a chance. "Does Lori know how her special friend died?"

Carolyn exploded. "Of course she doesn't for Christ's sake. Do you think I'm going to tell her that her boyfriend, or whatever, died because he loved her and she loved him? Get a life, Ed, for crying out loud!"

"No, Carolyn, I didn't think *you* would tell her anything of the sort. But then the world's problems don't rest on your shoulders do they?"

He held the phone away from his ear as she slammed down her phone.

Her mother heard the phone being slammed and quickly entered the room. "Are you all right, my dear?"

"No I am bloody well not," Carolyn shouted. "I have a friend who's...who's...less than bloody intelligent." She shook her head in frustration.

"That would be Mr. Crowe would it, dear?"

"Yes, Mother, it would be Mr. smart-arse Crowe."

Lady Stonebridge joined Carolyn, sitting on her bed. "Carolyn Ann, please don't give up on people so fast. He always seemed so basically common-sense to me. What did he do that has so upset you?"

It was a rare occasion her mother used both her names. Carolyn looked at the floor, then at her mother, then back to the floor. "I don't know, Mother. He just asked a common-sense question I suppose." She sighed. "Give me another minute please."

Ed ran back into his office and grabbed the phone on the second ring. "Dumb-assed Crowe speaking."

"It's dumb-arsed on this side of the pond," she said.

"Dumb-arsed Crowe speaking." He smiled and started to breathe again.

Carolyn held her head high and spoke clearly. "I'm sorry, Ed. That was rude of me, very rude of me. As usual my mother takes your side of things, and this one time she's right."

"I think this might be my first good night's sleep since Damascus, Carolyn."

She laughed. "Me too. I'll tell my mother I don't need the sleeping pill. I'll tell her I have good friends to keep me relaxed. Good night, Ed. And thanks."

"Good night, Carolyn. Regards to your mother."

They hung up.

Carolyn walked to and opened her bedroom door. Her mother was in the hallway waiting anxiously. "It's fine, Mother, I'll pass on the pill thanks. I'll get a good night's sleep now. And Mr. Crowe thanks you for taking his side – as usual." She kissed her mother's cheek and returned to her bed.

As Lady Stonebridge headed downstairs to pour herself and Lord Stonebridge a small port each she mumbled to herself: *To sleep: perchance to dream: ay, there's the rub.*

Ed grabbed the local newspaper as he headed for home. Iran had attacked Iraq yesterday. One hundred thousand troops had crossed the border, no doubt all in the name of God. He shook his head is disgust and headed to the pub for a beer. He promised himself that he would learn more about religion, particularly Islam. But for now; a beer.

CHAPTER THIRTY

THE QUEEN'S HEAD
FRIDAY 14ᵀᴴ FEBRUARY 1986
6:15 PM

E d felt better, more relaxed and happy to have had a busy and successful week at work. The increase in the number of large cruise ships joining the several fleets meant there were some fine deals as more clients were willing to accept the premise that cruising was not just for the tuxedoed and long-evening-dress crowd. He had used Vicky's comments from the report on her cruise as examples of the many activities now available on the new ships.

As he picked up his beer, he felt a poke in his back. "Hey, bloke, whatcha thinking about?" Vicky snuggled in between Ed and the others standing at the bar.

"Hey, Vicky! I was just thinking about you. What a co-incidence."

"Yeah, right."

Ed gave, and received, a quick hug. "What's new with you, Vicky?"

She moved closer to him and spoke quietly. "So what's with the PKK?"

Ed looked puzzled, and was just a tad concerned. "Excuse me?"

She moved closer. "And what about pissing your pants in Libya, bloke?"

"Whoa, Vicky, where are going with this?" Her questions touched on his first two operations with MI6. He didn't want to talk about them, certainly not here and not now.

Vicky smiled. "I'll tell you where we're going, Edwin. We're going to your place. Now slip me your keys, enjoy your beer and I'll be ready and waiting for you in half an hour."

Ed took his keys from his pocket and passed them to Vicky who slid them into her purse.

She stepped back. "Just wanted to drop by and say hello." She spoke loud enough for Seana behind the bar to hear her. She waved to both of them and left the pub.

"Where's she off to?" Seana asked.

"Dunno," Ed lied. "Busy lady."

Seana shrugged. "Don't forget we're on for tomorrow. We'll see you at your place at nine-thirty. Have you picked the book you're going to read yet?"

"Not yet," Ed replied. "I think I'll make it an early night and go find one."

He very slowly drank his pint of beer, left by the door closest to down-town, but headed straight home. He was curious, very curious.

As he reached his apartment door he could hear soft music playing. The door was slightly ajar, with little light coming from the room. He entered and closed the door behind him

Vicky was standing in the centre of the room wearing only her bra and panties, and for the two garments there was not a lot of fabric used in their creation. "Happy Valentines. Get over here, bloke," she said, extending her arms to him.

Ed quickly walked into her arms feeling the warmth and closeness of her beautiful body. He held her tight with his hands spread over the soft velvet skin of her back. "Vicky, about what you said..."

"Later, Ed, please...pretty please?"

He kissed her gently on her neck. "Vicky, I want you to go back into my bedroom, get fully dressed, then come back..."

Vicky's body sagged in despair. "Oh, Ed. Please don't do that to me, I beg..."

He squeezed her gently, slipping his hand into her panties. "Then when you come back to me, Vicky, fully dressed, then I will oh so slowly undress you. And as I oh so slowly undress you, I will lick, kiss, taste and touch you like never before."

"Oh God, yes," she chuckled, kissing his chin, "and I'll do the same to you. Please don't move, Ed. Not a muscle." She giggled as she walked backwards to his bedroom. "Well you can move one muscle, big boy, just one."

Ed waited until Vicky closed the door to his bedroom. He quickly walked to his stereo equipment, found his 'Phantom of The Opera' tape, and set it to the song he wanted.

When Vicky returned she was wearing a light blue two-piece business suit and a pair of three inch heels. "I hope you did as you were told," she winked.

"I moved only to enhance the evening's pleasure, pretty lady. Press play on the tape deck. Happy Valentines."

She pressed the button and walked quickly into his open arms and held him tight as the song began.

Night time sharpens, heightens each sensation.....

"Oh my God," she whispered, "you're going to undress me to, Music of The Night. That is so romantic. I love that."

Ed began to undress her starting with the six buttons on her top. "You are so beautiful, Vicky. I want so much to see you naked."

Any pretense of slowness slipped away as they groped at each other to remove their clothes.

As the song ended:

Help me make the music of the night

she stood again in just her bra and panties, and he in his underpants. She reached down and slipped her hand onto his now erect cock.

"I'll take this as a compliment," she smiled.

"And I'll offer it on a complimentary basis. Free as a bird, so to speak."

She took his hand and led him into his bedroom, closing the door behind them. She turned to him. "There are men in the ranks…," she said firmly. "Now, Ed, I want you to fuck me like we've never fucked before, and likely won't ever fuck again. And that, bloke, is an order."

With great pleasure, Ed did as he was told.

Vicky snuggled up to Ed from behind. She kissed him on the back of the neck. "It seemed rather appropriate," she whispered, "that we finished to, *Wishing You Were Somehow Here Again*. Was that planned too?"

Ed shrugged. "I couldn't hear it due to all the noise in the room….a sort of screaming."

She gently bit the back of his neck. "Smart-ass! You seemed to do alright for yourself in that area."

"It was wonderful, Vicky. You are a very sexy person."

She kissed him where she had bitten him. "Ed, if I ask you a question – about tonight, I mean – would you promise to tell me the truth?"

He knew he had no choice. "Of course I will."

"Have you ever used that music before – to make love I mean?"

He shook his head. "Never."

"Will you promise not to use it again, unless it's with me?"

He rolled over and kissed her gently. "I promise."

"Good!" she said rolling over and getting out of the bed. "Move your ass, bloke; we have a reservation at the Japanese restaurant in twenty minutes."

"But…"

She slapped his bum "No buts; except move that one."

Vicky drove carefully along Lakeshore and turned north on Kerr. She pulled up in front of the restaurant, put the car in park and turned to Ed. "One other promise?"

"Absolutely."

"You won't tell the girls about us, about tonight, will you? I know you're doing your reading trip to the States tomorrow with Seana and Steph. Promise?"

Ed Nodded. "Promise. Now about the...."

"In the restaurant, Ed. You'll hear all about it." She smiled. "I promise."

The restaurant was unusually empty for a Friday night with only the staff in sight. Vicky led them to the curtained area at the far end of the restaurant, and they sat across from each other. When the waitress opened the curtain, Vicky ordered a large tray of sushi, a glass of wine for Ed and a glass of water for herself. The order was delivered super fast, almost too fast for a Japanese restaurant Ed thought. They toasted each other and bowed their heads in thanks, Japanese style.

"I have to powder my nose," Vicky said, and with a wink left the table.

Several minutes later the waitress delivered a Bloody Mary in a large glass.

"We didn't..." Ed started.

"The lady ordered it as she left," the waitress replied, bowing slightly and disappearing.

Ed had to think about what was going on. Vicky didn't drink, and certainly no a Bloody Mary. It all became clear in an instant. He closed his eyes, crossed his arms over his chest and waited. Thirty seconds later someone moved into the spot across the table from him, and picked up the drink.

"Hi, Pat," he said, not opening his eyes. "Nice to not see you."

"Good evening, Edwin Crowe. How's your Friday evening going so far?" Pat reached over and touched his elbow. "You can open those peepers now."

Ed opened his peepers, reached over and shook her hand heartily. "How ya doin' me ol' china?"

"None of that London shite to me, matey. I'm marrying a damn cockney type. English please. Bet you didn't expect to see me this evening."

"That, my dear Pat, would be the understatement of the year. How goes it?"

Pat took a sip of her drink. "I'm doing wonderfully, thanks. However I'd do better if I got a hug from my old friend."

They slid out from the curtained area and gave each other a solid good-friends hug. They both felt better.

Pat spoke first. "So I'm here to talk business and pleasure. Take your pick."

"Pat, we're in an open restaurant here," Ed observed, pointing to the curtain and the walls that separated the stalls.

Pat shook her head. "No problem. The place is empty and the owners are across the street enjoying a fine Portuguese meal, compliments of the federal government."

Ed tapped his nose. "I should have known you had it all organized. Okay, let's go personal first."

Pat reached into her purse, placed a credit card report on the table in front of Ed and pointed at it. "Between The Queen's Head the LCBO and the local pizza joints, you don't do much in life lately. You look terrible, and you've put on weight. What's the deal?"

"Bloody Hell, Pat, there is a limit you know. You're not my mother for crying out loud."

Pat continued. "And Vicky asked me to apologize for her using the eff word. I sure hope it wasn't followed by 'off'."

Ed shook his head, wondering who could ever understand women. "No it wasn't," was all he could muster.

Pat pushed her drink away and leaned forward. "Ed, I'm here as a friend. Not as your MI6 and CSIS go-between contact person. Now I want to talk about you and Vicky."

Ed shook his head and raised his voice. "No bloody way, Pat. That is none of your business."

She raised her hand to lower the tone. "All I want to say is that she likes you. In fact she likes you a lot. I like you, Ed. Carolyn likes you…or more. But my point is that Carolyn and I are one hell of a lot more sure of ourselves than Vicky is. Please be careful with her feelings, Ed. That's all I'm asking."

Ed laughed. "Or telling more like."

"Whatever."

"Okay, I hear you. Thanks."

Pat pointed to the dish of sushi. "And this is better than a constant diet of pizza and bangers and mash. Okay, old friend?"

Ed nodded his understanding. "Got it."

They worked on the sushi dish, both of them struggling with the chop sticks. Ed took a break and a sip of wine.

"So tell me, Pat, how come you and Vicky got together for this pick-on-Ed Friday?"

"Good question. I was wondering when you'd get around to asking. Although I suspect it would be better described as Ed's good-Friday, eh?"

"No comment. Explanation please."

She picked up the last two sushi pieces, popping one in Ed's mouth and the final one in her own. "Well it's like this. You had mentioned that she was a life insurance agent, and a pretty good one. So I gave her a call and we met this morning to go over her thoughts on what Roy and my needs would be once we married." She stopped to smile. "That sounds great, eh? Me and Roy married. Me marrying your best mate, and then he'll be my best mate also….only different. Get it? Play on words."

Ed nodded, and waved her to carry on.

"So we met this morning and she did a super job…but to your point. When I mentioned you, well she was all aglow. 'Such a nice bloke', something about 'men in the ranks', and how you helped her in her major personal issue. She made you sound like you were the best thing since sliced bread." She shrugged. "Well, I thought I should set her straight."

"Thanks."

"Actually I mostly agreed with her, and then she said she wanted to see you tonight and didn't know how to get you to herself – as in out of The Queen's Head – without her friends who work there knowing."

"Well this time a real thank you. But what about…?"

"I told her nothing important. It seems she knew of your many visits out of the country as a result of a report her father had done on you. He sounds seriously concerned."

"Just protecting his daughter. Nice parents."

"Rich parents."

Ed chuckled. "Vicky's doing very well for herself without her parents' help, thank you very much."

Pat nodded with a quick grin. "Yes, I know."

"You know everything."

"Just doing my job."

Ed chewed on his lower lip, thinking of how to ask his next question. He came straight to the point. "So can you tell me why Carolyn is – for lack of a better description – pissed off with me?"

Pat sat up straight and pushed her drink away. "Aha, now that gets a bit tricky. It all comes down to politics, in this case international politics. And religion."

"How encouraging."

"Now hear me out, Ed; and that is not a request. The main issue between you and Carolyn is bad communication. Simple as that. Carolyn took a huge risk in letting Mr. Surbey proceed with his plan. She did not have the authority to do that. As you know both of you were to bring Surbey back to England, or kill him. His choice of death included the killing of Abu Nidal. Now to anyone with half a brain in their head, that would make sense. Nidal is all kinds of things; a murderer, a ruthless terrorist, likely a psychopath, and a drunk to boot. His only goal in life is to return Palestine to its pre 1947 borders. No Jewish state, no Jews, period. He, by design, has split the PLO into two very different branches. He hates Arafat and the feeling is returned. Keep in mind that Nidal was involved in the killing of eleven Israeli athletes at the Olympic Village in Munich in 1972. That was just the start, and I won't go into all the rest of his killings. The point, Ed, is that his goal is to not negotiate an inch, and in doing so he has given the PLO a black eye around the world. And here's the interesting but sad reality; it has given Israel an excuse not to negotiate with the Palestinians. In effect his actions have offered Israel a divide-and-conquer attitude, and they don't have to do anything but watch." She took a deep breath. "You with me so far?"

"Yes, but what's this got to do with Carolyn and me?"

"Hear me out. Good question. Now as I said Carolyn did not have the authority to go along with the plan, and I gather you didn't like it very much; but you followed her directions and I give you full credit for that. Indeed you became Crowe's bait as I understand it. Fine acting I'm sure."

Ed closed his eyes and shook his head. "Oscar material, no doubt about it."

"Now, Ed, here is the communication issue. Carolyn could not contact London or Lord Stonebridge to seek permission for Surbey's plan. To do so would have resulted in the plan being cancelled. Why you ask? Simple answer, but messy. Lord Stonebridge would have had to contact Washington. He simply could not have risked a UK-US political upheaval at this time. In the past, perhaps, but not with Thatcher and Reagan. The ramifications would have been too great; in fact a disaster. Lord Stonebridge didn't know, so the US didn't know, so the plan went ahead. Unfortunately, not as planned. Nidal didn't die, so the world continues to unfold as is. The US is happy."

Ed sat back, put his hand to his chin and closed his eyes in order to think clearly. He sat for several minutes, before opening them and looking directly into Pat's eyes.

He spoke slowly. "Are you telling me...?"

"Yes."

"Are you telling me that the US is happier to have the PLO divided, as it were, instead of being one organization to communicate with the world, the UN and everyone else to boot? Bloody Hell."

Pat placed her hands flat on the table. "That's what Carolyn thought, that's what I think, and that's what lots of knowledgeable people in the international community think but aren't about to say so publicly."

"And the main reason in the US is for the Jewish vote?"

Pat nodded. "Not too many Arab voters in the US are there?"

Ed cringed at the thought that the world worked in such a devious way. "Did anything good come out of this entire matter? I'd like to think so."

Pat gave a quick smile. "Maybe, Ed, maybe. We know Abu Nidal is now in Libya and keeping his head low; very low. The expectation or hope anyway, is that his being out of touch with his organization will reduce its activities. Time will tell. Gaddafi will protect him, but will not let him create any risk for Gaddafi himself by any direct activities that result in further deaths, at least that's the presumption. It would not take much for the US to pick on Gaddafi."

Ed stood to leave. "Okay, I'm out of here. If I stay any longer you'll be asking me to go back to Libya to nab Nidal, and I'll screw up like the last time."

Pat walked with him to the entrance of the restaurant. "That was no screw up, Ed. Your target died, and that was option B. Nothing to be ashamed of. Want me to drive you home?"

"No thanks, I need the exercise. You'll agree with me, I'm sure."

"Look, Ed," Pat said, holding his arm to prevent him from leaving, "I think Carolyn was a tad unfair in expecting you to come to the same conclusion as she did. She has way more knowledge in this area that you do, more than most for that matter. Why don't you let me give her a call in the next couple of days, and I'll update her on our conversation?" She smiled. "Just one part of our conversation, that is."

"I think we've drifted too far for that, Pat. Let's let it ride for a while."

Pat gave him a hug. "Okay," she agreed, "I won't make the call." She knew full well she would, but had no feeling of guilt in lying to him. She headed to the Portuguese restaurant to pay the owners of the Japanese restaurant for the food and rental. She turned after crossing the road and called to Ed. "And phone your mother. She hasn't heard from you in a while."

Ed acknowledged her comment and started his slow walk home. He knew Pat would phone Carolyn. He knew Carolyn would phone him; Pat would make sure of that. Pat seemed to have her way of getting things moving in her direction. He chuckled to himself; that was what he liked about her.

The slow walk home gave him an opportunity to think through where he was in his personal life. He loved Carolyn; that went without question. But no matter what small significance she placed on their obvious different levels in life, he knew it mattered. Maybe not to Carolyn on a one-to-one basis, however that would change as they surrounded themselves with friends and family. Mixing with gentry was not easy, he knew that. The class system was still thriving in England. He didn't see it as wrong, it had history behind it. But his mother visiting Stonebridge Manor for a weekend was not the same as being invited to Ascot to wear 'fashionable' hats. Of course she wouldn't be invited to Ascot. Lady Stonebridge knew his mother wouldn't accept the invitation, so she wouldn't make the invitation in the first place. Why put a friend in an awkward situation? No; he and Carolyn long term was awkward.

Vicky was a wonderful person, but he suspected not for him – or more realistically, he was not for her. He loved her in a way he could never explain to her. If they were a permanent couple, she would not be happy. He wanted to remain a travel agent, but more importantly he wanted to remain a consultant with MI6. It was in his blood. He enjoyed it – too much perhaps. He couldn't see himself heading off across the world, sometimes into danger, with Vicky wanting to spend the time at 'their' cottage on Lake Muskoka. It was never going to work.

Setting the thought process aside, he picked up his pace. He wanted to get home and sort out this evening's events.

It was nearly eleven when he arrived home. He hung up his coat, walked to the phone and dialed.

"Are you mad at me?" Vicky asked, knowing it was Ed phoning.

"Absolutely not, pretty lady, absolutely not. Whatcha doing?"

Vicky sat up straighter and moved a pillow behind her back. "I'm in bed reading a book."

"Whatcha reading?"

Vicky smiled as she answered. "'Saturday Night and Sunday Morning'. Have you read it?"

"Oh, yeah. Read the book and saw the movie."

"I don't like this bloke at all. Not at all like you is he?"

He couldn't help but chuckle. "No he's not like me at all. Thank God for that. May I borrow the book?"

"Sure. How do I...?"

Ed nervously licked his lips. "Will you bring it over tonight, Vicky? Will you stay the night with me?"

She lowered the book to think. "Ed, I don't want to, you know... again."

"Nothing like that, Vicky. Honest. I just want us to finish the evening. No personal stuff, just sleeping together. Please?"

"Promise?"

"I won't even ask to kiss your beautiful breasts. How could you ask for more than that?"

She shuddered at the thought. "Okay and I promise not to ask you to kiss them. I'll see you in twenty."

Twenty minutes later Vicky entered his apartment dressed in jeans and a tee-shirt. She held the book in one hand and a long sleeping gown high in the air in the other hand. She gave him a quick kiss then entered the bedroom to change. He waited several minutes and joined her in his bed, keeping his underwear on. They lay down holding hands, looking up at the ceiling.

She squeezed his hand. "You sure you aren't mad at me?"

"I like you way too much to be mad at you, Vicky. I like you a lot and I want you to know that. Now what shall we fall asleep thinking about?"

"Cruising," she replied. "I'm going to dream about cruising."

"Great idea, I'll join you...in the dream I mean."

"Good night, bloke."

"Good night, pretty lady."

CHAPTER THIRTY-ONE

SATURDAY, FEBRUARY 15ᵀᴴ 1986. 7A.M.

Vicky shook Ed awake, holding a cup of tea for him. "Wake up, bloke. I'm on my way home and you have to be ready in a couple of hours."

Ed sat up, took the tea and slurped down a long sip of nice hot English Breakfast tea. "Thank you, young lady. How was your sleep?"

"Not bad," she replied, "except for your snuggling up and talking in your sleep."

Ed cringed. "Oh my! Did you understand what I was going on about?"

"No," she lied easily. His mumbling about explosions and Islam didn't make sense to her, and she didn't want to know what he was talking about. She stood to leave. "Return the book sometime. I'll finish it when I want to know all about an angry young Englishman with a drinking problem. In the meantime I have you as a very nice friend."

Ed left that comment alone. "Thanks for coming over, Vicky, and we each kept our promises. I meant what I said you know."

"I know you did, Ed. That was nice to hear. Let's stay in touch." She leaned over gave him a quick kiss and left.

Ed sat back enjoying his cup of tea and her lingering sensual smell. He felt good about her sleeping over. He knew they had both made their point that they were attracted to each other on more than just a physical basis.

Ed was working on his second pot of tea when the phone rang. He looked at his watch. It was 9am, and he wondered if his reading friends Seana and Stephanie were cancelling. Vicky spoke before he could say hello.

"Okay, bloke," she laughed, "I can do the music thingy too. "Listen to this."

He recognized the song immediately. It was Johnny Mathis. He sat down to listen:

You ask how much I need you, must I explain?
I need you, oh my darling, like roses need rain.
You ask how long I'll love you, I'll tell you true:
Until the twelfth of never, I'll still be loving you.

After two more verses, Vicky spoke, not allowing Ed to interrupt.

"So there! Don't take it too seriously. Say 'Hi' to the girls. I gotta go. Bye, Ed." She hung up.

He sat thinking about what had just happened. He walked to the kitchen area. "This requires another cup of tea," he said aloud. "Maybe two."

Seana steered the car onto the QEW at nine-forty. They had their Tim's coffee; three large. That would get them to the US border.

"Vicky phoned this morning and asked me to say 'Hi'," Ed said, sitting in the back seat and taking a sip of his coffee.

"Did she say anything about last night?" Seana asked.

Ed shook his head. "No. Just sent her love and say 'Hi to the girls'."

Stephanie was sitting in the passenger seat, and turned to speak. "Maybe she had a date?"

"I don't think so," Seana replied. "If she had a date on Valentine's Day, we'd know about it for sure. She's been asked out a couple of times by some guys she knows, but she is still nervous about dating."

Stephanie shook her head. "That is so sad. She's such a lovely person." She turned to Ed. "Isn't she, Edwin?"

"She certainly is," Ed agreed, opening the book. "'Saturday Night and Sunday Morning'," he continued, "a book by Alan Sillitoe." He turned the pages:

> "*Nine hundred and fifty four, nine hundred and fifty bloody five. Another few more and that's the lot for a Friday*'."

"Bloody," Stephanie repeated. "Must be bloody English."

Ed nodded. "Right on. England in the early sixties."

"Do we get to meet 'Missus Brown's lovely daughter'?" Seana chuckled.

"'Fraid not. Way before the British Invasion. All very gritty and real."

"Not a comedy then." Stephanie added.

Ed replied with a strong northern English accent. "Not even close, ducky. Not even bloody close." He went back to reading the book.

The trip to the Peace Bridge crossing over the Niagara River took just over an hour and they waited twenty minutes as the line of cars entering the U.S. slowly moved toward one of the several Border Crossing gates. As Seana pulled the car up to the booth, Ed stopped reading and Stephanie gathered their passports from her purse. She handed them to Seana who smiled and passed them through the window to the guard sitting several feet higher in his booth. He nodded and turned his attention to the passports. Seana rolled up the window to keep out the cold.

The guard's eyes gave away the fact that something wasn't right. He motioned Seana to roll down the door window and spoke with authority. "Turn off the vehicle please, miss."

"Maybe he likes you," Stephanie whispered.

Seana didn't reply, keeping her eyes on the guard.

The guard was on the phone nodding and shaking his head as he spoke.

Ed kept a straight face and spoke quietly. "You ladies been visiting too often? It's all computerized now you know."

"Stop talking, you two," Seana said, trying not to move her lips too much.

Ed shrugged and went back to reading the book. He read for several minutes. It was an interesting part of the story.

"Shit!" Seana said.

"Double shit," Stephanie added.

Ed looked up. Two new guards walked up, one on each side of the car. Their jackets were pulled back, exposing the hand guns strapped to their belts. They didn't remove the guns from the holsters, but the message was clear. They directed that the four windows be lowered which was quickly accomplished. A guard opened the back door and pointed to Ed. "Outside please, sir."

Ed moved quickly out of the car, keeping his hands in sight, like he'd seen a hundred times on television. He followed the lead guard while the second walked behind him to one side. Entering a building a hundred yards away from the traffic, they patted him down and escorted him to a small windowless room. The furniture consisted on one chair and one table. There were no "Welcome to America" signs. He sat and waited. Knowing he had done nothing wrong, he wasn't overly worried. His greatest concern was what he would explain to the girls when he returned to the car, surely only minutes from now. Half an hour later -nothing. Now he was beginning to worry. Not to his surprise, he needed to pee.

Seana and Stephanie were still waiting in the car, parked close to the building they had seen Ed enter.

"What do you think?" Seana asked, biting her lower lip nervously.

"No idea," Stephanie replied, finishing her now cold coffee. "He's a boring old travel agent. What would they want with him?"

"None of the 'old' eh, he's only a couple of years older than us."

Stephanie nodded. "True. So he's a boring *young* travel agent!"

They laughed to relax, but inwardly they were nervous.

The door finally opened and the guard motioned Ed to follow. Ed wasn't about to give in too easily. He had his pride. "Excuse me," he said as walked beside the guard, "I need to see a man."

The guard turned. "What?"

Ed held his head high. "I need to see a man about a dog please."

"What the…?"

"A restroom. I'd like to use the washroom…please."

Shaking his head, the guard led him to the restroom and waited just outside while Ed relieved himself. Feeling physically and emotionally better he followed the guard along a grey empty hallway and was escorted into what was obviously a senior guard's office. The room was large with windows on two sides. To his left he could see Seana's car. In front of him was a large desk with the officer sitting talking on the phone. He was listening more than speaking. Ed declined the offer to sit. Once more he waited. The officer put down the phone and looked up to Ed with a large smile.

"Welcome to America, Mr. Edwin Crowe. We're not used to British spies visiting us un-announced: especially when they're dead."

Ed looked at the name plate on the desk, giving himself time to think. "You obviously have me confused, Officer Dan Kleemola. As you can see I am entirely alive. I am also a Canadian citizen as my passport makes clear."

Kleemola pointed at his phone. "That was a representative of the Foreign Office in Ottawa. Took some time to get hold of her, Saturday morning and all. I think it's fair to say she just took a strip off me and my associates. Friend of yours?"

Ed shook his head. "Don't know anyone in Ottawa."

"You can go," Kleemola said standing to give Ed the three passports and to shake hands. "And by the way, she asked me to remind you to phone your mother."

"Ahh!" Ed grinned. "I guess I do have a friend in Ottawa. Sorry about that."

"Have a nice trip. Your friends are waiting. We gave them a coffee each."

Ed walked back through the hallway, out of a side door, and quickly jumped into the backseat of the car. He picked up the book. "Now where was I?"

Seana turned the car and headed to Niagara Falls, U.S., turning right on the river road toward the retail outlet mall. "Forget the fiction, Ed. When we stop for lunch we want to hear what that was all about."

Ed continued reading. "Arthur walked into the pub…" He put the book down. "You ladies might be interested to know that I met a guy in The Queen's Head one time who told me that he left England in 1964 after seeing the movie of this book. Of course he didn't use the word movie; he said he saw it at the flicks. That's a funny English expression. Interesting, eh?"

Stephanie turned to Ed. "Lunch is on me. You talk, we listen."

CHAPTER THIRTY-TWO

TUESDAY FEBRUARY 18ᵀᴴ 1986 6 P.M.

"Victoria Kilgour speaking. How may I help you?"

"Hi, Victoria, it's Edwin Crowe. How are you today?"

Vicky looked at the phone as if it was speaking by itself. Victoria? Edwin? This sounded weird. "I'm fine, thank you."

Ed took the chance. "I was wondering, Victoria, if you would go out with me? Tomorrow?"

Vicky closed her eyes. Is this really happening, she wondered. "Are you asking me out on a date, Edwin Crowe?"

"Umm, yes, I suppose I am. But look, if, you know, it's not…"

Vicky interrupted. "Let me check with my parents, okay?"

"Yes, yes, I'll wait. Thanks."

She covered the mouthpiece with her hand and sat back in her chair grinning like a Cheshire Cat. She hadn't felt this silly and happy at the same time for years. She waited for thirty seconds before she spoke. "Yes, that would be nice, but I must be home by ten at the latest." She covered her mouth to stop giggling.

"Yes, of course, ten at the latest. Okay if I pick you up at five-thirty?"

She remembered the rules. "Let's make it at six, Edwin."

"Six it is. I won't be late."

"That would be nice. See you at six."

They hung up.

Vicky was almost crying with fun and laughter.

Ed was recovering from his very real nervousness.

Ed walked up to the main door of the Kilgour's mansion at exactly five-fifty-five. The door opened and Vicky slipped out and closed the door. "Let's move before my parents come and see who my date is."

He gently took her arm, escorted her down the five steps and they walked a short distance along the long driveway to his car. He opened the passenger door for her and she slipped in with a 'thank you' nod. Beneath her thin winter jacket she was wearing a white blouse and a dark blue skirt that was longer than the current style. She looked beautiful, but he kept his thoughts to himself.

Walking around the front of the car, he joined her in the car and they both did up their seatbelts.

To his surprise he was still nervous, but tried not to show it.

"I was hoping we could drive to Niagara Fall and see the lights," he said somewhat anxiously. "And I won't speed, honest."

"That would be fine, Edwin. May I call you Ed?"

"Great, yes, please do. And may I..."

"Yes. Vicky is fine."

He turned onto Lakeshore, heading east. "Would you like a Tim's coffee for the drive?" he asked.

She gave him a small nod. "That would be lovely, Ed. A medium with just cream please."

Fifteen minutes later they were heading down the QEW sipping on their coffees. Drinking their coffee allowed them the opportunity not to have to force a conversation. Ed broke the silence that was getting awkward.

"I've never seen the lights at the Falls, have you?"

"Once when I was a kid. It's really lovely."

"You be the tour guide, and I'll be the tourist."

"Absolutely," she answered with some authority. "Right now we're on the QEW, which stands for Queen Elizabeth Way."

They laughed and any nervousness dissipated. They were already enjoying their first real date.

They chatted about everything and nothing: everything that was insignificant and nothing that was personal. They agreed the weather wasn't too cold for February, the Leafs wouldn't make the play-offs, personal computers were going to change the world and Ed agreed he should buy one like Vicky's for his home use.

Arriving in Niagara Falls, they parked close to the actual falls. Being winter there were not the large crowds that were normal in the summer. The mist rose well into the air as the water poured over the drop. As it settled the mist froze on the safety bars at the river's edge and was more than an inch thick. Standing only feet way from the actual drop was exhilarating; and cold. Ed put his arm around Vicky to keep her warm, and after a few quiet minutes they entered the tourist shopping area for a bite to eat.

Happily, there was an A&W, and they both chuckled as they ordered a Teenburger each, with a side order of fries that they shared. As hungry as they were, they both tried not to eat too fast. They motioned to each other to take the last French fry and Ed won; Vicky took the last one, but then bit off half and popped the remaining half into Ed's mouth. Vicky motioned that they should head back outside to enjoy the light show.

Walking a hundred feet away from the drop allowed them to fully appreciate the magic of the lights that shone through the actual waterfall and the lights from the many buildings close to the falls that lit up the sky. It was a wonderful sight.

Ed carefully put his arm around Vicky, and she snuggled in closer. "Beautiful," Ed said.

"Yes, it truly is," Vicky smiled.

"I meant you, Vicky."

She laughed and squeezed in tighter. "Thanks. And thanks for the date."

The light show continued and they waited until they were cold enough to need the warmth of the car heater before they headed back. Ed took her hand as they crossed the road and didn't let go until he opened the passenger side door for her. They headed for home.

"We're back on the QEW now," Vicky said with a giggle, "and I'm your famous navigator."

"And my favorite," Ed added.

"So tell me, Ed," Vicky asked seriously, "what is your favorite hobby?"

"That's easy, favorite navigator; bird watching. I've been a bird watcher since I was a kid in England, and coming to Canada opened a brand new world for me."

"Wow, I'd have never guessed. I though bird watchers were funny little men that hid behind trees searching for the last of the Red Necked Double Breasted Chickadee or something with a strange name like that. But you....well I'll have to change my opinion now."

Ed was now able to speak with some authority. "Ah, now Chickadees! They're clever little things and will eat out of your hand. There are three species; the Black-Capped which we get here, the Carolina which is found south of us, and the Boreal which is found to the north of us and is very similar to the Black-Capped but smaller. Now it's funny you should mention a Double Breasted, since there is no such species of course, but they are all part of the Titmice family. Sort of a play on words on your part." He gave her a quick grin.

"Utterly unintentional, I can assure you," she laughed. "I'll never look at a Chickadee again without thinking of this trip. Most informative."

"And your favorite hobby?" Ed asked.

"You won't believe me."

"I'll believe anything you tell me."

"Crossword puzzles."

"Hey, that's great. Regular or cryptic?"

She raised her head a little higher. "Both."

"Okay, try this; 'Be here by six, Edward'."

"Easy peasy. The answer is 'Invited', and that's what you did tonight…you, Ed, were at my place by six. That's amazing!"

Ed laughed. "I didn't see that one coming myself. You are obviously very smart as well as, you know, beautiful."

"Just drive, Ed. You keep talking and you'll have me totally embarrassed." She licked her lips. "But thanks. You say the nicest things."

Ed did as he was told and kept his mind on the road.

Ed turned into her parents' long U shaped driveway, and parked halfway to the house. He wanted to walk Vicky home. She understood and waited for him to open her door. She slipped out with a nod of thanks. Slowly they walked toward the front entrance of the massive and well lit home of the Kilgours. Ed walked Prince Phillip style with his hands held behind his back.

"You can hold my hand if you like," Vicky said stopping and turning to face him.

"I would love to," he replied. He took her hand, kissed it quickly and they walked on very, very slowly.

No matter how slowly they walked and how often they stopped to look at the stars shining on a cloudless sky, they reached the front entrance. Ed looked at his watch; nine-fifty-five, five minutes early.

Vicky took his other hand and held them. She looked him in his eyes, and fluttered hers nicely. "You know, Ed, that is the loveliest date

I've ever been on, and you are a true gentleman. Thank you so very much. I…"

The front door opened narrowly. "Time to come in soon, dear," Mrs. Kilgour said quietly.

Ed squeezed her hands. "Best date…until the twelfth of never, Vicky. You are a beautiful, beautiful person. May I phone you sometime?"

She leaned forward, gave him a quick kiss on his lips and stepped back. "That would be nice, Ed. That would be very nice." She turned and entered her home. She waved good night to her parents, with a wink of thanks to her mother, and almost floated her way up to her bedroom.

Ed drove slowly home, driving past The Queen's Head and not even thinking of stopping for a beer. He wanted to remember tonight over a cup of tea and with a clear head.

Vicky opened her diary. She hadn't entered much lately, either too personal or too boring. She wrote today's only entry;

> First _real_ date with Ed.
> Wonderful, wonderful, wonderful
> A new beginning.

Removing her makeup carefully Vicky knew she had to say it out loud: "Bye, Ed." She felt better now, knowing she would get a good night's sleep.

CHAPTER THIRTY-THREE

SATURDAY, FEBRUARY 22ND 1986 12 NOON.

With his maps and bird book spread across the table, Ed was looking forward to adding more birds this spring to his list of 'seen and correctly recognized'. The Tim Hortons was busy, but not full, and he enjoyed the companionship of fellow coffee drinkers. Some he recognized and waved 'good morning', but he had never spoken to any of them. He was totally shocked when he looked up and saw Vicky enter and walk toward him. She was speaking quietly into her cell phone. Ed stood as she arrived at his table.

"Vicky, I er…"

She put her finger to her mouth to stop him from continuing and held the phone out for him. "There's a lady who would like to speak to you, Ed. Better take it outside."

Taking the phone he walked outside and turned into a side lane.

"Hi, Pat," he whispered, "what's happening?" There was a slight pause.

"Ed, it's me; Carolyn. Can you speak freely?"

"Carolyn! Yeah, sure. I'm in a back lane. Where are you?"

"At the manor. Listen, Ed, we need you to come to England immediately. Any major problems?"

He had to think quickly. "No. Just work."

"I'll look after that." Carolyn spoke with authority. "There's a plane waiting for you at Hamilton airport. You need to get there right away."

His head was spinning. "I need my passport, my…"

"Victoria has all of that in her car. She'll give you more details. Let me just say that Pat is currently in the air flying to England to see Roy and his family. Nothing to do with your flight. Okay?"

"Sure, sure. What does Vicky know?"

"Nothing whatsoever, but she has great faith in Pat and it was Pat that put me on to her. Listen I'll give you the quick overview of why this is happening." She took a deep breath. "Pat phoned you this morning about nine to get you moving. No response at home and you mobile went to message."

Ed cringed. "Shit. Sorry."

"Victoria has your mobile too. Please turn on, just in case."

"Got it."

"So we took the chance and Pat contacted Victoria. Pat had to catch a flight, so I took over. Victoria has been amazing. Done lots of things, no questions asked…except how much underwear you would need"

"Oh God," Ed groaned.

"Buy her a coffee and get to the airport as soon as possible, Ed. I'll see you in about seven hours."

"Looking forward to it."

Carolyn smiled. "So am I."

Inside the Tim's, Vicky had collected all of Ed's materials and waited for the nod from Ed. She knew better than to listen in. She was excited and enjoying the situation.

Following Carolyn's advice he bought them each a coffee and they headed off to the airport in Vicky's car. They waited until they were on the QEW before either spoke.

"You're not mad at me are you?" Vicky asked, keeping her eyes on the road.

"Not in a million years, Vicky. If I may say so, I would say I'm proud to know you. And thanks."

She gave him a quick wink. "Thanks. Ask away."

"Where did…"

"Where did I get your key from? I knew that would be your first question." She grinned. "Pat left it with me. Left it with me, not gave it to me. She wanted to leave it somewhere close at hand in Oakville, and who better than her life insurance agent. Now she told me she had it for business purposes, and who am I to question that?"

"Never question Pat."

"Exactly. Anyway she was off to Jolly Old, as she calls England, and asked me if I could, and I quote here; 'do some funny, awkward stuff for and about our friend Ed Crowe?' So I said yes, and then she told me I would hear from Carolyn, and then I did. Nice lady that Carolyn."

"Very nice. You'd like her."

"So to make a long story short I went to your apartment, packed you up for a week's trip, and then had to find you."

"Which you did."

"Well I was getting worried. That was the third Tim Hortons I had visited. The option was an all-bulletin's call to the police and no-one wanted that."

"You done good, Vicky! Now your questions."

She shook her head. "None."

Ed nodded thoughtfully. "Thank you. I appreciate that."

"However."

"Oh oh."

"I will ask you to let me know when you get back from Jolly Old, or wherever, that you let me treat you to a Japanese lunch some time – as you life insurance agent that is - and finally…"

"Oh oh."

"And finally, that you take me bird watching one day; as my travel agent that is."

"You're a tough bargainer, but I agree to all of your requests."

They pulled up at front of the main door at Hamilton airport. Ed moved to get out, but Vicky held him back and turned to face him.

"So listen, Mr. Edwin Crowe; when we go for that Japanese lunch, I'm going to ask you a few questions. You won't have to answer them, in fact I'm sure you won't answer some of them, but here's a small sample. Why do Pat and your lady friend in England know everything about your apartment? Why do they know, for example, that your passport is hidden in with your underwear, and more specifically that it's under the second pair of white underwear? Why did the US Border people pull you over last Saturday? I don't believe the story you told the girls, at least not after today I don't. Why do you have what looks like a bullet wound on the left side of your stomach? And speaking of your lady friend in England, why did she know so much about me, such as she knew I'm a life insurance agent, with an MBA? And on that point, did you tell the complete truth on your application for life insurance? And the big question, Mr. Edwin Crowe, is why was your Canadian passport issued four years before you came to Canada?"

Ed rubbed his chin. "Hmmm, interesting questions, Miss Victoria Kilgour. I guess I'll have some time to think those questions. I must say you are very observant in addition to being intelligent, positive, with a great sense of humor, and very, very pretty. I will ponder those questions and will address them at the Japanese lunch that I am very much looking forward to."

They got out of the car; Vicky opened the trunk and gave Ed his travelling bag. "Lots of underwear," she said. "Have a safe trip."

They shook hands, and Ed entered the building.

Vicky watched through the glass door as two men in pilot's uniforms met Ed. The three introduced themselves and left. "Well," she said aloud, "that was a good start to the day."

CHAPTER THIRTY-FOUR

SATURDAY, 11:30PM HALTON AIR BASE, ENGLAND.

The corporate jet's engines were shut down and Ed waited for the co-pilot to wave him off. He grabbed his bag, stepped down and walked toward Carolyn who was standing by her car some thirty feet away. As he approached she held out her hand.

Ed shook his head. "I'm not shaking hands with you, young lady."

Carolyn shrugged. "Okay, give me a hug then."

"Nope!"

"Oh for God's sake give me a kiss, but make it fast."

Ed took her in his arms and kissed her gently, but held her close after the kiss. She pressed her head against his chest and returned the hug. They didn't need to speak for a while; their silence said it all.

"Sorry," Carolyn said.

"Me too," Ed replied, giving her an extra squeeze.

She took his hand, walked him to the passenger side of the car, and held the door open for him. "This is the extent of my apology," she smiled.

He threw his bag into the back seat and got in. "Home James," he said with authority. She didn't move. "Wherever you say, Miss Andrews. You're the boss." She nodded and closed the door. Nothing else was said on that subject.

They passed through the limited security as they left the airfield and headed west. Ed noticed they were in a new and very fancy car. "Nice car," he nodded. "What is it a VW?"

"Try again," Carolyn said, tapping the dashboard that looked more like an airplane's.

"Hillman?"

Carolyn pulled a face. "Hillman! They don't make them any more. It's a Jag for crying out loud. And before you ask, it's mine and I paid for it." She paused. "Okay, my father had to co-sign, but it's mine."

Ed spent some time looking at its features. "Nice car. Suits you."

Carolyn looked sideways at him. "What exactly does that mean?"

"Well it's classy, in good running order, probably expensive to look after, and given the speed we're travelling at, I'd say it needs extra maintenance once in a while."

"Hey, listen here…"

"But mostly it's what I would choose if I had the choice."

Carolyn thought on that for a while. "Okay, that sounds better. But having a baby like this is a two way street; I look after him and he looks after me."

"Gotcha."

The drive continued through small country lanes, and Carolyn stopped several times and looked back through the rear-view mirror.

"I suppose you know you drove down this road ten minutes ago?" Ed asked.

"Yep! Just being careful."

When she was positive they were not being followed, she picked up speed and moved onto wider roads.

Ed looked out at the hedges and farmland they were passing. "May I ask?"

"Stonebridge Manor, Ed. We have a twelve-thirty meeting with Lord Stonebridge and the General. No sleep tonight, Mister." Her use of his departmental name set the stage he was anticipating.

"As you say, Miss. No sleep tonight. Do you know what's up?"

"Can't tell you."

"Will I be travelling out of country?"

"Can't tell you."

"Will we be working together?"

"Can't tell you."

"What can you tell me?"

Carolyn thought for a moment. "I like Victoria. She was very helpful, and once she understood how important it was for her friend, that would be you, she followed orders with no questions asked. Very nice to speak to. Obviously intelligent."

"Yes she is."

Carolyn gave him a quick look. "What else can you tell me about her?"

Ed was waiting for that very question. "Same as I told her about you...nothing."

"Good answer, Ed. Good answer."

As they pulled into the grounds of Stonebridge Manor a light rain began. Rain in February in England was far from unusual, but it did cast a bit of a dull atmosphere for the meeting and work ahead. There was important work ahead, of that Ed was sure. The rush to bring him to England, including getting a non-ratified citizen involved, left little to the imagination as far as timing was involved. But the closer they got to the manor, the more the dullness cleared. He was happy to be back in England; happy to be meeting with the head of MI6, and particularly happy to be close to Carolyn again. Her presence alone made the trip worthwhile.

"What are you grinning at?" Carolyn lightly laughed.

"Why you, Miss Andrews. You."

She let the comment go, and pulled up and parked in front of Stonebridge Manor.

As they walked up the steps to the large double-door entrance, Carolyn stopped and took Ed's arm. "Look, Ed, before we go in, I want you to know that I lied to you on the phone the last week."

Ed rubbed his chin. "Well you didn't tell me you loved me..."

"No, I didn't did I." She smiled, but decided to stick to her point. "The truth is I didn't tell Surbey's wife that he was a suicide bomber." She took a deep breath. "I did tell her that he had arranged the explosion and that he pressed the button, but I didn't use those two words. I'm sorry."

"Apology accepted."

She held his arm tighter to stop him from entering. "I used those words, Ed, to make myself appear tougher than I really am and I used them, and this really bothers me, to upset you. I don't know why, I just wanted someone to get mad at, someone to argue with. And you were an easy target." She shook her head. "And then you told me I was a 'tough lady' to say those words. You're a good man, Ed Crowe, a good man."

She let go of his arm and they entered Stonebridge Manor.

Neither Ed nor Carolyn was surprised to see Lady Stonebridge standing at the centre of the very large reception area. She was dressed to receive the Queen and was obviously happy to see them together. "Well, Mr. Crowe, how nice to see you. What brings you to the old country at this time of year?" She held out her hand for Ed to shake.

"Well now, Lady Stonebridge that is a mighty fine question. What does bring me to Jolly Old in rainy and dreary February? Perhaps your most charming daughter might know the answer." He turned to Carolyn with a smile.

Carolyn gave a quick shrug of her shoulders and pointed upstairs. "What do I know, I'm just the driver. If you'll excuse us, Mother?" She gently pushed Ed toward the stairs.

Lady Stonebridge stood aside. "I shall have some tea sent up. I'm sure Mr. Crowe could do with a good cuppa, isn't that so?"

Ed gave a nod of acceptance as he was escorted up the stairs without comment. When they got to Lord Stonebridge's office Carolyn reached for the door handle and stopped. "Okay, Sunshine, give me a quick kiss and answer me one question."

Ed kissed her quickly and waited.

Carolyn stood up straight to add authority. "Did you give Victoria a quick kiss when she drove you to the airport?"

Ed held back a smile. "Absolutely not. We shook hands."

"That's okay then," Carolyn said and opened the door.

Lord Stonebridge and the General stood to welcome Ed. There was a quick catch-up of how everybody was doing and then Lord Stonebridge invited everyone to sit. He took his seat at his large desk and spread his hands. "It seems we have a challenge, ladies and gentlemen," he said seriously. "I will ask the General to bring us up to date and then we will come up with a plan to address the matter at hand.

Before the General spoke, there was a tap on the door and, to everyone's surprise, Lady Stonebridge rolled in a tray of tea and crumpets. "Well we are English," she stated with a grin and immediately left the room.

"Priorities must," Lord Stonebridge declared, and they helped themselves.

The General put down his cup and saucer and took control. "We have a simple problem but there is, I'm afraid, no simple or safe answer. You will recall, Ed, not long ago while you were in the embassy in Damascus, taking a rest on the floor, so to speak, you met Jo-Ann Gisel. The ambassador introduced her as his Director of Communications; which of course she is not. In fact she is a very senior officer of this department. She has made some very good connections with the Syrian government; not an easy task at the best of times. We now wonder if the connections were too good. She is being held by the Syrian Republican Guard, or more likely by retired officers of the Guard. The Guard is the only army unit allowed in the city of Damascus, and its main role is to protect the President and the city." The General took a sip of tea. "Now this is where it gets confusing, so bear with me. The Guard was, at one time, led by Rifaat al-Assad, the president's brother. In 1983 when the president was sick, Rifaat tried unsuccessfully to take over the government. The two of them have not been on good terms since then. It is difficult for us to know exactly what is going on, since our best contact person with the Syrian government was Miss Gisel herself. What we do know is our embassy in Damascus has received written notice that she is being held as a result of the shooting, and more specifically, Ed, your death. The message from the captors makes it clear that they don't believe what Miss Gisel has told them, and instead they think that we were party to bringing Abu Nidal to Damascus in an effort to embarrass their government. No government, especially the Syrian government, wants to be associated with Nidal. To be in any way associated with him means the U.S. is your number one enemy. The thinking goes that the U.S. will use any excuse to attack supporters of Nidal."

Ed raised his hand. "And is that true?"

"Probably," Lord Stonebridge replied.

"I'm lost," Carolyn admitted. "So what do we do? If the captors are themselves not happy with their government, what's the point of taking Miss Gisel hostage?"

"Thanks for asking," Ed added. "I was wondering if I was the only one lost in the process."

The General chuckled. "I understand. But here is what we think. And I stress 'think'. If the captors can prove that we are part of the Nidal issue, then that would be an embarrassment to their government, and would enhance the tarnished reputation of Rifaat al-Assad, to the detriment of his brother, the president."

"So Miss Gisel is being used a pawn in the politics of Syria," Ed asked.

"Absolutely," Lord Stonebridge replied, "but it gets worse. Please continue, General."

"The plot thickens," the General continued. "Does the name Oleg Gordievsky mean anything to you?"

Ed shook his head.

"Of course," Carolyn answered. "Our famous double agent."

Lord Stonebridge nodded. "Exactly; our famous double agent. Now, Mr. Crowe, I am reluctant to tell you too much. The less you know the better, as is often the case in our business. Suffice to say that Mr. Gordievsky was a Colonel with the KGB, who worked at the U.S.S.R. embassy in London. In fact he had been working for us for many years and was a great help in our understanding of what went on in Moscow. He was caught by the KGB in May last year, tortured and imprisoned. In July he managed to escape to the Finish border where he was met by our people and eventually returned to England where he now lives a free man. He has since been found guilty of treason by the Soviet authorities and sentenced to death in absentia."

Ed got up and poured himself more tea. "That clears everything up," he muttered.

The General laughed. "I'm sure it does. Clear as mud no doubt. The real issue here is that Miss Gisel was Gordievsy's main contact in London. At the present time Syria and Moscow are on very good terms. Most of the military training and weapons of the Syrian army are special gifts from the Soviets. In fact the only naval base the Soviets have in the entire Mediterranean is in the Syrian port of Tartus. Suffice to say that if the Soviets find out about Miss Gisel's work with Gordievsky, then the political relations between us and the Soviets would suffer, but more importantly the risk of Syria transferring her to Moscow is very real and very dangerous. If the captors, not the Syrian government find out her prior role, and *they* send her to Moscow, then all hell breaks loose in Damascus, Moscow, and London."

Carolyn finished the last drops of her tea. "So speed is the issue. We need to get Miss Gisel back to the U.K. as quickly as possible?"

Lord Stonebridge nodded. "And do it in a way that doesn't disrupt the balance of power in Damascus or our relations with the U.S.S.R. Gordievsky had identified many years ago a certain Mikhail Gorbachev as a future Soviet leader. He, of course, was recently appointed as the General Secretary of the Central Committee of the Communist Party and therefore de facto leader of the U.S.S.R. He has a plan, to be announced on Monday, just two days from now, to make significant changes to the Soviet economy. He is introducing two new concepts to his people; glasnost, which translates into openness, and perestroika which roughly translates into restructuring. We cannot let anything disrupt our relations with him. Mrs. Thatcher believes he will change the face of the world; economically, militarily, and politically. We don't want the Gordievsky matter to raise its head. We need Miss Gisel back safe and sound. It is a priority of the highest level."

The General looked at his watch. "That would be one day from now, sir. It's Sunday."

"I'll make some more tea," Carolyn offered.

"I'll help," Ed said enthusiastically. "Can't beat a good cup of tea to work out a plan to save the world."

Lord Stonebridge rubbed his tired eyes. "Youthful enthusiasm," he muttered. "Thank God for that."

Ed followed Carolyn to the kitchen area. "I think I've brought too much underwear," he said.

"I think you're correct, Mister," she replied using his operational name, "and I don't like the sound of that."

Ed started washing the cups and saucers. He leaned over and gave Carolyn a quick kiss on the cheek. "There are not a lot of choices when it comes to our operational plans for tomorrow, are there?"

Carolyn shook her head. "Nope. Just two. It's we do it, or we don't do it."

"Will you be there with me?"

"As far as I can go, Ed. As far as I can go."

Ed pushed the tea trolley into Lord Stonebridge's office and motioned for Carolyn to sit. "I will play mother," he bowed and proceeded to pour and deliver.

As Ed performed his task with skill and bluster, Carolyn spoke for the two of them. "When do we leave for Damascus? *We* being Mr. Crowe and me. Do we phone Ambassador Wood now or later? I assume we do not take our guns, and I presume that the meeting with the captors can be set up for today?"

Lord Stonebridge took a long sip of his tea then nodded to the General. "Great minds think alike it seems?"

The General raised his eyebrows. "And fools..."

"Exactly," Lord Stonebridge interrupted, turning to Carolyn. "You both leave immediately, but only Mr. Crowe attends the meeting. I will phone Ambassador Wood as you head for the plane. Do not take any weapons; hand guns in this situation would be like taking a pea-shooter into battle. And the meeting must be held today or we cancel. That will be the message to the captors: No messing around with Britain." He escorted them to the door. "And remember Sergeant McAleese will still be in Damascus. Use him if need be."

Not entirely to Ed's surprise Carolyn's travel bag was packed and ready to go. They shook hands with Lord Stonebridge and the General and had left the manor before Lady Stonebridge was aware they were leaving.

Carolyn drove directly to the Halton Air Base and directly onto the airstrip where their RAF plane awaited. They were directed to a huge jet plane sitting at the end of a runway. The three crew members ushered them into the rear of the plane where they sat in a most uncomfortable seat on one side of the interior.

"What kind of plane is this?" Ed asked looking around.

The senior officer replied with a smile. "It's a Canberra PR7. And I'm sure you know that makes it a bomber. Not built for passengers I'm afraid, but we were told to get you there ASAP. Buckle up. It's noisy and fast. We'll be there before you know it."

The take-off was extremely noisy where they sat and they covered their ears until the plane leveled off. It was still noisy, but they could hear each other speak.

Ed spoke close to her ear. "You're still lead, right?"

Carolyn nodded unenthusiastically.

"Perfect," Ed added, leaning back to relax.

Carolyn punched him in the arm. "You know this is dangerous don't you?"

"Of course I do, Miss. But I have you to look after me, and that makes it just a little safer."

Carolyn snuggled closer. "The operation hasn't started yet, Ed. Put your arms around me please."

Ed did as he was told, and they held each other close for the three hour flight.

CHAPTER THIRTY-FIVE

DAMASCUS, SYRIA
SUNDAY, FEBRUARY 23RD
1986.
6.15A.M.

A mbassador Wood was waiting for them along with the Syrian airport authorities. They were whisked through security and customs with almost a smile. They spoke little on the trip from the airport to the British Embassy. Ambassador Wood drove as quickly as he could through the busy city as it awoke to another busy day. Food sellers were already on the streets and many people, mostly men, were starting their day at work. Sundays were not regarded any differently by most Syrians, but for the small Christian minority it was their day of rest and prayer.

The embassy was busy when they arrived. Security was heavier than normal and the staff were already busy working the phones, fax, and telex machines spread throughout the building. Ed and Carolyn followed Ambassador Wood into his office where, to no-one's surprise, there was a hot pot of tea ready to pour. Ed and Carolyn served as the ambassador looked through some messages on his desk. Ed thought that the ambassador looked like he hadn't slept in days, and that turned out to be the case.

"Here is where we are at," the ambassador started explaining. "Miss Gisel was taken from her residence without incidence according to her neighbors. She made no resistance as our rules require. Several hours later we received a letter, delivered by hand, telling us that she is being held as a spy on the basis that she has been involved in espionage; which of course she has. But their basis is that she, we, assisted in bringing Nidal to Damascus in order to tie Nidal to Syria and in doing so set the U.S. against them. No-one in this part of the world likes the U.S. but they certainly don't want to be regarded as enemy number one of Washington. Our assumption, and that's all it is, is that she was identified by Lori Quinn some time ago, and the captors are using whatever information Miss Quinn gave them. They want a ransom of fifty-thousand pounds paid for her release. It's the amount that has us thinking that it is not the Syrian authorities that are behind this. Fifty grand is a lot of money, but not enough to risk a breakdown in relations between the two countries."

Carolyn raised her hand. "But that makes it even more complex, surely."

Ambassador Wood nodded. "Absolutely. But here's the most important aspect of what we're about to do. We must, and I stress *must*, act as if we believe we are dealing with the authorities. To do anything differently would only delay any activity and we cannot afford that. We need to sort this out before the Soviets get involved. Gorbachev has already visited both Canada, where he met Prime Minister Trudeau and the U.K where he met and got along well with Mrs. Thatcher. He also had a brief meeting with President Reagan last November in Geneva. They also got along quite well and no doubt Reagan's charm rubbed off on him. Gorbachev wants to make changes that many in his own party don't agree with. We cannot, absolutely cannot, have this whole Gordievsky-Gisel relationship issue come to light."

Ed stood and poured more tea. "So what is the plan, sir?"

"We get her back, and we do so today." He opened his desk drawer, took out a newspaper and handed it to Ed. "That 'dead person' on page four is you. We have to make it clear that you are not dead, that we were not involved with bringing Nidal to Syria, and, in fact, we were aware of the bombing that almost killed him."

Carolyn spoke quickly. "But won't they think we were part of the bombing, not just aware of it?"

The ambassador closed his eyes and shook his head slowly. "Not us, Miss Andrews; not the U.K. that is. Mr. Crowe is Canadian and Mr. Surbey was American." He shrugged. "So we point to America and their friend to the north."

"Oh shit!" Ed gasped.

Carolyn couldn't believe her ears. "You're kidding….sir?"

"Not in the least, Miss Andrews. It makes sense. America would do anything to have Gorbachev succeed in his plans, and when we tell the American's - as in President Reagan - what we did, they'll be happy to go along with our story. At least that's Mrs. Thatcher's opinion. And *she* is not a woman to argue with."

"Amen," Ed chuckled. "Get it? Ah…men."

Carolyn shook her head. "Forgive him, sir. He hasn't slept for a while."

The ambassador scratched his un-shaven face. "I understand fully. Now let us proceed. Time is not on our side."

Carolyn and Ed moved their chairs closer to the ambassador's desk. Notwithstanding the dangers involved, Ed could not help but get excited about what they were about to do. Being a travel agent simply did not, could not, compare.

"One question," Carolyn asked, raising her hand. "Will we pay the fifty-thousand under any circumstances?"

"Not in a million years," Wood replied with certainty.

"What if they capture Mr. Crowe?" she continued.

Ambassador Wood sat back in his chair, not expecting such a question. "Let's say not in a hundred years, shall we. How does that sound, Mr. Crowe?"

Ed gave a quick grin. "Very kind of you, sir. I do appreciate your special consideration."

Carolyn rolled her eyes. "They'd probably ask for less anyway."

The ambassador reached into his desk draw and held up a document. "This is their letter and offer for release. It includes a mobile telephone number for us to contact."

"All mod cons," Ed noted.

"Exactly. Now what I plan to say is that we would like to send someone to speak to them about their offer. No explanation, just we want to meet. Further, this will be the only offer we plan on making; take it or leave it."

"But there is no offer, sir," Carolyn commented.

"But of course there is, Miss Andrews," Wood replied. "They return Miss Gisel, or we - the United States of America – will break off diplomatic relationships with Syria on the basis that we now believe they were involved in the October 1983 bombing of the U.S. Marine Barracks in Beirut. That is to say, it will have nothing to do with their current holding a British diplomat."

"Were they involved?" Ed asked.

Wood nodded. "Probably."

Carolyn wrung her hands. "This is getting messy."

"Everything in Syria is messy," Wood added. "Now let's get down to the details of our work today."

Ambassador Wood spoke into his phone with authority. "He is about six feet tall, medium length dark hair, and will be holding a newspaper in his right hand. He will not be carrying anything else except his passport. His name is Crowe. He will be standing outside the front entrance of the embassy at nine, forty minutes from now. I suggest you listen to what he has to offer." He paused and listened. "As I said, listen to him. He speaks with authorization." He hung up.

Ed asked the question. "What did they say?"

Wood shook his head. "They now want a hundred thousand."

Carolyn closed her eyes briefly before she spoke. "One further question, Ambassador. Mrs. Thatcher has approved this, correct?"

"Yes she has, Miss Andrews. And so has Prime Minister Mulroney. He's aware we're putting a Canadian passport in play, and the risks involved politically."

"There you go," Ed offered enthusiastically, "what can go wrong, eh?"

"I'll get us some more tea," Carolyn responded.

"That's the spirit," Ambassador Wood agreed.

Ed stood outside the embassy gate with the newspaper in his right hand. It was chilly but he wore as little as he could get away with. More clothes meant more security concerns for the enemy. He was beginning to worry if anyone would show up as he stamped his feet gently to keep himself warm.

The Jeep turned onto the main street from a back alley a hundred yards away and drove quickly up to him. The back door was opened from inside and Ed got in. Both the driver and the man next to him were wearing uniforms that Ed guessed were army, but it didn't matter. Seeing them uniformed relaxed Ed somewhat. To be held for ransom by non-military personnel would have been a greater risk. His relaxation waned quickly as the drive was fast and bumpy and too much tea was moving inevitably to its ultimate location.

The Jeep pulled up in front of a large double gate that opened as they arrived. They drove in and parked in front of what was a large house anywhere but surely massive for a private home in Damascus. He followed the driver and guard into the home. They waved him into a large room that was Western in nature with the exception of the large number of carpets that covered both the floors and the walls. At the far end was a beautiful wooden desk, at which sat a soldier with a significant number of medals and military paraphernalia. He smiled and motioned Ed to take a seat in front of the desk.

The man was big, but not in any way fat. When he stood to walk to a small table, his six-foot frame and immaculate uniform made it clear he was a most senior officer. "Would you like some tea?" he asked Ed.

"No, thank you very much. Too much tea already this morning." He paused. "In fact, could I..."

The officer motioned to a room. Ed stood, put the newspaper on the desk and moved speedily to relieve himself. He returned to his seat with a nod of thanks.

The officer reached across the table, palm up. "I am General Mohammed Safavi, and I am told by your ambassador you are Mr. Edwin Crowe. Your passport please."

"He is not my ambassador, General. As you can see I am Canadian." Ed gave him the passport and watched as the general read it at great length, nodding as he reviewed the visas and stamps on Ed's passport. He looked up at Ed and returned the passport. "You get around," he said, looking Ed straight in the eyes. "What requires such travel for a young man?"

"I'm a travel agent."

The general laughed aloud and slammed his fist on his desk. "A travel agent! Now that is funny." But the laughter died quickly and he leaned forward with a stern and humorless expression. "Where is the money, Mr. Crowe? If you want her back, then we want the money. And we want it now."

Ed counted to ten. "General Safavi, please let me respond to your concerns regarding both Miss Gisel's role at the British Embassy and the circumstances surrounding the matter of Abu Nidal's recent visit to Damascus. Now I know that you believe, quite incorrectly, that we were party to encouraging Nidal to visit your lovely city. In fact the truth is quite the opposite. It was us that bombed the meeting where Nidal met, and it was one of us that died in doing so."

General Safavi waved him off with a flick of his hand. "Do you take us for fools, Mr. Crowe? You arranged to have Nidal visit Syria with the full intention of his organization recruiting members from our citizenry with the goal of turning the U.S. against our country. You were not part of the bombing, that was some crazy man, and a crazy man that did not succeed. Now give us the money, or leave before we keep you too."

Ed pointed to the newspaper. "Sir, with respect… If you would look at page four of the newspaper you will see the photo of the dead man who was killed by your 'crazy man' at the British Embassy. It was this killing that allowed our man, your 'crazy man', to enter the meeting where Nidal sat. Certainly Nidal still lives and is currently in Libya, but please, sir, review the photo."

Reluctantly the general opened the newspaper and studied the photo. He took a one-second look at Ed, and then went back to the photo. He kept his head down and rubbed his chin in thought. Ed waited, not wanting to be the first to speak.

"This means nothing," the general said, as he folded the newspaper neatly. "So you played dead. I don't see where this fits into your lady friend not being a spy for MI6."

Ed chose his words carefully. "Sir, that photo was taken at the request of the CIA. The man that entered the Nidal meeting was a member of the CIA, and, sir, I was asked by the CIA to be shot and 'killed' by their man in order for their man to gain entry into the Nidal meeting. General Safavi, the CIA is going to kill Abu Nidal, and will go to any length to do so. They have the full support of the PLO and many other Palestinian organizations. The CIA will attack and bomb wherever they locate Nidal, be that in Syria, Libya, or Palestine. They are committed."

Safavi shrugged and motioned a lack of interest. "So Nidal is in Libya and if they kill him, so much the better."

Ed nodded his understanding. "Yes, he is in Libya. You know that, the CIA knows that and the British MI6 probably knows that. But, sir, if you don't release Miss Gisel, then Prime Minister Thatcher will inform President Reagan that Nidal is back in Damascus as a guest of President al-Assad. And as I said, the CIA…"

General Safavi was around the desk in a matter of seconds. He pulled out a revolver and forced it into Ed's mouth. "You will die in a minute, Mr. Crowe. Do you have anything to say to your CIA friends?"

Ed closed his eyes shut tight. He couldn't think. He knew only that he needed to take a pee yet again. He shook his head, not wanting to see his killer's smile. He heard the sound of a safety being released as General Safavi shouted in Arabic. Then the sound of a door opening, people running, and finally the explosive sound of a gun being fired.

The gun was still in his mouth, and he could only hear and feel a dull ache in his head. He kept his eyes closed tight. He would have prayed, had he known how.

"Open your eyes, Mr. CIA Crowe," General Safavi said quietly.

Ed saw the look of disgust in the general's eyes, and the second gun in his other hand. Smoke curled slowly from its barrel.

Slowly, menacingly the general took the gun out of Ed's mouth. "Here is a message to your CIA friends." He grinned, and then with all his strength smashed the smoking gun into the right side of Ed's face. Blackness and pain ruled.

CHAPTER THIRTY-SIX

TUESDAY, FEBRUARY 25TH 1986 DAMASCUS

T he sound of voices seemed a long way off. He knew he was alive, but where and when was lost on him. He didn't move; he had to understand where he was. He listened, finally realizing he was hearing sound only with his left ear. *Of course; the gift from the general. Listen, Ed, listen.* Ah, the sound of music: a softly spoken Scottish accent.

"Hello, Mac," Ed managed. "How ya doin'?"

"Dinna worry about me, laddie. The doc will be here in a few minutes. Dinna move yer head. Yer on more drugs than a rocker in the sixties. Stay calm and carry on." He laughed. "Always wanted to say that."

Ed opened his eyes but saw little. His right eye was partly covered with a thin bandage and his left eye was watery and wouldn't focus. He was looking at a ceiling, but it was fuzzy. He gave up and closed both eyes.

"You're doing fine, Mr. Crowe," Ambassador Wood offered. "We'll have you home in no time. Well in a couple of days for sure."

Ed gulped, scared to ask the obvious. "What happened?"

Ambassador Wood pulled up a chair, sitting close to the bed. "Miss Gisel was dropped of at the embassy on Sunday at noon. She was, and is, fine. They simply dropped her as if they were running a taxi service. We sent her back to England that day. She's home with her family."

"And Carolyn...er... Miss Andrews?"

"She went with Miss Gisel, and reported back to London and Stonebridge Manor."

Mac spoke slowly. "They dropped yer off yesterday. That would be Monday."

"How's my face?"

There was a slight pause before Ambassador Wood replied. "Mac said he thought you'd be kicked by a horse...a Clydesdale no less. The doc said your eye will be fine. You're on a lot of medication."

"Okay, everybody out," the doctor ordered as he entered the room. "I want to give my patient a quick once-over. The NHS doesn't pay me to lose patients. Out you go."

With the shuffle of feet and a closing of a door, the doctor took over. Ed relaxed and waited for the prodding and questioning.

Twenty minutes later the doctor left and Ambassador Wood and Mac entered. They waited for a diagnosis.

"Fit and ready to go home, the doc says," Ed beamed, slowly putting his shirt back on.

The ambassador took over. "Good. Now please tell us what happened that resulted in the safe return of Miss Gisel, and the not-so-safe return of you?"

Ed relayed the story in as much detail as he could, trying not to miss a word. He shrugged when he got to the end of his story. "But what I don't know is what happened to me from Sunday until I was dropped off yesterday. How was I dropped of anyway?"

"Dumped from a moving car," Mac replied quickly, "but they were nice enough to cover yer head with an old bag."

"We thought you were dead," the ambassador added. "However, to the future! You are positive they think you're attached in some way to the CIA? This is important."

"Definitely."

The ambassador turned to Mac. "Let's do what we talked about please."

Mac nodded and left the room.

Ed waited while the ambassador ordered tea and biscuits. "And bring a travelling flask for our Mr. Crowe please." He put down the phone with a smile.

"Going somewhere am I" Ed asked.

"You're going home, Mr. Crowe, and you're going home as a guest of the U.S.A.F. And while you are flying home would you please write out your report in complete detail from when you left the embassy on Sunday. You will get word as to where to send it."

"Not via England?"

"Oh no! You're a CIA contact. You're going home with your associates. You will be driven to the airport in an ambulance. We want the officials here to see you leave, and see who you are flying with. That will be important. In the meantime I will report back to Stonebridge Manor, and then without a doubt Lord Stonebridge will contact Prime Minister Thatcher." He chuckled. "And there is no doubt in my mind she will be on the phone to President Reagan within minutes, happy to explain how we used his agency to save one of our own, but more importantly to ensure Mr. Gorbachev has an uninterrupted Communist Party gathering."

The tea and biscuits arrived and Ambassador Wood was more than happy to play mother.

Mac entered the room and helped himself to a cup of tea. "The plane will be ready in an hour."

Ambassador Wood picked up his phone. "I'll phone for an ambulance. Enjoy your cuppa, Mr. Crowe; you've got a long trip to North America.

CHAPTER THIRTY-SEVEN

WEDNESDAY, FEBRUARY 26ᵀᴴ 1986. HAMILTON AIRPORT 4AM

E d thanked the crew, grabbed his bag and walked down the metal gangway directly onto the tarmac. It was cold and dark and the wind blew snow across the open area. But he was home and looking forward to a good night's sleep in his own bed.

The trip from the embassy to the airport in the ambulance had been noisy and fast. He had worn additional bandages around his head as he walked to the ambulance with Mac's assistance. He felt he had played his part well, and Mac suggested he should be nominated for an Oscar. The flight was amazingly fast and at a height he had never flown before. There was lots of coffee but, alas, no tea.

The airport was all but empty and the agent barely looked at his passport. The man just nodded and waved him on. Ed was wondering if there would be a taxi this early, as he exited the control area.

Ed couldn't believe his eyes.

"Hi, bloke," Vicky said as she gave him a hug and took his bag. She was wearing jeans and a warm winter jacket. "I'm here to get you home at the request of your two very concerned friends Pat and Carolyn."

"Wow, Vicky, you didn't have to…"

"Yes I did. Now bundle up, it's cold out there."

Vicky drove carefully. She didn't want her special package to end up on the side of the road due to her normal fast driving. "Welcome home, Ed. How are you doing?"

"How do I look?"

"Ugly as sin. But we'll get those bandages off you when we get home and I picked up some medication that was recommended by your doctor in never-never-land; or wherever you just came from. You're off work until next Monday. Pat's updated your boss."

"This isn't fair to you, Vicky."

Vicky laughed. "Pat said you would say that and she said to remind you that life ain't fair."

"Did you speak to Carolyn?"

"She asked me to tell you that she'll be in touch, and that she was worried sick about you for a while."

"Thanks."

Vicky pulled off the QEW and headed for Ed's apartment. "You know," she said thoughtfully, "I really do enjoy helping you and your associates out like this. I know I can't ask any direct questions, and that's part of the fun. Honest."

Ed opened the door to his apartment and turned to Vicky. "Thanks, Vicky. I really do…"

"Not yet, bloke. You get showered and ready for bed and since I packed you, I'll unpack you."

Vicky pushed him toward the bathroom. "Get cleaned up; take off the bandages before you shower, and don't come out naked please."

"What have we done to you?" he mumbled, walking into the bathroom as ordered.

Ten minutes later Ed was sitting up in bed. Vicky applied the cream carefully to his face, doing her best not to hurt him.

She spoke quietly. "That should do it for a while. Now get some sleep. I'll be in the living room doing some paper-work."

"Pat and Carolyn should not have asked you to do this, Vicky. You have your own very busy life."

"Oh, they didn't. They just asked me to pick you up, drive you home and get you safely unpacked. The home-care is my idea. Get some sleep." She turned to leave, but changed her mind. She gave him a quick kiss on his left cheek. "Get some sleep. That's an order."

Ed did as he was told.

He felt the gun in his mouth. He couldn't breathe. Sweat poured off his face and he struggled to speak.

"Ed! Wake up!" Vicky screamed. "For God's sake, wake up!"

He sat up, gulping for air. He was wet with sweat and breathing in gulps. "Shit, I'm sorry. Christ! What an awful dream. Look I'm sorry."

Vicky grabbed a handful of tissues and began to wipe his face and chest. "Calm down, Ed. You're okay. I'm here. Relax please."

Ed took a deep breath. "God I'm glad you stayed, Vicky. I owe you one."

She smiled. "Yes you do. Now can I do anything? Please let me know."

Ed thought for a moment. "Yes, please. Just trust me." He took Vicky's right hand, moved it to his mouth and took her thumb fully in his mouth. He closed his eyes and enjoyed the sensation. After a minute he smiled and removed her thumb. "Thanks. That'll help next time."

She gave him a strange look. "I was getting worried there, thinking you were getting naughty."

Ed smiled. "I'll explain sometime. What time is it, Vicky?'

"Just gone ten, bloke. Time to get up. The kettle for tea is on." She stood to leave.

"You're a wonderful person, Miss Kilgour. Truly a wonderful person."

"Yeah, yeah," she replied leaving his room. "Tea in five minutes."

They sat around the kitchen table enjoying a very hot pot of tea. They could have been an old married couple. He hadn't shaved for a couple of days and was wearing just his housecoat – tied tightly at the waist at her request. She was in her jeans and loose fitting top and, unusually, without any make-up.

"I unpacked for you," Vicky motioned to a dirty pile of clothes in the bathroom.

"Thanks." He sipped his tea and smiled. He was enjoying their new and emerging relationship.

"And I read your document."

Ed almost spilt his tea. "Oh shit, that was supposed to be…"

She grinned. "Not that one. Not the one in the U.S.A.F. envelope. I could see it was some form of report. It's in with your knives and forks: unread."

Ed relaxed. "Then which document?"

"'Callie the cat'. Carolyn added it to your luggage 'while you were away'. I must say she writes better than you. Longer sentences, better descriptions of places, and much better punctuation."

"Oxford education perhaps?"

"No. Just male versus female. Life is simple." She got up to leave. "When did you eat last?"

Ed thought for a second. "Well I had tea and biscuits at the embassy and coffee and cookies on the plane."

Vicky's eyes lit up. "Really! Now which embassy would that be?"

His eyes closed and his head dropped. "The Embassy Hotel in London," he mumbled, "…er…er…Bloomsbury area."

"Er, er is correct, bloke. Maybe I'll look it up on the internet. It may have its own web page. That's the new way."

Ed grimaced.

She walked to the door to leave. "Don't worry I won't look it up. Never, ever. And for what it's worth I didn't look at your passport since last night. Your trip is all yours. Honest."

"Thanks. I owe you again."

"Yes you do. I have to go home, clean up and I have a twelve o'clock appointment. Why don't I pick you up downstairs at one-thirty and we'll do a late lunch. Your treat and we'll talk about anything but you."

Ed laughed. "You are magical, Vicky. One-thirty downstairs. My treat and my pleasure."

She nodded and left.

Ed walked out of his bathroom wearing just a towel around his waist as Vicky let herself into his apartment. He looked at the clock, it just one-fifteen. To his surprise Vicky looked relaxed to see him half naked.

"What's up?" Ed asked.

"Where you been for twenty minutes?" Vicky replied, turning her back to him. "People have been phoning you."

Ed laughed. "I took a long shower, for God's sake. Don't worry; I won't drop the towel. Besides…" The phone rang.

Vicky waved him off. "I'll get it. Get something on."

Ed turned and headed to his bedroom.

She waited for the fourth ring. "Crowe residence," she answered. "Who may I say is calling?" Her eyes popped wide open, just as Ed ran in from his bedroom wearing a pair of pants and a tee-shirt. She held the phone out to Ed. "The White House," she mouthed.

Ed took a deep breath. "Crowe speaking."

A lady's voice spoke: obviously American. "Is this Mr. Edwin Crowe?"

"Yes, Ma'am."

"Please hold for the President of The United Sates of America."

"The President. Yes, Ma'am."

Vicky was beside herself, not sure whether to laugh, cry, or leave the room. She headed for the door. Ed waved her back. He motioned it would only take a minute.

The President came on the line. "Mr. Crowe, we speak again."

"Yes, Mr. President. It is very nice to hear from you…again."

Reagan chuckled. "It seems to me the last time we spoke I was thanking you for saving some of my fellow countrymen, and now it seems you are getting me into trouble with Syria."

"Yes, sir. Sorry about that, sir."

"Not a problem, Mr. Crowe. We will get Abu Nidal and his people. Have no doubt about that. It will take time, but it will happen. More importantly at this time are the changes going on in Moscow. We need Gorbachev to succeed for the world to be a safer place."

"Yes, sir. Our best wishes for Mr. Gorbachev."

"Now Mrs. Thatcher tells me you had to be *killed* by our Mr. Surbey, and she also told me that you were *killed* by Gaddafi in Libya last year. Now at the risk of sounding heartless, I would have to say that sounds like…a murder of Crowes to me." He laughed loudly and Ed joined him.

"A murder of Crowes, it is, Mr. President. Thank you. I hadn't thought of it like that."

Vicky stood motionless, not believing what she was hearing and who was saying what to whom. Her friends would never believe her, but she knew she could never tell anyone anyway. Her life would never be more fun or interesting. Deep in her own thoughts she missed the final comments from Ed, and he hung up the phone.

"I'll get changed for lunch," Ed said walking into his bedroom, acting as if he spoke to the President of the United States of America every day. He had a wide grin on his face, but didn't let Vicky see it.

"Gorbachev? A murder of Crowes?" Vicky asked, standing in the centre of the apartment as Ed returned from his bedroom.

Ed shrugged. "A gaggle of geese, a pride of lions, a…"

"I know all about collective nouns. I went to university, remember? What about a coven of spies? But that wasn't the intent of my question, was it?"

Ed reached for her arm. "Let me buy you that lunch I promised you. And since we will not be talking about me, perhaps we could talk a lot about you?"

The phone rang.

Vicky stepped back. "I am not answering that!"

Ed picked up the phone. "Crowe's nest."

"Did you get the call?" Pat asked.

"Just hung up. Had a regular old chat. Nice guy."

"Don't be smart."

"I'll get my report to you. I'll pop it in the mail tomorrow."

"Fine. No rush. Listen…I have to tell you something." She sounded cautious.

Ed waited.

"It's Carolyn. I spoke to her at length the other day. She isn't doing very well. She's feeling down, having a few bad days, you know?"

Ed waited, smiling at Vicky.

"She wants me to tell you that she needs some time to herself. She's taking a few months off work and relaxing at home. Maybe a trip to the south of France." She stopped talking.

"By herself?"

"With her mother. No-one else. I wouldn't lie to you, not about this anyway."

Ed nodded. "I'm sure she needs a rest. Say 'Hi' from me next time you chat."

"I will, Ed. I'm still in England. I'll phone when I get back to Ottawa. We'll chat."

"Perfect. Thanks." He hung up.

Vicky looked nervous. "Everything okay?"

"Never better, young lady, never better. Let's go to lunch and tell me all, or most, about yourself that I don't already know."

She put her arm around his. "Looking forward to it, mister."

He took her arm and they left for lunch.

When they arrived at Vicky's car, she turned to Ed shaking her head. He knew something was wrong.

"Look, Ed, this is weird. I don't know who you really are, if you're for real, what you do and don't do on your trips around the world. We met just a couple of months ago, and within a couple of hours of meeting you, you've got me half naked…and I loved it. You find my ex-fiancé within a couple of days as if that's your full time job. Then you have me running around going on about 'men in the ranks'. We become lovers, although somewhat reluctantly on your part, and I'm very glad we did. Then you're all over the world on last minute trips, finally returning beaten up on your last trip...and I'm there to help you - at four o'clock in the morning! You chat to the President of The United States like an old friend, about things I know nothing about. I simply don't feel comfortable. Let's forget about lunch today, okay? Give me some time to sort things out. Sorry."

"Not a problem, Vicky. I understand. Maybe you could drop me off downtown and I'll grab a bite to eat."

She agreed and they got into to her car. To his own surprise he was comfortable with the changes. He certainly had some things of his own to sort out. They shook hands as he exited her car.

CHAPTER THIRTY-EIGHT

FRIDAY, FEBRUARY 28TH, 1986 THE QUEEN'S HEAD 6:00 PM

The pub was unusually busy. There was a break in the temperature and some of the snow on the sidewalks was actually melting. Winter wasn't so bad after all. The customers were happy and talkative.

Ed stood at the bar relaxed after a few days off work. The matter at hand was where to eat. He was not sure if he would eat at the pub or head home for a pizza delivery. He sipped on his beer, pondering such important matters. What it really did was take his mind off Pat's conversation about Carolyn, and his now confusing relationship with Vicky. Pat hadn't phoned from Ottawa, so he was left guessing as what had been said between her and Carolyn. He took a large sip of beer and went back to thinking of food.

Seana was working the bar and stopped to chat a little from time to time as she moved quickly to keep up with orders. She moved toward Ed, but was looking over his shoulder. "Vicky, what are you doing here?"

Vicky stood next to Ed, nudging her way in. "Just dropping by to say hello. I've got a date later on, but wanted to touch base with everyone." She was wearing a fashionable long blue dress under a fur-trimmed black leather jacket, and was wearing a stunning necklace that Ed assumed was set with real diamonds. She turned to Ed. "Nice to see you."

"Do I know your date?" Seana asked as she pulled a pint of beer.

Vicky shook her head. "Not likely. He's a bit of a loner. The quiet and unassuming type."

"Have fun," Seana added as she moved on.

"Nice to see you," Ed said, "and if you don't mind my saying so, you look very lovely. With that charming blue dress and your cheery smile, you look and smell like the first day of spring. And a little twinkle from your baby blue eyes would melt any young man's heart." He bowed his head slightly. "I do hope you enjoy your evening, Vicky."

"Thanks, I'm sure I will." She turned to leave, but only went half a step before she turned back and leaned into Ed, speaking softly. "I've sorted things out. I will be at your place in half an hour. I will wait exactly fifteen minutes, and then go home if you don't show. I love you, and I want to be your girlfriend. Not you fiancé. Not your wife. I just want to be your girlfriend." She kissed him on his bruised cheek and left the pub.

Ed turned back to his beer. There was only a small amount left. He finished it and put the glass on the bar.

"Another pint?" Seana asked.

His world felt a whole lot better. "Just half a pint please. I've got a busy weekend."

AUTHOR'S NOTE

This novel is fiction but is based, in part, on actual events. There were terrorist attacks at Rome and Vienna airports on December 27th 1985, the work of the militant Palestinian splinter group, the Abu Nidal Organization; named after its leader Abu Nidal. At the time of these and many other attacks that he organized, he was described by the U.S. State Department as the world's worst terrorist. He died in August 2002 of gunshot wounds.